Strange Bedfellows

Rett MacPherson

Word Posse

Dedication
To the most amazing group of people I've ever had the pleasure of knowing:
Thomas Drennan, Laurell K. Hamilton, Deborah Millitello, Marella Sands,
Sharon Shinn, and Mark Sumner.

From Word Posse
Bad to the Bones, Rett MacPherson
Sleeping the Churchyard Sleep, Rett MacPherson
Pandora's Mirror, Marella Sands
Fortune's Daughter, Marella Sands
Restless Bones, Marella Sands
The Angels' Share Series, by Marella Sands
Escaping Normal Series, by Marella Sands
The Water Girl, Deborah Millitello
The Mourning Dove, Deborah Millitello
The Wizard and the Warrior, Deborah Millitello
Do Virgins Taste Better? And Other Strange Tales, Deborah Millitello
Thor McGraw and the Ice Man Murder, Tom Drennan
The Naturalist, Mark Sumner
On Whetsday, Mark Sumner

Visit us at www.wordposse.com

ISBN-13: 978-1-944089-22-1

I

January and bitter cold. As Emma drove on the dark two-lane road, she realized with mild panic that she hadn't seen a building in the past five miles. Not another sign of civilization anywhere. Just three-foot-high snowbanks and large pine trees that hugged the side of the road like protective ancient spirits. The heater was on full blast, but her teeth still chattered. The backseat and trunk were filled with most of her possessions. When she'd stopped two hours ago to use the restroom, her nostril hairs had instantly frozen and her eyeballs had nearly evaporated. If her car broke down now, she was convinced that her body would turn to ice in sixty seconds. She'd be found in April by the Minnesota Department of Transportation with her fingers still clutching the steering wheel.

She'd left Missouri fourteen hours ago. When she'd started talking to the GPS, she knew she was seriously road weary. The GPS lady had a very nice soothing voice, and more than once Emma had thought about making a wrong turn just so she could hear her say, "Recalculating. Recalculating."

This is nuts, she thought. *Nuts, nuts, nuts. I'm driving in a blizzard! This is the craziest thing I've ever done!*

Well, okay, maybe not.

Emma Gordon had certainly done some crazy things in her life, but, like a cat, she usually landed on her feet. When she was fourteen, she was expelled from St. James Catholic School for writing graffiti on the side of the school wall: *Count your blessings.*

With lots of little hearts and swirls and crosses, except she'd been in such a hurry that she'd accidently left out the 'o' in count. It was reported that one of the nuns had passed out cold on the parking lot and got a concussion. That had definitely been a low point in Emma's life, and she'd spent a full forty-five minutes in the confessional. She'd tried not to be too hard on herself over it, because in all fairness her frontal lobe had not been fully developed at the time. Papal forgiveness and lobe issues aside, her craziness had just been getting started.

Like the time she married that community theater actor without knowing he was already married. Or the time she rescued a bag of cats from a watery grave. She'd been at a friend's lake house for the weekend and came upon a group of teenage boys at a nearby river, who thought it was fun to stuff nine cats into a bag and throw it off of a bridge. Emma had been on the banks of the river, dived in, almost drowned, but ultimately saved the ferocious felines, and then drove like Speed Racer down dusty dirt roads trying to outrun the perpetrators. The cats had clawed her arms to pieces, tore up the interior of her car and infested it with fleas so badly, that she'd almost had to sell it. The fleas chowed on her ankles every time she drove the car, and she worried that she would develop cancer from all the ineffective chemicals she'd used on the seats. So when winter arrived she opened all the doors and froze the fleas to death.

Sometimes on quiet, lonely nights, she still wondered if those fleas had suffered when they died.

Picking up hitchhikers was another crazy thing. She knew she wasn't supposed to, but she couldn't help it. She always thought if she were walking on the side of the road, she'd want somebody— who wasn't a serial killer—to offer her a ride, and so every time she saw a hitcher she'd stop. Every time she'd tell them, "I have mace." Every time they'd look at her like, "Lady, I don't care. I just want a sandwich and a ride to the liquor store." And every time she would hear her grandmother's words. *"They'll kill you and rape you. In that order if you're lucky."* And so to heed her grandmother's warning, she'd drive with one hand on the steering wheel and the other holding up the can of mace, but by golly, she did her humanitarian deed.

And there was more. Lots more.

But right now, she really needed to concentrate on the current crazy thing that she was engaged in. Just how had she gotten herself into this mess?

She knew the answer to that before she even asked it. Desperation. Desperate people did desperate things. Her latest business venture in Colorado had gone belly-up, and at twenty-eight, Emma had dragged herself home to St. Louis, only to discover that her mother had sold the house and moved to Belize with Ted. Her mother had left Emma a few boxes of belongings in her cousin's garage. Emma had suddenly found herself homeless and jobless. She'd resorted to sleeping on her ex-boyfriend's ex-girlfriend's couch with a poodle that had fecal incontinence. You couldn't get much more desperate than that.

Which was why she found herself driving on snow-packed roads in eastern Minnesota at two in the morning, heading for a house that she'd bought sight-unseen with money that had come, quite unexpectedly, from her granny's estate. She was relieved to not have to sleep with the poopy poodle anymore.

According to the information that she had from the realtor, the house was located nine point two miles past the turn-off. That turn-off had been the junction of two state roads about a mile outside of town. She was almost there. If she could just stay on the road and not freeze to death.

She looked down at the odometer. She should be coming up on Lady Slipper Lane. "Turn right in point two miles," the GPS said. Her heart did a flip-flop, and she turned right onto what appeared to be a gravel road. She couldn't be sure because of the snow cover, but her tires immediately began to jostle. Off to her right she could make out the big sprawling expanse of some sort of farm. Big barns, outbuildings, and a large house were nestled back from the road.

"Nice place," she said to the GPS. Her excitement mounted and, despite the cold, her palms began to sweat.

"In twenty feet, make a left-hand turn to your final destination," the GPS said.

She took a deep breath, closed her eyes...*final destination*...opened them again and made the turn. Tomorrow was the start of her new life.

At first she couldn't see anything. The driveway was about a quarter of a mile long and lined with trees. But then, at the very end, she saw the house.

And there was a horse in the front yard.

"What in the...?"

The horse wore a blanket over its back and didn't bother to move as her car approached. It just looked up at her and snorted. She stopped the car, but kept it running. It was pitch dark. She couldn't see anything except what was directly in front of her headlights. And what was directly in front of the headlights was an old two-story home with a porch that was missing half of its railings.

"Well, it could be worse," she said. She decided she'd wait until morning to pass judgment. Sunlight always made things look better.

Stepping out of the car, she was immediately smacked in the face by brutal arctic air. She went to the trunk to retrieve her flashlights and made sure she kept the driver's side door open in case she had to make a hasty retreat. Out of her pocket, she pulled the house key that the realtor had mailed her when she signed the papers. She made her way warily past the enormous horse and it snorted at her again. She unlocked the door, stepped inside and shone her flashlight around the room.

In the darkness, the beam of light landed on a large empty room with a crooked chandelier to the left and brick fireplace to the right. She made her way into the kitchen and tried the switch. Nothing. *I know I called the electric company! I know I did!* She moved down the hallway looking for the thermostat and then realized that if there was no electricity, the furnace would not kick on, even if it was a gas heater. Whoever invented that system hadn't thought too far ahead, now, had he?

In the kitchen, on the counter, she found a letter that read: *Due to blizzard and power outages all over the county, the electric company could not make it out to turn on your service. I left you my horse. – Your neighbor.*

"Is the horse an electrician?" she said in the darkness. What good was the horse going to do her?! And it was 2017, couldn't somebody somewhere just push a button? She tried not to panic. In the survival pack in the car that her cousin Jackie had packed for her, there was a lighter. Jackie was a smart woman. Smarter than Emma. Definitely more cautious.

The next half hour was filled with a flurry of activity. Emma tried desperately to find firewood. Even though she'd never started a fire in her life. Well, not intentionally, anyway, and one thing she knew for certain was that accidents were rarely repeatable. She never did find any firewood, but there was a sketchy-looking shed out back that she refused to go in. Serial killers, you know.

She'd carried her belongings into the house, keeping a watchful eye on the horse. She'd only brought what could fit in her car. Her cousin Jackie was going to send the remaining boxes in a few days. She decided that her only recourse was to go back to town and try and find a hotel for the night. On her last trip back out to her car, she leaned against the door trying to get a signal on her cell phone. And realized she'd just locked her keys in the car. And it was running.

The snowflakes were getting bigger and fatter even though Emma couldn't understand how that wasn't possible.

She turned to head back into the house to make one more search for something to burn, even if it meant going upstairs into those big empty bedrooms. The horse was no longer on the front porch, and this panicked her for a moment. Maybe her neighbor came back for his horse and *he* was a serial killer?

Seriously, she had to get a grip.

Then she heard the horse make some noise from within her house. He'd just walked into her house. Like he'd been invited. She wasn't even sure how he'd fit through the door.

She stomped her feet.

"I am an idiot."

She took a deep breath, wincing from the pain of the cold in her lungs. Of course, she realized that this was all her fault. She should have triple checked to see if there was power at the house. She should have left Missouri earlier so that she would have arrived in the daylight. When businesses were open. She shouldn't have stopped in Iowa and helped that Amish guy get his buggy out of the ditch. That had really sucked up some time. Almost two hours. Stupid Amish guy. Now here she was with her keys locked in her car with the engine running, no power, no heat and a horse *in her house!* Where was that Amish guy now? Huh?

He'd been so grateful for her help, though. And he'd even posed for a selfie with her. She'd posted it on Facebook with the caption: *Check out me and the Amish dude in Iowa.*

But she knew there was nobody to blame but herself.

In the end, she yanked a few rotten porch railings off, along with some of the stair railings in the house and burned them in the fireplace after googling how to build a fire.

Note to self: Purchase unfashionable but practical coat. And boots.

Then, in utter exhaustion, she slumped to the floor and cried.

The horse nudged her head with his nose. Then he lay down next to her on the floor with such a thump that Emma thought for a moment the floor had given way. She covered herself with his blanket that had been draped across his back. She wiped tears and snot onto her gloves and glanced over at the horse. "Are you sick?" she asked. She thought she'd read somewhere that horses only lay down if they were sick. "Please don't puke on me. I don't think I could take it if you puked."

Indeed, vomit of any kind was her Kryptonite.

Rummaging through her emergency kit, she found a bottle of water, a bag of ranch-flavored Doritos, dark chocolate, a flare, batteries of all sizes, and condoms. What in the world Jackie thought she was going to do with condoms in an emergency, Emma didn't know.

She began to get drowsy then, and she leaned back on the horse's belly. He was warm. She vaguely wondered if she was being asphyxiated by the varnish on the burning rails, but she didn't care. Mr. Horse was fabulously warm. She curled into his belly, gave a fleeting thought to fleas, and fell fast asleep.

2

Emma opened her eyes to find an extraordinarily hairy man with shining blue eyes staring down at her. She screamed, startling the horse, who whinnied, jumped up and trotted over to the front door. "Who the hell are you?" Emma said, backpedaling on all fours and trying to stand up.

"Your neighbor. Across the way," he said.

"How'd you get in?" she asked. She pushed herself to a standing position while trying not to let the stranger out of her sight.

"You didn't lock the door. We don't have much in the way of crime around here, but you should still probably get in the habit."

She caught her breath and straightened her coat and then realized that she'd slept all night with her hat and shoes on, too.

"W-what's your name?" she stammered.

"Clancy Stephens," he said, bending over to retrieve the horse's blanket.

"W-what do you want?"

"I came to get my horse," he said in such a snooty tone that it made her want to stick her tongue out at him.

"Oh. I thought maybe he came with the property," she said.

Clancy was about six foot with lots of shoulder-length amber-colored hair and a beard of the same color covering most of his face. But it was his eyes that were the most striking feature. Partly because they were almost all she could see of his face, but also because they were at once piercing, keen, and yet kind. He wore a red sock hat pulled down over his ears and one of those khaki-colored one-piece cover-alls. The kind that mechanics wore.

"Hardly," he said. He glanced around the room and took note of the fireplace. "Why don't you have a fire going?"

"Uh, well, I did. But I couldn't find any wood," she said, scratching the back of her neck. "And I ran out of stair railings around four this morning."

Clancy cut his gaze around to the big, double wide staircase that spilled like a wooden water fall into the living room.

"There's wood in the shed," he said, gesturing over his shoulder in the general direction of the outbuildings. "There's plenty out there. I waited for you until ten o'clock. Thought maybe you weren't coming or you got a hotel room somewhere, so I went home."

"Waited for me? I don't understand."

"Your real-estate agent wanted me to let you know that you didn't have any power. Which was kind of dumb, since I figured you'd realize that soon enough on your own."

"H-how did you know I didn't have power?"

"It's a small community. My buddy's wife works for the electric company. They had a massive power outage over in the next town so they couldn't make it out here. Power lines are down over most of the county."

"So, you just left me over here, knowing there was no power?" The hysteria rose in her voice.

He shrugged. "You were late. I couldn't wait all night."

"Well, there was an Amish guy in Iowa!" she yelled.

"What?" he asked.

"You have no idea how cold it was over here last night! I could have *died!*"

His eyebrows shot up. "There was no way you'd die. I left you Roy. And a blanket. And firewood in the shed."

"Roy?" she asked.

"My horse," he said.

"You left me your *horse*?! What was I supposed to do with him, go all Han Solo and cut him open like a Tauntaun?"

"Are you speaking English?" he asked.

"Yes, I'm speaking freakin' English!"

"Did he or did he not keep you warm?" Clancy asked.

She took a deep breath and glanced over at the horse who stood with his head down, staring at the doorknob. He probably had to pee. Because, God knew, she had to. "Yes, he kept me warm."

"Then I don't see the problem. How was I supposed to know that you'd rather burn your staircase than go out to the woodshed and bring in the wood?" he said.

"I didn't know there *was* a woodshed!"

He rolled his eyes and said, "It was nice to meet you." Only the way he spoke the words told her he meant the exact opposite. He spat them out at her like they were hot coals on his tongue.

"Yeah, nice to meet you, too," she said in an equally haughty tone, just as he was turning to leave. "Don't let the door hit you in the ass on the way out."

He stopped, clearly exasperated. "Fine, next time I won't leave you my horse," he said. "Come on, Roy."

Like there would be a next time.

As Clancy got to the bottom step on the front porch he said, "Oh, by the way. Ned, the guy who used to live here, did a great job of insulating the pipes, so you've got water. However, the toilet isn't working."

She just stood, tapping her foot, arms crossed, glaring at him. She hadn't thought to check the toilet last night. She'd been too cold and too tired to pee, anyway. And besides, Mr. Jenkins had assured her everything was working! That the house was move-in ready. Totally livable.

Maybe Minnesotans had a different idea of what "livable" actually meant!

"So, you have to use the outhouse," he added with the slightest hint of a smile.

He's screwing with me! He has to be. Right?

"You enjoyed telling me that, didn't you?" she said.

"Lady, I don't care where you take your tinkle."

As Clancy and Roy reached the snow, the horse stopped and looked back at her. He snorted. Clancy pulled on the rope, but the horse didn't move. He kept looking back at Emma with a doleful expression. "Let's go, Roy," Clancy said to him. But still, the horse wouldn't budge.

Clancy sighed and said, "He wants you to say good-bye. He thinks you're mad at him."

Emma gave Clancy a condescending look.

"I swear. Just pet him on the rump and tell him he's a good boy," Clancy said.

The horse snorted again and Emma's heart melted. The horse really was worried that she was upset with him. Well, after all, they had spent the night together. They'd bonded. She stepped into the brilliant sunshine and ran her hand along the length of his back. "Thank you, for keeping me warm, Roy. I appreciate it. You're a good boy."

And then the horse turned and walked down the driveway, seemingly happy with her approval and dismissal.

What a jerk! She thought. Clancy, not Roy.

She had to get into town and get the power turned on. She realized suddenly, her keys, and clothing were locked in the car which was now out of gas and her cellphone was most likely dead. She glanced up the driveway to see Clancy and Roy almost to the road. "Wait! Wait!" she called after them.

One thing Clancy Stephens had learned in his thirty-three years was that most women wanted something. They never did anything without an ulterior motive. They also never hesitated to ask for favors that they could never repay. And none of them were above lying to get what they wanted. Except Caitlin, of course. His eight-year-old niece was perfect. Well, and her mother, his sister Peri, was pretty close to perfect as well. At least now that she was past the age of playing tricks on him and eating all his Frankenberries.

And Mrs. Osborne, his first-grade teacher, was an angel. He still sent her flowers on her birthday. How could he not? He'd been a gangly boy with a terrible lisp and no friends, and she helped turned his life around. All by giving him an extra half an hour of her time three days a week for speech therapy.

But take for example, his new neighbor, Emma. First she insulted him and his horse, told him not to let the door hit him in the ass and then ran down her driveway asking for him to take her to town because she'd suddenly realized that she'd locked her keys in the car the night before and was out of gas!

He'd called a locksmith for her so she could retrieve her purse from the front seat. And the only reason Clancy had given in and driven her to town was because he was going in that direction anyway, and because Roy had slapped him in the face with his tail and farted on him when he'd hesitated. Damned horse was no judge of character.

So here he was driving in his pick-up truck with a total stranger who didn't like him—but needed him for something. What was he supposed to talk about? He glanced at her out of the corner of his eye. She was dressed completely inappropriately. Those tennis shoes were not waterproof in the least. What kind of idiot came to Minnesota the first week of January in tennis shoes? She removed her hat and wild, curly, butterscotch-colored hair pinged out in every direction. It wasn't necessarily long hair, maybe shoulder length, but the curls gave it such bounce that it seemed like she had enough hair for three people. She swiped a handful behind her ear and he noticed that she had about eight silver studs piercing the cartilage all the way up.

He was just thinking about how she wasn't going to last too long in that house over there when she said, "Wow, this is really pretty in the daylight." She stared out of the window at the tall snow-covered pines and the deep blue sky. "I've got to buy myself a proper coat and boots today. Where's the nearest place I can do that?"

Okay, so she wasn't completely without sense. She realized she wasn't dressed properly. But still, what was her story? She didn't seem like the type of person who wanted to live in the country or on a farm. And lately, a lot of the property around Quail Bottom was being sold to people from the Twin Cities. They wanted a weekend getaway that wasn't all the way in Duluth or in the Boundary Waters. And Quail Bottom was about halfway between the two places and it rested on the St. Croix River and Odin Lake. A hunter and fisherman's paradise. Usually those types of people had families that they wanted to expose to the country way of life a couple of days out of the month. Unless she had a hunting husband and a brood of kids hiding somewhere, he predicted that she'd sell out and move back to the city within a year.

"Reynold's Boots up in Winchester Hollow," he answered. "He's got snowsuits and coats, too. Along with snowshoes, skis, that sort of thing."

"Oh, good," she said. "Thanks. And thank you for taking me to town to get gas. I really appreciate it. Do you mind if I charge my phone?"

He glanced over and saw that she had one of those gadgets that allowed you to charge your phone in the car. "Go ahead," he said.

Pleasantries were out of the way. Now what was he going to talk about? He was terrible at small talk. And wasn't it amazing how she could behave nicely to him when he was doing her a favor but just earlier she'd been rambling on at him about an Amish guy and Han Solo?

"So, what do you do on your farm?" she asked.

"I breed horses."

"Oooh, like thoroughbreds?"

He smiled. "You follow horse racing?"

"No," she said. "But I spent some time in Kentucky, and well, I'd just as soon forget about Kentucky, but I knew this guy...he'd just talk about horses all day. He told me once that he'd sell his mother for an ounce of the perfect horse semen."

Clancy smiled. He knew guys like that.

"He's in jail now," she said. "He got caught stripping copper wire out of office buildings. I guess to buy horse semen. Personally, I could find other things to spend my money on. But Roy, your horse, he's really something. You teach him to behave like that?"

"Roy is a special horse," was all he said. Which didn't really answer her question, but he wasn't sure how to explain Roy, because even he didn't completely understand Roy.

"What kind of horse is he?" she asked.

"A Suffolk Punch," he said.

"What's that mean?"

"It means he's a draft horse. So, not built for speed or for war. Built for agriculture mostly."

"Is that what you breed?" she asked.

"No, Roy was a rescue. Found him chained to a wall in a barn of a house that was for sale."

"I don't understand," she said.

"The people moved, put the house on the market and just decided to leave the animals. It wasn't until the real-estate agent went out to look at the property, she found them..." His voice trailed off. What he and Zoe had found there was enough to make even the most hardened person cry. Clancy had been called out to help remove the animals because he had enough trailers to transport them. His first reaction was to gag. Then he'd choked up and cried and had to walk away from the barn. Then he got angry. If the owners of that house had come walking up the drive, he would have beaten them to a pulp right then and there.

"I don't get why people do that sort of thing. Personally, I've never had a pet. My mother wouldn't allow it. But I could never tolerate people mistreating animals. There was this one time I went to a friend's lake house for the weekend..."

Clancy took a deep breath. He might not be one for small talk, but apparently, she was. He only listened half-heartedly. Something about cats and fleas.

"Anyway, you were talking about your farm," she said.

"Oh, yeah, we breed a couple of different kinds of horses. Belgians, which are also big draft horses. We use those for clearing logs and debris from the forests. That's another side job that we do. We also breed Appaloosas and quarter horses."

"Wow, sounds nice," she said. "Do you send your studs out or do they send the mares to you or is it mechanical? You just ship the semen?"

Okay, so she'd learned something about horses. Probably from that guy in Kentucky. "People send us their mares or we do it mechanical. We don't send our stallions out."

"Who's we?"

"Me and my dad," he said.

"So you guys would know all the folks around here who have horses?" Emma asked.

He shrugged. "Maybe not everybody."

"What about the rodeo?"

"There are rodeos and horse shows and barrel racing all over the state pretty much every weekend when the weather's good," he said. "Are you interested in one in particular?"

"Hmmm," she said. "Not really." He got the feeling that there was more to that subject, but let it go. Because he really didn't care.

Even if she did save nine cats. The less he knew about her, the less he had to play "friendly neighbor."

He glanced over at her again. She was really pretty in that wide-eyed gypsy sort of way. Her hair might have been butterscotch, but her eyebrows were dark brown and her eyes were...well, they were orange in the center fading out to green on the edges. She wasn't pale but she didn't look fake-baked either. God, he hated that fake-baked look. The best word he could come up with to describe her skin was olive.

He pulled into the gas station and she filled up her gas can while he filled up his truck. "I have to pee like nobody's business," she said, apparently thinking it was Clancy's business. "I'll be right back."

Then she disappeared and came back a few moments later with a coffee in each hand and a box of those powder-covered donuts under her arm. She handed a coffee to him as they got into the truck. "Black?"

"Uh, yeah," he said.

"That's what I thought. I can usually tell." She opened the box of donuts and offered them to him. He took three.

"I just have to drop this paperwork off with my farrier, then I can get you back to your car," he said, as he started the engine.

"Okay," she said. After a moment she added. "I think if I'd waited another hour for this coffee I would have killed something."

Clancy chuckled.

"So what's your mom do?" she asked.

"She's dead."

"Oh, sorry. Got any other family?"

"A sister and a niece."

"You married?"

"Nope," he said. And in spite of himself he found himself asking, "What's your family like?"

"Oh," she waved a hand. "Well, I'm from Missouri. My mom recently sold everything she owned and moved to...I can never remember. One of those exotic places down around the equator with a guy named Mario. Or was it Raul? No, it was Ted. How could I forget? I never met my dad. No siblings. That I know of. I've got some cousins that I'm real fond of, though."

He nodded. He really didn't want to ask her why she'd never met her dad because then she'd tell him. And, again, he didn't want to know his new neighbor that well. Especially since he was certain she wouldn't stay long.

She continued talking. "I mean, I get it. It's warm and exotic down south. Personally, I love Mexico. One time, when I was like three, we were on vacation and we somehow wandered into Tijuana—if you knew my mother, you'd understand what I mean when I say 'wandered'—and there were these Mexican hat dancers performing in the square. I tried to leave with them. All those beautiful skirts and that amazing music. I just wanted to follow them around for the rest of my life."

Clancy smiled.

Emma laughed, a deep and throaty, natural laugh. "Mom was so angry. Mostly because she spent three hours looking for me."

"I can see how that would be stressful for a parent."

"Oh, yeah, but the best part was like two years later, I jumped in a UPS truck and the driver didn't know I was in there for like, ten miles, and when he did find me, I asked him to mail me to Tijuana. My mother was *livid* that time. Mostly because she had to leave work to come and pick me up at his next stop. The driver was freaking out. Thought he was going to get fired or sued." She smiled at the memory. "So, I understand the allure of exotic places. Really, I do. I just..."

"What?"

Emma glanced out the window. "Nothing," she said. "Listen to me. You couldn't care less, could you?"

Just then, they passed old Marty Pepper, dressed in his donated Army coat and boots, huddled on the corner. Clancy pulled into the parking lot for the insurance office. It looked as though somebody had made a donation to Marty's pot this morning because the guy had managed to buy an egg sandwich from the drive-thru right off the interstate. "Oh, who's that?" Emma asked.

"Local homeless guy. Seems like every town's gotta have one, right? He's totally harmless. He'll take whatever donation you give him, but he won't steal. My dad says he's actually a pretty upright kinda guy."

"How long has he been homeless?"

"Long as I can remember."

Emma was quiet. Reflective.

"So..." Clancy ventured. He knew he shouldn't, but he had to ask the obvious question. "What brings you up here?"

"Oh! That's the best part!" she said and slapped her knee. "My dad's from up here. I've come up to start a relationship with him."

Don't ask her. Leave it alone. You don't want to know. Clancy most likely knew the man, and this was going to be awkward.

"My mom met my dad at a rodeo up here. Back in 1986."

"Oh, interesting," he said. And he was quite proud of the fact that he'd not asked the next obvious question, which was her father's identity.

Clancy pulled around the back of the building and parked, relieved to get out of his own damn truck. "I'll be right back," he said.

Inside he found Bradly, his farrier and best friend, sitting behind the desk. Brad was a part-time insurance salesman in addition to his other business ventures.

Clancy and Brad had known each other all their lives. Went to school together, played soccer together, and they'd hated each other until they were about twelve. Clancy had not been the most athletically adept child, whereas Brad was a natural at sports and he had picked on Clancy and made fun of him. Then one summer they'd been partnered up at a 4H horse event and their roles had been reversed. Clancy was the one who knew everything about riding, and he'd showed Brad the ropes. That was when Bradly Halverson had fallen in love with horses. His friend was what a person thought of when they thought of a typical Minnesotan. Blond, blue-eyed and big. "How's that new mare doing?" Brad asked.

"Just fine. She's a beauty," Clancy said. He handed him the paperwork he'd brought. "Zeus is gonna need shoeing soon. Got any ideas on how we're going to get to him?"

"Tranquilizer dart," Brad said and smiled.

Clancy said, "I'm being serious."

Brad shrugged. "That horse should be put down, Clancy. You know that and I know you don't want to hear it. The vet can't get near him. The dentist can't get near him. I can't get near him. Even the other horses can't get near him. You're gonna have to do something."

Clancy just looked away and worked his jaw.

"He kicked the crap out of me last time, Clancy. Not sure my shoulder is ever gonna be the same. I won't go near him unless he's drugged," Brad said. "Have you tried one of those animal psychologists?"

Clancy rolled his eyes at the suggestion. Zeus was a broken horse. He hadn't been the same since the accident. But Clancy could not bear the thought of putting him down and so if drugging him was what they had to do to keep him healthy, then for right now, that's what he'd do.

"I'll think on it," Clancy said. And he would. He valued Brad's opinion because Clancy wasn't in the business of training horses or breaking them in or fixing them. Sure, he knew the basics of training and he knew how to take care of them, but aside from riding for his own pleasure and aside from logging, he just bred the horses and then handed them off to somebody else to do the hardcore training. He'd never had any reason to keep a horse that was unmanageable. But Zeus wasn't just any other horse. And truth be told, he was in over his head where Zeus was concerned. He'd brought in expert trainers and veterinarians who'd been in business for decades and not one of them had managed to even get in the ring with him. "I've got to go. Ned's old place sold, and I've got the new owner out in the car. She came in late last night, totally unprepared. No power, which wasn't really her fault, but still. She doesn't even own a decent pair of boots. Anyway, I've got to get her back out to her house. So, we'll talk more later."

"You betcha," Brad said.

Clancy came out to find Emma kicking the excess snow off the wheel wells of his truck. He decided that she may have been wearing a ridiculous coat and shoes, but there was nothing ridiculous about her jeans. In fact, they looked just fine. Soft and faded in the right places. "No need for that," he said as he got back in the truck.

She climbed back in and made "brrrr" noises and rubbed her hands together. Then she plopped another donut in her mouth. "These things are completely devoid of any nutrition, but I'll be darned if I can eat just one of them. I should have bought a banana."

"Glad you didn't," he said, and took another donut. "I hate bananas."

She smiled. He turned the truck around to head back to the house so she could put the gas in her car and eventually get her power turned back on. And leave him alone.

"You know anybody who can do some handiwork?" she asked.

"Like...?"

"Like, getting my toilet fixed. Fix the porch, maybe do some painting? Oh, and the railing on my stairs..."

"What are you paying?"

She shrugged. "I don't know. Whatever the going rate is, I suppose. I just need it done fast and I don't want to get cheated."

"Actually, my cousin Brandon could use some work," he said.

"Great. Have him call me. Can I get your cellphone number?"

He gave it to her and she dialed it from her phone and the phone in his pocket rang. "There, now you've got mine, too."

After Clancy had dropped Emma off at the house, she filled her gas tank from the red can and gave a sigh of relief as it started right up. She glanced at the clock on the dashboard. It was almost noon. She had a lot to do before dark.

On the way back to town she called and begged the electric company to please bump her to the top of the list, but they gave her no guarantees. She stopped and filled up her tank and filled up the gas can, too. Then she went up to that Reynold's place in Winchester Hollow, which was about half an hour north of Quail Bottom. There she bought boots, a decent coat, some thermal underwear, candles, a kerosene lamp, a sleeping bag, and a gas-powered heater. That heater would in no way heat her whole house, but she could put it in the bathroom long enough to take a shower. Her total came to just under $700.

She needed a job. Granny's money wouldn't last forever. But she'd worry about that next week.

After she went to the grocery store, she went to the office of *The County Reporter,* which was housed in a little tiny building right off the main street in Quail Bottom. It was next to a place called Luella's Cafe. The smell coming out of the cafe was sinful. Not to mention distracting. Grilled onions, garlic, something with lots of butter. Was there a more crippling combination of smells in the world? She shook her head and reminded herself that she could eat there any time she wanted. She was now a resident.

At the newspaper office, she placed an ad in the paper that was to run for the next two weeks. It read: *Attention: If you slept with*

Helen Wiesnewski in the year 1986 at a rodeo, congratulations, you could be my father! Please contact me. I don't want anything from you. Just hugs.

The reason she had to place the ad was because Emma did not know who her father was, because neither did her mother. After Helen had left for an exotic retirement, she'd mailed Emma a letter that said, *"Dear Emma, I still cannot remember the full name of your father. But he lived in a town called Quail Bottom, Minnesota. I think his name was Doug or Tug, or maybe it was Larry. Forgive me, it was the eighties, darling. We met at a rodeo, but I don't remember exactly where the rodeo was. But I remember the name Quail Bottom because it made me laugh. I think he may have had a sister who was a famous gospel singer. I do not know why that sticks with me. Maybe it's because I shouted a lot of Hallelujahs that month. Maybe if you go there, you can find him."* Along with the letter was a grainy 3x5 photo of her big-haired mother, wearing a shoulder-padded Western shirt, and a man with a lasso and a big ol' belt buckle and a cowboy hat that covered half of his face. On the back of the picture her mother had written: *Me and that cowboy. 1986. Minnesota.*

Emma gave her contact information to the woman behind the counter, whose desk plate said Shirley Umbridge. Shirley had nicotined-stained hands and burgundy hair piled on top of her head and big squishy bags under her eyes. She looked worried as she took Emma's money. "You're not from around here, are you?" she asked.

"No," Emma said, cheerfully. "But I will be from now on."

3

By the time Emma had finished all her errands, it was almost dark. The sun set sooner up here than it did down in Missouri, which meant in the summer, the days must be noticeably longer. She'd never put much thought into that before. Summer must be pure heaven up here.

She carried in all the stuff she'd bought, including a cooler that held milk, orange juice and eggs. She finally just set the whole cooler out on the front porch because the food sure as heck wasn't going to spoil. She scarfed down the pepperoni pizza and a bottle of tea that she'd bought at the pizzeria. She wanted to unpack her clothes and hang them in the bedroom closet but she hadn't even had a chance to see which bedroom she wanted, so she just left them packed. She was fairly certain that she wasn't going to be spending much time upstairs unti l the power was on. It was too far away from the heat source.

When Emma went outside to get wood out of the woodshed, she almost tripped over a dog sitting on the front porch. At least she thought it was a dog. It was scruffy and mangy with one blind eye. When he stood he looked to be about the size of a retriever. In fact, the more she studied him, the more she thought he actually was a golden retriever.

"Oh, goodness," she said. She squatted down to his size, took her glove off and stroked him between the eyes. The dog's tail slowly began to wag back and forth. "Where'd you come from?"

She pulled out her phone and texted Clancy: *U missing a dog?*

Then she went to the woodshed to bring wood into the house. The last streams of daylight streaked across the sky in frosty pink and gold runnels, and it turned the snow that had collected on the evergreens a soothing salmon color. Her breath caught for just a second at the sight of it. And for the first time she noticed the stillness all around her.

She kicked the side of the woodshed, just to make sure there was nothing hiding in there and waited ten seconds. There was a giant pile of wood, a couple of old buckets and a shovel leaning against the wall. She gathered as much wood as she could carry and dumped it in the bin on the front porch. She made four more trips and each time the dog greeted her with a hopeful expression and a slight lift of his tail, only to have his excitement wane as she went back to the shed. When she was finished with her chore, it was completely dark.

She gazed up at the sky and gasped. Never in her whole life had she seen so many stars. So many clear, crisp pinpoints in a pitch-black swath from one horizon to the next. Not in Colorado, not in Arizona, not in Kentucky.

"Wow," she said.

Emma gave one last glance at the dog before shutting the door. An hour later she had a roaring fire going in the living room and one going in the kitchen stove. She wouldn't use the gas heater unless she had to. For the first time since she left St. Louis she could take off her coat and change her clothes without the threat of freezing to death!

She needed a shower, but she was exhausted and didn't want to even consider hauling her new heater in the bathroom. Besides, she just realized, if there was no electricity, the water heater wouldn't work, would it? She checked the water in the kitchen. The hot water ran and ran and ran, but it remained frigid. The water was so cold that it hurt. How was it not slush?

Her phone buzzed. It was Clancy. *No missing dogs here.*

As if on cue, the dog on the porch began to whine.

She made her bed on the floor in front of the fire and was about to put on her jammies when she heard the dog again. "Oh, for the love of Pete," she said. She went to the kitchen, got him a few slices of bread and headed for the porch. She opened the door just a crack and placed the bread outside. The dog just looked at her and whined.

She shut the door.

She texted both of her cousins to let them know she was alive, barely. *No power. Cold as a witch's tit in a brass bra. But, for some reason, I like it.*

The dog whined again and she opened the door. "You cannot come in here. You're filthy. I do not know what's living in your fur." He cocked his head to the side and raised his paw toward her.

She shut the door.

He had to be freezing out there, but he was a dog, right? Weren't dogs wild animals at one time? Like, you know, animals. Animals lived outside. Couldn't they survive winter? Of course they could.

But what if he couldn't?

Five minutes later she found herself running across her yard to the woodshed where she remembered seeing a bucket. The dog perked up, but she didn't look at him. *I can't believe I'm doing this.* She left him on the porch and went straight to the sink. She filled the bucket with water and set it on the stove. It wasn't a skillet or an actual pan, but she thought water would warm in it just the same. When steam came off of it, she poured it in the sink, added a little of the frigid water to it to get it the right temperature and shook her head. *I cannot believe I'm doing this!*

She opened the door and let in the dog, who lowered his head and stepped cautiously over the threshold. "Come on. Bath time. You are so not sleeping in here with your coat looking like that."

She got her shampoo out of her duffel bag and a brush. Luckily for her, she had two brushes. The dog was much heavier than she anticipated, but even so his bony ribs nearly poked through his fur.

She set him in the sink and he just looked at her.

"Oh please, make this easy on me."

She ran warm water over the dog's back with an empty tea bottle. "Come on, that's it," she said. Finally, he sat as best he could in the sink. She scrubbed and scrubbed, and the water turned brown from the sludge and debris caught in his coat. There were a few carcasses of some sort of bug floating around in there, but she ignored them.

There are no dead bugs in my sink. There are no dead bugs in my sink.

"Say cheese," she said. Then she raised her phone and snapped his picture. She posted it to Facebook with the status: *My bedfellow for the night.*

When she finished shampooing him, she realized that she had no way to rinse him, except with the cold water from the tap. He wasn't going to like that one bit. But what was she supposed to do? He couldn't keep Pantene in his hair overnight. She wasn't even sure if it was safe to use human shampoo on him in the first place. She turned the water on and used the spray handle to rinse him. He yelped and squirmed and she shushed him as best she could. "Stay!" she said, firmly.

He wriggled and wrestled and finally she took him by the muzzle and made eye contact with him. "Just give me a minute," she said, soothingly. "I just need a minute."

Finally, the bath was finished. She realized then she had no towel to dry him on, so she used the sweatshirt that she'd been wearing earlier. *I so need to go shopping!*

She lay down on her sleeping bag, suddenly exhausted and overwhelmed by everything she had to do and everything she'd already done. She texted her cousin Jackie requesting that she ship her the rest of her things. It wasn't enough stuff to have warranted renting a U-Haul, but it had been enough that she couldn't fit it into her car.

Emma looked at the dog then, who sat in front of the fire with an expression of pure bliss. She was tempted to take a bath the same way he had. How was it that the dog was cleaner than she was? She changed into her flannel jammies, almost too tired to raise her arms over her head. She made sure the stove had lots of wood in it and cracked the oven door to let the heat into the house and she put what she thought was a safe amount of wood into the fireplace for the night and settled into her sleeping bag.

And then the dog whimpered.

She opened one eye and looked at him. His chin was on the floor, his paws out in front of him. He inched forward on his belly and stopped. She opened both eyes and he inched forward some more. "Oh my God," she said. "You're killing me."

He moved forward, little by little, on his belly until he'd reached Emma's sleeping bag. "Stop right there. You're still wet."

He mostly listened. His body curled up to the sleeping bag, but just as Emma dozed off, he rested his head right on her abdomen and went to sleep.

4

The next morning Emma awoke to a paw in her face and an extinguished fire.

Really? She had to get up and start a fire before she could do anything else? How did the pioneers survive? Then she thought about the fact that her toilet didn't work, and she almost cried right then and there. *If I were a pioneer, I'd live in a nudist colony in Mexico,* she thought. *To heck with this frontier farmer bullshit.*

When she opened the door to let the dog out, a giant horse nose was eye-level with her and Emma gave a little squeal. "Roy!" she exclaimed as the dog ran through the horse's legs and out to the yard. "What are you doing here?"

He shook his head.

"You're not coming in," she said, shutting the door. She found her phone and realized that she needed to go to a library or someplace with electricity to charge it because it was almost dead.

She texted Clancy: *Roy is here. Did you leave him here for a reason or did he just find his way?*

She scarfed the rest of those powdered donuts and another bottle of tea and gave a brief thought to the fact that if she didn't eat real food soon, she would die. She was in the middle of daydreaming about soy chicken and mashed potatoes and steamed asparagus when her phone buzzed. The text from Clancy read: *I'll be right there.*

She managed to get her teeth brushed before Clancy came riding up her driveway on a big black horse. He was in the middle of arguing with Roy when she opened the door. "Uh, hello," he said. He looked her up and down from beneath his white cowboy hat.

He must never have seen a woman in flannel pajamas before. "Hi," she said. Was he really just going to take his horse home and not even speak to her? The cowboy hat looked good on him. In fact, it magically lent him an air of competence. Before he was just some yahoo who lived across the road. Now he looked like a bona fide somebody. And sitting atop of that horse made him look...in charge. Downright...sexy. She shook her head.

"He's refusing to budge again," Clancy said, dismounting.

"Well, what's he doing here?" she asked.

He shrugged. "I don't know."

"What's that on your hat?" she asked. She pointed to what looked like a little beaded flower stuck in the hat band.

He reached up as if he'd forgotten. "Oh, that's a pansy that one of our neighbors beaded for me."

And he wore it. This big, gruff, bearded horse breeder wore a beaded pansy on his hat band. That hat was woven with testosterone and it must have shivered at the presence of the little delicate flower. It made her sort of like him. A little.

"How'd he get out?" she asked.

"Oh, Roy can get out of anything," he said. "Except chains. I'm afraid you're going to have to encourage him to go. For some reason he must think he owes you something."

"Why?" Emma asked.

"I'm not sure," he said. "Just do like you did yesterday. Rub his rump and tell him he's a good boy."

"Well, okay," she said and did as he asked. The horse flicked his tail at her and then nudged Clancy in the back.

When Clancy had mounted his black horse, he pointed to the dog and said to Emma, "Is that the dog you found?"

"Well, he found me," she said.

"Looks well taken care of."

"Oh well, I sorta gave him a bath."

"You did what?" he asked.

She shrugged. "So, shoot me for being a softy."

Clancy smiled at her and said, "Just don't name him. You'll never get rid of him then."

"Right," she said, shivering.

As Clancy and Roy were leaving, Emma said, "Um, I was wondering..."

Clancy's back stiffened.

"Would you mind terribly if I used your bathroom? I could really use a shower. I promise, I'll clean up my mess. I just...I don't know when the power is going to be on and I'm disgusting."

For a moment she really thought he was going to say no. Even if he wanted to say no, even if he absolutely did not want his household and his day disrupted, how could he say no? He'd look like a total jerk, right? And unfriendly to boot. Of course he would say yes.

"I'd rather you didn't," he said.

Emma was speechless. "Oh," she managed.

What a jerk! Of all the, well, she didn't know him well enough to think of proper adjectives for him. Maybe it was just as well. He could be a serial killer and she would have been walking into his lair. Funny though, Granny had been completely silent on this one, and she couldn't remember ever hearing of a cowboy serial killer. Although, it wasn't as if Emma was an expert on the subject like her Granny had been.

She glanced over at the outhouse and she squeezed her legs tighter. She would just drive to town to pee. Maybe one of the gas stations had showers like she'd encountered in Iowa. Or maybe she'd have to get a hotel room somewhere just to be able to bathe. But the closest hotel was an hour away and what would she do with the dog? Maybe she'd just squat behind the house. That seemed easier and quicker and less scary than the outhouse. Down and up and she'd be finished. Oh, but then she'd have splatter on her pants and what if she dribbled?

I ought to go pee in Clancy's front yard, she thought as she watched him and Roy saunter on up the driveway.

Just as she was about to go back in the house, a snowmobile came roaring down her driveway. At first she thought the driver was a little kid, but when the person took off the helmet, she realized that it was in fact, a tiny little old lady. "Hi!" the woman said. "My name is Aurora Lee and I'm your neighbor up the road."

Emma blinked at her.

As Aurora drew closer, Emma could see that she was indeed, about a hundred and eighty-five years old. Her face had so many wrinkles that the only smooth part Emma could find was on the woman's nose. Her hair, however, was still mostly black, with just a salting of gray throughout, and Emma thought, *native nationality*. The woman couldn't have been more than five foot, if that, and when she extended her hand, Emma noticed that it was half the size of her own.

Emma smiled at her and shook her hand. "I'm Emma Gordon."

"I noticed Clancy leaving," she said. "So, you've met him."

"Yes," Emma said.

"Heard you don't have any power," Aurora said.

"No," Emma said. "I don't."

"Oh jeez," she said. "And with that big outage over in Brunswick, who knows when you'll get it back on."

"Right," Emma said, her spirits sinking.

"You want to come to my house and at least get a shower?" she asked.

Tears welled in Emma's eyes. "Oh. My. God. Yes. I'll just be a minute."

Grabbing clean clothes and toiletries, she shoved her feet into her new boots and pulled on her coat, without giving a second thought that she was still in her pajamas. "I'll follow you," she said to Aurora. As she opened the door to her car, the dog jumped in and settled himself in the passenger seat. Her bladder was too full for her to argue with him.

Aurora's home was a humble log cabin with a big front porch. Inside, it was warm and decorated in a weird cross between shabby chic and Native American. She owned eyelet lace curtains and fancy doilies and tablecloths, but she also had an Indian drum that sat in the corner, and animal skins of various kinds hung on the walls and floors. Elaborately beaded bags of some sort and bead embroidered pictures hung on the walls. This was probably the neighbor who had made Clancy his pansy.

Aurora showed her the bathroom, and a few minutes later Emma lost herself in the glorious feeling of hot water. She washed her hair twice, just in case she wouldn't get another shower for a few days. When she finished scrubbing everything, she just stood under the stream, warming her skin for a while. She emerged twenty minutes later to find that Aurora had made tea for them along with homemade chocolate chip cookies.

Feeling human again, Emma sat down at the table and said, "I am so grateful for that shower. You have no idea."

"You're quite welcome," Aurora said and sipped her tea. She wore a long black woolen dress that hung just below her knees over black leggings. Around her neck she wore more of that fabulous beadwork, and silver bangles clanked on her bony birdlike wrists.

"Do you live here alone?" Emma asked.

"Sometimes," Aurora said. "I have many grandchildren who come to stay off and on. My son lives in Mille Lacs, one daughter in St. Paul and another in Grand Marais."

Emma drank her tea, ate a cookie and immediately wanted another. They were still warm and gooey! "Are you Native American?"

"I am Anishinaabe. Also known as Ojibwe."

Emma had no idea what either of those words meant.

"Chippewa," Aurora said.

"Oh, Chippewa," Emma said. She could see the living room from the kitchen, and she glanced at the various objects, but her eyes kept going to the large, beaded bag hanging over the fireplace. "Did you make that?" she asked, pointing to it.

"Yes," Aurora said. "It's known as a bandolier bag. Made with *manidoominens*."

"Maniwhominens?" Emma asked.

"Seed beads," Aurora said. "The straps are so it can be worn over the shoulder and the bag then settles at the hip."

"The flower design is gorgeous. The colors are amazing. How can you see to do that?" Emma asked.

Aurora smiled and said, "Sometimes I think it is the only reason I can still see. When I stop beading, I will die."

"Oh," Emma said.

"I saw your ad in the paper," Aurora said.

Emma had been taking a drink of her tea and she nearly spit it. "Oh, goodness," Emma said. Even though she'd put the ad in the paper for the very reason of finding her father, it made her heart flutter a little bit to realize that it was actually *in the paper*. And people would read it. Hopefully, her *father* would read it. "Well, there's no going back now."

"Tell me your story," Aurora said. Her voice was crackly but strong. "How did you come to be here?"

"I've never met my father. I only know that he was from Quail Bottom. He and my mother met at a rodeo—my mother had gone through a spell where she wanted to be a cowgirl and had spent several summers traveling to different rodeos, so who knows which one. All I know is that she spent the summer of 1986 in Minnesota, so the rodeo that I was conceived at was somewhere in this state. She said that my father talked a lot about the town that he was from. She remembered specifically that it was Quail Bottom because she thought the name was so funny."

"You don't know his name?"

"Apparently it wasn't as funny," she explained.

"I've lived here my whole life. I might be able to help."

Emma swallowed. The idea of her father had long been a fantasy. This man who would turn out to be a great person, who—had he known of her existence—would have been there for her. Would have saved her from loneliness and the onslaught of the seventeen different boyfriends that her mother made Emma pretend to like. Harold with the garlic breath. Monty with the greasy hair and the Elvis pants. Rinaldo the Italian heir to a vineyard who turned out to be a con artist who stole all her mother's jewelry. Helen had only married one of the various boyfriends, Ken Gordon, and that was who had given Emma her last name. They divorced a year later. So Emma's last name, the name she'd been known by her whole life, had belonged to a man that she had no connection to whatsoever. Yes, Dear Father would have saved her from all of that. She imagined that he was tall and blonde with eyes like hers. She imagined that he was a history professor who wore tweed jackets and smoked a pipe and knew everything there was to know. Somebody who had all the answers.

And she was counting on her father to remember her mother's name, even if Helen could not remember his. Because that's the kind of guy her father would be. Decent. Responsible. Sentimental.

And then she heard Granny add, *"Which is why he spent a wild weekend with a woman he met at a rodeo."*

But now? The whole drive up here she'd tried not to think about it. It was like one part of her was doing what she always did. Plowing forward at lightning speed, regardless of consequences, chasing after that blasted bull so she could pull on the ring. So she could *own* that stupid ring. But then the other part of her was terrified. What if she actually found him? What if he didn't like her? What if he wasn't likeable? What if he was worse than greasy Monty with the Elvis pants?

"I have one picture, but his cowboy hat covers most of his face. From what I understand, they spent the weekend together. I think she knew his last name at one point but has since forgotten it. Or maybe she forgot it right after it was over because his name is not on my birth certificate either. The only other thing I know is that his sister was a gospel singer or something like that," Emma said.

An expression crossed Aurora's face that indicated she was considering something. Emma ate another one of those warm, gooey cookies and hoped Aurora didn't notice.

"Well, you might visit Luella Sampson," Aurora said. "She owns a café in town and she's the head of the choir at the UCC church. She might be able to give you the names of some of the choir members from the eighties. That's the only church in town. There's a Lutheran church and a Catholic church up in Winchester Hollow."

"Oh, good idea," Emma said. "Do you not think that my father will answer the ad?"

Aurora shrugged. "He could be dead for all you know. Plus, you just never know who's going to answer or why."

"True. I'll go see her tomorrow," Emma said.

There was a knock at the door and as Aurora got up to answer it, Emma snuck another—a third!—one of those sinful cookies. In the other room, she heard Clancy's voice.

"Aurora," he said. "Just want to let you know that Brandon said he's finished fixing that back fence of yours. You shouldn't have any more problems with your llamas getting out."

"Well, good," Aurora said. "Would you like some cookies and tea?"

Emma decided to step around the corner then. He glanced up at her and cleared his throat. She leaned against the wall, hands hooked in the loops on her jeans and smiled at him.

"I didn't realize you had company," he said.

"Yes, Aurora here *offered* to let me use her shower," Emma said. "For which I am eternally grateful."

Realizing she had chocolate on her upper lip, she licked it off and tried to act nonchalant.

The jerk at least had the decency to blush.

"Well, you sure look a lot better," he said, eyeballing her from her head to her toes.

"Thanks," she said. "I think. Are you saying I looked bad before?"

"You looked like hell," he said.

"Oh, wow," Emma said and silently cursed herself that all she could think of was "oh, wow." She so desperately wanted a funny retort. Finally, she said, "Well, you needn't concern yourself about it. It's not as though I took the shower for you."

That was better, wasn't it? *No, I just sound stupid.*

Aurora cleared her throat. "Thank you, Clancy. Tell Brandon I'll get him the money for the repairs next week."

"No problem," he said. Then he said to Emma, "Are you expecting somebody? Because there's a car in your driveway."

Emma sped down the road because all she could think about was maybe it was her father answering her ad. Of course, she'd forgotten the dog who'd not been quick enough to make a run for the front seat. So at the end of Aurora's driveway, she backed up, retrieved the dog and then made a beeline for home.

She pulled into the driveway just as a man was getting ready to get into his vehicle and leave. She knew instantly he couldn't possibly be her father because he wasn't wearing a tweed jacket, nor was he blond. Instead, the man had long salt and pepper hair with a big ol' bushy mustache and a five o'clock shadow that was going on midnight. He wore waders and a thick red-and-white plaid flannel shirt. And his truck was ancient, rusty and smelled like fish.

Even in her car she could smell the fish.

She got out, hands sweaty, and said, "Can I help you?"

"My name is Sam Sherman," he said. "And I'm answering your ad."

5

There was no way this man was her father. Just not possible. Not once in all of her fantasies about him was the pungent odor of walleye so thick that she couldn't get near him.

She'd invited him in and realized that she had no place to sit and hadn't built a fire yet, so it was cold. Sam brought in more wood for her as she got a blaze going. The only place to sit was on the ledge of the fireplace and so they perched there with their backs to the flames. Emma's heart raced. She stared at his face, long and hard, and tried to discern if any of her features could be found, but there were too many whiskers everywhere and she couldn't *find* his face. He was nearly as hairy as Clancy.

"I uh..." He cleared his throat. "Well, shoot, I don't know what to say."

She smiled. "How did you know my mother?" she asked.

"Girl, when I saw your ad, the bottom fell out of my stomach. That whole summer was a special summer, but there was one week in particular that I could never forget. I met this woman at the rodeo up by Fargo..."

"What did she look like?"

"Light brown eyes, reddish hair."

"Tall or short," she said.

"Medium," he said. "And her name was Helen."

Emma's heart leapt. "You're sure? What was her last name?"

"We never exchanged last names," he said, looking down at the floor.

He'd described her mother to a T. Could this be her father? The name Sam didn't sound like Doug or Tug or Larry, for that matter. "Do you have any siblings?"

"I got two sisters and a brother," he said.

"Are either of your sisters gospel singers?" she asked.

He paused a moment. "Well, I mean, Maggie sings in the church choir, but she's never been a professional, if that's what you mean."

Her mother never said if her father's sister was famous or a professional or if she was just your average run-of-the-mill alto like everybody else. But she got the feeling from the way she'd said, "His sister was a gospel singer," that it had meant more than just singing in the church choir.

She looked at his hands as he picked at his nails. They were rough, beaten, weathered. "What do you do for a living, Sam?"

"I'm a fisherman," he said. "And I own a bar out on the wharf at the lake."

"How many women have you picked up at rodeos in your life?" she asked.

He looked at her then and her heart warmed. His eyes were so blue they could compete with the winter sky. His face was nearly as weathered as his hands. He ran his fingers through his thick hair that had once been dark. "Once or twice," he said. "But in 1986, Helen was the only one I met at a rodeo."

She wasn't sure what to think. It was just shy of noon. He probably got his paper early, around five. He'd responded to her in less than eight hours. She hadn't expected that. And how had he known where she lived? The contact info had been her cell phone. *Things work differently in small towns.* She knew that from experience. St. Louis wasn't a small town, but she'd been in enough of them to know.

"So, do you think you're my father?" she asked.

"Maybe," he said.

"So, why are you here? Why'd you answer that ad so quickly?" she asked.

"I thought about it all morning. I've got a son in Texas. We haven't talked in years," he said. "But I can say that I was there for most of his upbringing. Can't imagine what it must have been like for you not knowing. I knew my father well. So, I guess I was curious to see what you'd be like. And to answer any questions you might have, because if I am your father, it didn't seem right to keep you in suspense any longer. I figure you've had enough wondering."

Was he her father? She wasn't convinced. She looked nothing like him, that she could tell. But she didn't look all that much like her mother, either. So, if she didn't look like either of them, who did she look like? She always thought she'd just automatically know when she'd found the right man. Like there'd be some sort of psychic connection between them. Without words being spoken, they'd see each other and just *know*.

But looking at Sam she didn't know anything. Or feel anything. Other than respect for coming forward.

"Do you own a tweed jacket?" she asked.

Two hours later, Sam headed back to his lake and left Emma with his phone number and a confused feeling. They'd promised to get together again. He even offered to take a DNA test, which Emma thought was a good idea. Somehow, the whole thing had been so anti-climactic. She'd moved in and in less than 48 hours had accomplished what she'd came here for. Nothing was ever that easy for her. Never.

And her power still wasn't on.

She went into town and bought a package of cheap plastic cups, some dog food and a lawn chair that was on clearance from last summer. She was tired of sitting on the floor. Then she went to Luella's Café and sat down at the breakfast bar.

A black woman came up to the counter and said, "You need to see a menu?"

"Yes, please," Emma said. She glanced at the name tag. It said Luella. "Oh, you're just who I was hoping to see."

"Really, how so?" Luella had latte-colored skin and she wore her hair pulled up in a Scrunchie, the loose black curls hanging down her back. Her lower lip was pierced and she wore blue cat eyeglasses. She was of medium build, almost athletic. It was impossible to say how old she was. There was no discounting her age lines or the stray gray hairs around her temples. If Emma had to guess by looks only, she would have guessed her to be thirty-five, but the experience that radiated off the woman said she was much older.

"Uh..." Emma hesitated. How to word this? She decided to order first instead. "I'll have the lumberjack breakfast. You do serve breakfast all day, don't you?"

Luella nodded.

"Eggs scrambled, bacon, biscuits. Hash browns on the side."

Luella nodded. "So why were you looking for me?"

"Um, I was wondering, this is going to sound weird, but are there any famous gospel singers who live around here?"

Luella looked at her over the top of her glasses. "Now why would you ask a question like that?"

"Well, Aurora Lee said you might know, since you're in charge of the church choir," Emma explained.

"And why are you looking for a gospel singer?" Luella asked.

"Well, I'm really looking for my father, who had a sister who was a gospel singer."

"Why don't you just call him?"

"I don't know his name."

"Ask your momma," she said.

"She doesn't know it either. The gospel singer was one of the clues to his identity. He was from Quail Bottom. Aurora said you might be able to help me get a list of singers from the mid-eighties."

"You're the one who put that ad in the paper," she said.

Emma nodded.

"I tell you what, you come out to the church tomorrow, say around three, and I'll see what I can come up with, but I don't think I'm going to be of much help. I'm the only gospel singer around here."

"You?" Emma said. "Well, you can't be my aunt."

"Why not?" Luella said.

"Well...you're black."

"You don't say," Luella said.

"And I'm not," Emma said.

Luella laughed.

"You have any brothers?" Emma asked.

"Lots," Luella said.

"Really?" Emma said, wide-eyed. Maybe Luella was her aunt.

"You got something against black people?"

"No, not at all," Emma said. "It's just my mother never said anything about it."

"Well, my daddy was white," Luella said. "So, I'm only half."

"I don't think that matters. She never once said that my father was black or mixed or anything like that. You'd think that she would have mentioned it," Emma said.

"Well, then, maybe your mother got her stories mixed up with some other guy. Maybe your father had a ballerina for a sister," she said. "Still, the offer stands."

Emma nodded her head and thought about it a minute. What if nothing her mother told her was true? What if all those designer drugs she took in the eighties had fried her brain and she couldn't remember one guy from the next?

Her breakfast arrived and Emma ate like she hadn't eaten in years. She paid her bill, left Luella a big tip with a promise of coming to see her the next day.

When she got home the dog was waiting on her front porch. "Hello, mutt," she said to him. "I got you some food."

She looked up in time to see a black cat running across the snow toward the porch. The dog barked, the cat hissed, and Emma scolded them both as she tried to unlock the front door while holding her shopping bags. As she opened the door, the cat just scurried right on in like it owned the place. The dog, however, hung his tail and whimpered just outside the door.

"Come on," Emma said. "Get in here."

But the dog whimpered some more and looked at the cat. Emma picked the cat up, who immediately started to purr. The dog barked. "Please, get in here. It's cold."

Finally, the dog reluctantly entered the house, tail down, and face sagging. Emma looked at the cat and said, "Where did you come from?" The cat had no collar. It was sleek and shiny black with green eyes and was...Emma turned it over...a female. She sighed and set the cat down. It immediately arched its back and hissed. The dog went to the fireplace and sat down. Then he barked at the indignity of whatever it was that insulted him. She couldn't be sure.

Emma poured the food out onto the floor and even the cat ate some of it, which did not make the dog happy. He growled. "Hey, Mutt," she said. "You have to share."

If she wasn't mistaken, she'd just named the dog. Great.

There was a knock at the door. She opened it and there stood Roy. She glanced left and right, but no Clancy. How in the world had he knocked? And why was he on her porch? Again. "Oh, good God," she said to the horse. "You do not live here."

She glanced back at Mutt and the cat and said, "I'll be right back."

6

Clancy drove a nail into a 2x4 with his hammer and then cussed as he missed on the last swing and smashed his thumb. He'd been irritable all morning. Ever since he'd read the ad in the paper that his neighbor had posted about trying to find her father. So was that her game? Was she trying to find some old guy who was half dead so she could move in and lay claim to his property? He could think of no other reason why a woman like her would buy a house out here and then put that ad in the paper. There had to be something monetary in it for her. Most women didn't just do things without a payoff.

And did she really think the guy would come forth anyway? He hoped his friends and neighbors weren't that dumb. Maybe this scam had worked on some other guy in some other town. Maybe this was her *modus operandi*.

He drove another nail and watched Zeus out of the corner of his eye. The horse was a buckskin Appaloosa, at one time tall and proud and Clancy's soul mate. He stood in the pasture with his back to the woods and one eye on Clancy. He would never turn his back on a person. Not anymore. And if you were smart, you wouldn't turn your back on him, either. He was unpredictable, aggressive, and barn sour. All Clancy could manage to do for him was put water and feed out and that was it unless he was drugged. This had been going on since the accident with his dad back in

November. But he just couldn't bring himself to euthanize the horse. At first his father had held on to hope that Zeus could be rehabilitated but then, reluctantly, last week he suggested that the horse be put down. Clancy said no. In fact, they'd almost come to blows over it. Reuben had said, "That horse is miserable, Clancy. And he's going to get sicker and sicker. You have to let him go."

Clancy had railed against him, wanting to say, "*Zeus wouldn't be in this situation if it weren't for you!*" But there was no point in saying it. Reuben already knew it. What he *had* said was, "I'll decide when it's the right time to put him down. He's *my* horse. And I'm his person."

"Clancy," his father had said.

"Look, Zeus didn't give up on me when I was lost, I owe him this much." Which was true. A troubled and lonely kid, Clancy had been on the verge of tumbling down the path of self-destructive behavior, until his Grandpa had walked into the barn with Zeus, a weanling with skinny legs, a brilliant coat and an eagerness to please. While Clancy had been surrounded by plenty of horses as a child, many of them were only at the ranch for a short time. And none of them had belonged to him or been his sole responsibility. Until Zeus. And later when Clancy had wanted to run, when he'd wanted to lash out and he'd wanted to hurt things because he'd been hurt, his horse gently reminded him that he was there. And that he needed Clancy. With Zeus, he'd always had a reason to do the right thing.

He was the only horse that Clancy's Grandpa had ever bought him, and his Grandpa was gone now. Killing that horse would be like killing his Grandpa. And killing his very best friend.

Yes, but if your best friend was begging you to let him go, would you force him to live for your own selfish needs?

He drove another nail and was distracted by the sound of Roy. Only the noise was coming from the wrong direction. The hammer slammed into his finger this time, as he looked up toward the drive and saw Roy walking home, escorted by Emma. Why did that horse keep going over there? Clancy stood up straight and let out a long exhale, shaking out his left hand that was now throbbing. Well, he was slightly relieved to see that Emma wore a big heavy coat and proper boots. Not because he was worried about her getting cold, but because earlier, at Aurora's house, when she'd come around the corner wearing low-rise skin-tight jeans and a white, long-sleeved, form-fitting shirt and no shoes, he'd damn near choked. Her hair had still been partially wet and she'd looked too good to ignore. And he wanted to ignore her because...well, he didn't need the complication of a smokin' hot neighbor who was here to find a sugar daddy. But he wasn't a dumb old man with lots of money, so he was pretty sure she wouldn't be interested in him anyway. But still, she'd looked really good. Like, really good. And that really ticked him off in a completely irrational way.

"What in the heck is wrong with you, Roy?" Clancy said as they approached.

"I think your horse likes me," she said, smiling up at him. She was even better looking in the bright sunlight. Those eyes were hypnotic. That hair like a buttery halo around her face. To his dismay, he suddenly had the desire to run his fingers through those corkscrew curls. Too bad he wasn't in the market for a woman like her. Of course, he wasn't in the market for *any* woman. "Thought I'd return him for you."

"Well, thanks," he said.

"You missing a black cat?" she asked.

"No," he said, taking the rope from her.

"Have you talked to your cousin about doing some work for me?"

"Yeah, I did. He said to let me know when you get power and he'll come out and you can go over what needs to be fixed."

Emma paused and took in the view around her. "This is a gorgeous place."

"Yes," he said. He forgot sometimes just how beautiful their ranch was. He saw it every day and a person could become complacent. He watched her gaze as it went to the various red stables and barns, the dark coniferous forest behind them and the undulating snow-covered hills in the distance. The appreciation on her face made him like her just a smidge, in spite of himself. Then she looked over at Zeus. He added, "Well, thank you." Which meant, *you can leave now.* "And I'm sorry he keeps bothering you." Which meant, *whatever it is you're doing to him, please stop.* "I don't know what's getting into him. I'm just gonna go put him away." *Go. Home.*

"Okay," she said. She gave a little wave and said, "See you later."

He put Roy in his stall and said, "Listen here, you little bastard, stay on this side of the road. You got me? This side of the road. Don't know what in the world is wrong with you."

As he came back outside and picked up his hammer to resume his work, his heart all but stopped. He looked into the corral and there was Emma petting Zeus. That woman was standing right next to him, one hand on his neck and the other petting his nose. She was about six seconds from being dead!

Clancy wasn't sure what to do. If he yelled out her name and spooked Zeus, the horse could turn on Emma in a second. If he went in the pen with them, the horse would most likely react the same way. But yet, he couldn't just stand there and watch her get mauled and trampled. *Stupid woman!* What was wrong with her? What kind of person just walked into somebody else's corral without being invited, anyway?

But the more he stood there, the more he realized that Zeus was not afraid of her. Zeus wasn't being aggressive. His tail swished back and forth like he didn't have a care in the world. He was relaxed. Almost sedated.

If Clancy could have gotten his hands around that horse's neck, he'd kill him! Why would Zeus let Emma near him but not Clancy? Not Reuben or any of the hired hands who knew the horse well? It wasn't fair.

Clancy's father came up behind him then and when he saw what was happening, he said, "Good God, get her out of there!"

"Shhh," Clancy said. "I don't know what she's doing but look at him. Zeus hasn't been that relaxed since the accident."

Reuben had been around horses his whole life and he'd told Clancy last week that he'd rarely seen a horse as far gone as Zeus ever make it around the bend and back to a normal life. So Clancy understood when his father took his hat off, scratched his head said, "I'll be damned. Who is that woman?"

Clancy shrugged and looked down at his father, whose stern face and intense eyes were widened in wonder. "Our new neighbor."

"Horse trainer?"

"No," Clancy said. "I'm not sure what she does for a living."

"Well, put her on the payroll."

Emma glanced over her shoulder and her brows knit together as she looked at them. They must have looked like idiots, Clancy realized, as they were both waving their hands wildly at her, motioning for her to come to them. "Come here!" Clancy said. "Slowly."

She looked back at Zeus and whispered something in his ear and then walked toward them. She turned her back on Zeus and Clancy held his breath. The horse took a couple of steps toward her, the furthest he'd been away from the barn in ages, and Reuben must have thought the horse was coming for her, even though Clancy knew that Zeus was just following her. But not in time. Reuben stepped into the corral to grab Emma by the arm, and when he did Zeus charged toward them. Emma turned around, threw her arm up in a protective stance, and Zeus reared up on his haunches and came down hard, just as Reuben pulled her out of the pen. His hoof hit her thigh but missed everything else. Emma cried out as they pulled her the rest of the way through the railings.

Zeus went wild, bucking and kicking and thrashing into the side of the stable. The other horses in the other buildings reacted to Zeus with angry noises of their own. Clancy, Reuben and Emma just stood there and watched until Zeus had finally spent all his energy and backed himself into the corner of the corral, protected by the stable on one side and the woods and fence on the other side. There was nothing else they *could* do.

"What just happened?" Emma said.

"Are you okay?" Clancy asked.

"I can't feel my thigh!" she said. "Which is kinda sorta freaking me out!"

"Let's get you in the house and take a look at it," Clancy said.

"Oh, my God," she said. She looked at Reuben. "That horse must hate you. He was doing fine until you stepped into the ring. What *happened?*"

"A miracle," Reuben said.

7

"Sit down. On the couch," Clancy ordered her. Emma figured that was no problem since she could barely stand. He disappeared for a second and then came back with a pair of scissors.

From the couch Emma said, "What are you going to do with those?"

"Cut your pants. I need to get a look at that thigh."

"*What?!*" she said. "Oh, no. You're not cutting my two-hundred-dollar True Religion jeans!"

He blinked at her.

"Well, I didn't pay two-hundred bucks for them. I got them at a resale shop for twenty. They had no idea what they had."

"I have to see your leg, Emma."

"I will never find another pair of these jeans for twenty bucks. Never. And I don't really even care about the name, they just make my butt look good. So, no. You're not cutting them."

"Well, then drop your drawers," he said.

That shut her up for a minute. "What do you mean?"

"Take your jeans off. Emma, that leg is gonna swell. If you don't get those pants off, you'll be cutting them off, anyway. Your choice."

Emma glared at him but figured he wouldn't try any funny stuff since, the man she assumed was his father was standing right there. Unless they were a father and son tag team of perverts. She waited a moment to see if she would hear Granny's voice. But nothing came. Granny had been strangely quiet since Emma had come to Minnesota.

Both men stood there, arms folded, waiting patiently. Finally, Clancy said, "I have to look at that leg. I've seen horses snap bones in people with what looked like just a tap. Either take them off, let me cut them, or let me drive you to the ER for an x-ray."

"Oh fine," she said, only because she hadn't met the deductible on her insurance. "Turn around. Both of you." With exasperated sighs they turned around, and she took off her coat, unbuttoned her jeans and pulled them down below her knees. She was not about to take them all the way off because then she'd have to take her boots off and that was just too much work. And besides, if she had to make a mad dash for it, she wanted her shoes on. She wrapped her coat around her hips.

"Ready," she said.

"Sit down," Reuben said.

Emma dropped onto the sofa and got a good look at her leg. A large round red spot appeared on her thigh where the horse's hoof had made contact, and deep purple gouges scarred her in a vertical pattern. It didn't really hurt, because it was numb. Later, when that wore off, she would be in a world of pain. In the few seconds that she'd been sitting there, the red mark had started to swell and the purple marks were darker.

The older man went to get something out of the kitchen, while Clancy sat on the coffee table facing her and put her feet in his lap. She was so happy that she'd taken a shower earlier this morning because otherwise Clancy might have mistaken her for Bigfoot's sister. But thanks to Aurora, the legs that now rested in Clancy's lap were smooth and soft, freshly shaven. She tucked the coat tighter around her hips so that neither of them could get a peek at her pink polka-dot underwear. Wait, was her bikini line a jungle or not? She couldn't remember. Now she heard Granny, "*Always wear clean underwear, dear. You never know when you'll be in an accident."*

He ran his hand along her calf and said, "Any pain down here?"

"No," she said. "But like I said, it's sort of numb."

He massaged the calf gently and she stared at his rough hands as they worked magic. Slowly she could begin to feel the sensation of little pin pricks. He moved up her leg and his palm rested on the inside of her thigh. *That* she could feel with no problem. He turned her leg slightly inward so he could inspect the whole thigh. He twisted her leg and moved it up and down, but none of that hurt, which she assumed was a good thing. Finally, he rubbed his hand lightly over the discoloration and whistled.

"What does that mean?" she asked.

"It means you're going to have one hell of a bruise," he said. "Serves you right, too. You don't just go wandering into corrals. Zeus is an extremely dangerous horse."

"Well, how was I supposed to know that?" she said. "He looked friendly enough. In fact, he's downright gorgeous. Majestic."

Clancy looked into her eyes then, with his palm resting against her inner thigh, and her heart did an annoying double beat. She met his gaze without faltering, even though she was fairly sure that he was engaged in lewd thoughts at the moment. He slid his hands around and felt for anything out of the ordinary and a wave of dizziness overcame her. It had to be from the adrenaline dump she just experienced, right?

"When did you have your last tetanus shot?" he asked.

"Uh...two years ago, I think. In Kentucky."

"Was it routine or did you get hurt?"

She pulled her sleeve up to show him the scar that ran along her forearm. Of course, she had little flowers and such tattooed all along it to disguise it now, so it was hard to make out at first.

"You got a tetanus shot because of a tattoo?"

She ran her finger along the scar. "No, the scar."

"What happened?"

"I was in Kentucky in a tree stand with a pregnant woman. Got struck by lightning, flipped over the edge, gouged my arm on a nail on the way over. Landed in the lake. Almost drowned. Again."

He blinked at her.

She blinked back.

"Well, technically," she said, "the tree got hit by lightning, not me. But I still count it."

"Okay, well, then you won't need a new tetanus shot," he said and shook his head.

"Good. I hate needles. And vomit. And ticks."

"Well, lady, Minnesota is tick capital of the world."

"Really? Shit," she said and rubbed her eyes. "Why didn't somebody tell me that?"

"I just did."

"Before I bought a house up here."

"Would that have made a difference?" he said.

She had a fleeting vision of a tiny tick embedded in her back and sucking all the blood out of her until it was the size of a hedgehog and she was a shriveled corpse like the one at the end of that Indiana Jones movie. "It might have," she said.

He got up then to retrieve something. Taking off his coat, he headed into the kitchen and said, "Stay." As if she was a dog.

When he returned, he had an Ace bandage, and the older man had a bottle of whiskey and three glasses. He poured two fingers worth of the brown liquid into each tumbler and handed her one. She just stared at it. What time was it? Three in the afternoon? She couldn't drink this now. She'd be out like a light for the rest of the day. Of course, maybe that wasn't such a bad thing.

"I'm Reuben Stephens," he said and raised his glass to her. He took a nice long sip of his drink. "Clancy's father."

She raised her glass back to him but didn't drink from it. She was too busy concentrating on Clancy's hands. Clancy wore a thermal shirt that fit way too snugly and she could see the shape of his biceps beneath it. He wrapped the Ace bandage around her leg with great care and when he was finished, he grabbed his glass from the table and chugged it back.

"I'll get you some ice," he said.

"No, really, I can't drink this."

"Not for your drink, silly," he said. He went into the kitchen and returned with an ice pack. "For your thigh."

"Drink up," Reuben said.

"Will this help my leg?"

"No, this is to calm your nerves. And mine," Reuben said. "And it's also to celebrate. Go on, drink it. You're going to wish you had, later. That leg's gonna hurt like a son-of-a-gun. Eat lots of pineapple and citrus. Maybe even some leafy greens."

"W-why?" she asked. She took a gulp of her drink. It burned going down and she sucked a quick intake of breath as her eyes watered.

"Compounds in those foods help bruises heal faster," Clancy said.

Emma had found herself in weird situations before. Being stuck in an elevator in Miami with a Brazilian drug lord who was experiencing a nervous breakdown because his very Catholic daughter had just married a Jewish man. That was weird. And there was that whole being up in a tree stand during bow hunting season in Kentucky with a pregnant woman who went into labor. Emma remembered how angry Donna had been because a contraction had made her miss the deer, but in actuality Emma had thrown a rock to scare it off. Then Emma spent two hours trying to convince Donna to climb down and go to the hospital. Partly because of the labor and partly because of the storm that had come up. And that was when the Powers That Be decided that out of all the trees in Kentucky, the one Emma happened to be in needed to be hit by lightning. Donna had made it to the ground a good thirty seconds before the lightning strike and ended up delivering a ten pound healthy baby boy an hour later, but Emma—in addition to nearly drowning and slicing open her arm—was mentally scarred for life. And there was the time she was on her way to work and the guy on the corner was naked and doing the helicopter dance and Emma had been so distracted by it that she rear-ended a cop. Only the cop hadn't seen the pervert and there was Emma left to explain a) what a helicopter dance was and b) how that contributed to her plowing into his vehicle. Yes, plenty of weird situations. But she couldn't remember a time that she ever sat on a stranger's couch with her pants around her ankles, chugging whiskey with a father and son.

No, Emma could very proudly say that any time her pants had ever been around her ankles, she had either been sitting on the toilet or making out with one guy only.

Clancy sat across from her on the coffee table and his dad stood next to him. They both stared at her like she was the latest exhibit in a zoo. Maybe that was because of the whole pants situation. Then a gigantic dog with lots of hair came bounding into the living room and jumped onto the couch and sat next to her. She stared at the dog and it barked. She chugged the last of her whiskey and didn't feel the burn so much this time because her esophagus was already numb.

"You're going to need rice," Reuben said.

"Rice?" she asked. It felt as though her brain was on board a boat during a hurricane.

"R. Rest. I. Ice. C. Compression. E. Elevation," Reuben explained, ticking them off on his fingers.

"Oh, okay," she said feeling warm and relaxed. She looked over at the dog, which resembled a big ball of dingy white yarn, and he licked her face.

"So, how did you do it?" Reuben said.

"Do what?" she asked.

"How did you get close enough to Zeus to touch him?" Clancy asked.

She looked from one man to the other. "I just stepped in the corral, walked up to him and petted him."

They both blinked.

"No magic..." she said, wiggling her fingers. Wow, her head was *really* swimming now. "I swear."

"Nobody's been able to get near him since the accident last November," Reuben said. "Nobody."

"Except you," Clancy said.

She wasn't sure what they expected her to say. She hadn't done anything special. She just talked to him and, well, just the normal stuff she did when she approached an animal. She looked over at the mop sitting next to her.

"Are you a vet?" Reuben asked. "A trainer?"

"Look, I've never really even owned a pet, unless you count the snails that I smuggled into my bathroom when I was seven," she said. "My mother wouldn't allow it and once I grew up I never stayed in one place long enough to con...con...consider it." Animals had always liked her, though, except for the nine cats that she'd rescued. But, given their situation, Emma could understand how the first human they saw after being plunged into a lake would take on the personification of evil. As a child, when she would spend the night with her girlfriends, their pets always slept next to her and followed her around. She'd had an instant rapport with them.

Clancy looked crestfallen, but Reuben was not so deterred. "Would you like to come over a couple of times a week and just get in the pen with Zeus?"

"Dad," Clancy said.

"Maybe just you being around him would get him used to people again. You don't have to do anything special. Just talk to him."

"Dad, it's too dangerous," Clancy said.

"We have to try," Reuben said. "We have to. There's a chance now, Clancy. A real chance that we won't have to put him down."

Emma put her hand up and they both looked at her. "Can I put my pants back on now?"

"No," Clancy said.

"No?" Uh-oh. *Come on Granny, where's my warning?*

"No offense, but they fit like they're painted on. Getting them up over your leg is going to be really painful. I'll get you an old pair of sweats or something."

Clancy was being really nice to her, she realized. Nicer than he'd been since she met him. All she'd had to do was get kicked in the leg by a one-ton horse to accomplish it. She just realized what he'd said, that he'd get her a pair of his sweats. That meant she would have to take these boots off anyway. Ugh.

Her vision blurred as she untied the laces. She was certain that there was only one lace per boot but it suddenly seemed like there were three or four. Finally, she got them off and she stood, pulled her pants all the way off, and her coat slipped to the ground. Then she fell, rather unceremoniously, back onto the couch. "Be careful there," Reuben said. "Can I help?"

"No, no, I got it," she said.

"I'm going to go check on Zeus," he said, and headed for the door. "See if he hurt himself when he had his fit."

Emma rested her head on the back of the couch, wondering how in the heck this had happened. It was all Roy's fault. She was going to kick his butt as soon as she was sober, even if she had to stand on a stool to do it. She glanced over at the dog and he licked her face again.

"Really?" she asked.

It whimpered.

Clancy came back with pants for her and as much as she tried to get up on her own, she just couldn't manage it. Her legs were wobbly, the room spun, and her spine was relaxed like a Slinky. And her leg freakin' hurt! Finally, after watching her maneuver like a cockroach for several moments, Clancy helped her up. "You okay?" he said.

"Yep," she said. She tried to get her foot into the pants leg, but the pants kept moving on her. She added, "Nope."

"What can I do?" he asked.

"Just let me hold onto that big rock of shoulder there and I should be fine."

"Okay," he said, smiling down at her.

"And don't do that."

"Do what?" he asked.

"Smile."

"Fine, I won't smile," he said.

"Good. Because that's magic, let me tell you."

"All right."

She put her hand on his shoulder and held onto the sweats with one hand, but no matter how many times her leg did ballet moves she could not get her foot to hit the hole to save her life. At one point her leg ended up over top of her arm and she was certain that there was evil magic at work here. She'd been dressing herself since she was three. This shouldn't be that difficult.

"You need me to do something else?" he asked. "How about if you sit down on the couch? Sitting would be better."

"No, no, I can do this. If I can't do this, I'm just gonna give up on life."

"Okay, fine," he said. "But I didn't take you for a quitter."

"All right, how about you hold the pants," she said. He chuckled and she said, "No smiling! I told you."

"I'm not smiling," he said. "I'm laughing with a straight face. I swear to you."

He held the pants while she held onto his big, hard, warm shoulders and tried to put her foot in the hole without thinking about how those shoulders had bulging biceps below them. *Point toes. Raise leg. Oh crap, that was his arm this time. Goddammit. Breathe. Reset. Lift leg. Point toes...* She watched her foot and it just kept going in weird directions. "Are you moving those pants around on me?" she asked.

"No," he said, laughing. "I swear."

"Good, because...yeah." She was drunk. *Note to self: Stick to beer and wine.*

Finally, one foot made it through the goal and mentally she sighed with relief. After a few seconds the other foot found the correct pants leg and she raised her hands over her head and cried out, "Score!" That threw her off balance and she fell into Clancy's chest and he was so surprised by it that he grabbed her butt to steady himself.

She looked up into his sparkling blue eyes and said, "I know you probably don't mean anything by it, but your hands are on my rump."

"Right," he said and removed them.

"Okay," she said. "Well, that was fun! But I gotta be going."

"Uh," he said. "I think you should stay here for a few hours."

"Why?" she asked.

"Until the whiskey wears off."

"Nope."

"Emma. There is no way you'll be able to get your shoes tied."

Oh man! Those stupid boots. They had laces that had to be tied and stuff. She almost rallied but had visions of being hogtied with her own bootlaces and finally just said, "But, my dog. And my cat. I didn't put out any water for them. And they'll freeze! Because everything up here freakin' freezes because it's like the freakin'

North Pole only farther south. Like a mid-North Pole. Whatever. Please save my animals from the winter wasteland that is my living room. *Please?* I know you're kind of prickly and don't like me, but don't take that out on my animals."

"I'll take care of it," he said.

He gave her a small shove and she plopped onto the couch and felt her head wobble and then fall back onto the cushions. The next thing she knew somebody moved her feet around so that she was lying horizontally. Not an unpleasant feeling. Then there was a soft blanket and tucking involved. The warm couch cradled her, and her head stopped spinning. Then the unmistakable smell of dog breath lulled her to sleep.

8

Emma woke to see a face that could have been the model for a porcelain doll. A little girl with long silky brown hair and huge brown eyes clutched a stuffed horse and stared down at Emma with intense scrutiny. The little girl smiled when she noticed Emma was awake and she said in a pixie voice, "Is your hair being bad?"

Emma tried to sit up but there was a massive fur ball lying on top of her. She shoved it and it reluctantly moved. Her cat tumbled down off the back of the couch and when she swung her legs around, her feet hit Mutt in the head. Poor dog. The room spun as she sat up and the whole debacle with the horse flooded back to her. She buried her head in her hands. *Is there any way I can get out of here and retain my dignity?*

The little girl stood waiting for an answer. Emma said, "No, my hair is always like this."

"Always?" the girl smiled.

"Pretty much."

"I like it!" the girl said.

Emma smiled back at her. "I like yours, too."

"My name is Caitlin Christine Michler. I'm eight."

"I'm Emma Rose Gordon, and I'm twenty-eight."

"My mommy is twenty-eight, too! When's your birthday?"

"Uh..." Emma had to think for a minute because, well, her synapses weren't firing this morning. At least not as well as Caitlin's. "March seventh."

"My mommy's is March second!" Caitlin said. She held up her stuffed horse. "This is Chester."

"Oh, nice to meet you, Chester," Emma said. She hunted around for her boots and as she knelt down next to the couch a cramp clenched her left leg and she grimaced. She found one boot under the couch but the other was across the room lying by the miniature Wookiee. Emma stood to retrieve it, but pain like red fire burned her entire thigh. She winced and hobbled across the room. When she turned around, Caitlin stood right behind her and Emma almost tripped over her.

"My Grandpa says that you can work magic. That you might be able to save Zeus."

"Oh, really?" Emma said. *I have to get out of here now!*

"Yes, and Uncle Clancy says that you wouldn't know your bum from a hole in the ground, but Grandpa said he didn't care. That what you did with Zeus was amazing."

Emma stopped and stared at Caitlin. "Your uncle's such a pleasant man, isn't he?"

"Oh, yes. I love my Uncle Clancy. His last girlfriend was really mean to him but I told him not to worry. When I grow up I will take care of him. He doesn't need a wife."

"Well, good luck, kid," Emma said.

"I haven't seen my Grandpa this happy in months. All because of you and Zeus."

Panic rose in Emma's chest. She was not a horse whisperer. In fact, she'd never even heard of the term until she saw that tear-jerking movie. Reuben Stephens was getting his hopes up and she was going to let him down.

"Because, you know, Grandpa was the reason for that accident."

Emma stopped. "He was?"

Caitlin nodded. Her big brown eyes grew bigger with each nod. "He went chasing after Grandma..." her voice trailed off. "In the snow..."

Emma's heart pounded in her chest.

And then the tears started. Caitlin said, "Oh, Emma, if you can save Zeus, even a little bit, I'd get my Grandpa back. He just hasn't been the same. And I want my Grandpa back."

The next thing Emma knew she was down on her knees hugging the little girl, wondering, *Where is your mother?*

And then the back door opened and a young woman walked in from the cold, bringing snow on her boots as she did so. "Caitlin! What are you doing?"

Caitlin wiped her eyes and said, "Mommy, this is Emma. The lady who is going to save Zeus."

"Oh, don't say that, Caitlin," Emma said. She turned to the woman who also had brown hair and eyes and said, "Hi, I just moved in across the road."

"Oh, nice to meet you," she said. "I'm Peri Michler. I'm Clancy's sister. We live up in Cloquette. We try to come down as often as we can."

The two shook hands and Emma suddenly felt really uncomfortable standing in the living room wearing Clancy's sweatpants. She looked out the window and was confused by the daylight. She knew she'd had to have slept a few hours or she wouldn't be sober with a pounding headache, so it should have been dark. "Oh, my gosh. Is it tomorrow?"

"It's never tomorrow," Caitlin said. "That's a pipe dream. It's always today."

Emma blinked at her and Peri said, "She's a little melodramatic."

Suddenly Emma burst out laughing and Peri joined her.

"I really have to get going. I've got places to be today. And hopefully I'll get my electricity turned on," Emma said. It had been four days since she'd slept in a real bed. She needed to buy one. She needed to do a lot of things. "Um, give your dad and your brother my thanks for everything."

"Oh, sure," the woman said. Peri was taller than Emma by about three inches or so, but she somehow still came across as petite. Small boned. "Um, what Caitlin said to you is true, though, all drama aside. I haven't seen my dad like this in a long time. If there's anything you can do with Zeus. I mean, even if you just show up and try."

Emma took a deep breath and remembered that horse rearing up and his nostrils flaring. Good thing Reuben and Clancy had pulled her out of there when they did. "I, well, of course," she said. Because how could she say no? She firmly believed that if you had it within your power to make somebody else's world better that you should do it.

Emma excused herself and went to the bathroom where she put her jeans and boots on with clenched teeth. Her leg hurt. A lot. On her way out of the bathroom she found her jacket and checked the pocket for her phone and said, "Do you know if anybody has seen my phone?"

Caitlin grabbed it from the end table and handed it to her, fully charged. Clancy or Reuben must have had the same brand of phone and used their charger. She looked down at Caitlin, whose expression was akin to a puppy dog, and said, "Nice meeting you, kid."

"Nice meeting you," Caitlin said. And then she curtsied.

Emma wasn't about to attempt a curtsy back, but instead hobbled out of the house. Mutt and the cat followed on her heels. Her leg throbbed to the point of distraction. But she'd be damned if she asked either Clancy or Reuben for a ride. She would barely be able to make eye contact after yesterday's events. Passing out like that!

Her face reddened as she thought, *Clancy groped my butt!*

"To keep you both from falling over, you lush," her Granny's voice said.

Clancy was driving nails again when he looked up in time to see Emma walk down the driveway back to her house with her dog and cat trailing along behind her. Her white hat with the fluffy ball on the end of it bounced with each step. It didn't surprise him to see her limping. Not after that hoof to the thigh. Coming up behind him was Roy and he walked right past Clancy without a care in the world as he headed down the road after her.

Clancy whistled and Roy stopped. "Can you at least *pretend* like you can't get out of your pen? For me? Just humor me," he said. Roy shook his head and Clancy added. "Go on. Get back to your pen."

Roy looked back down the road after Emma and then for whatever reason decided to obey Clancy's request. *Probably because he'll just go over there later,* Clancy thought. *What kind of juju does that woman have going on, anyway?*

He'd thought about her soft thigh and her pink polka-dotted underwear all damn night long, just like he thought of them now. He remembered the perfect curve of her calf and her insanely gorgeous olive skin. He'd thought about the feeling of her butt in his hands. Way more than a handful. She wasn't one of those teeny-tiny skinny things shaped like a fourteen-year-old boy. She was nicely padded where she was supposed to be. But even so, even after getting a taste of all of that, the thing he really wanted to do was run his hands through her hair. Basically, he thought about her way too much and was more than irritated to realize that he'd spent half of the night lying awake with his mind wandering down to the woman snoozing on his couch.

And why did he think of that right now?

Because she was working juju, that's why.

And she'd stolen his dog, too! Brandi always slept in his room. But not last night. She wouldn't leave Emma's side. Brandi even braved Emma's cat to sleep near her.

Maybe he should just go for it. Sleep with her and get it over with. Not that she'd be willing. But if she would be willing, then the mystery would be gone, and he could get back to his regularly scheduled program of mare ovulation and stallion semen. It said a lot about the state of his life when his horses had more sex than he did. Well, that wasn't entirely his fault. His ex-fiancé had something to do with that. She'd made him like Zeus. Gun-shy.

No, he wanted nothing to do with his neighbor. Besides he wasn't very good at meaningless sex. He didn't have to be in love, necessarily, but he had to have some feelings for the woman involved. Otherwise, it left him feeling hollow.

Soft, warm, perfectly toned thigh.

He cleared his head by thinking of the piles of poop in the stalls that he'd need to clean out later and drove another nail home and thought better of going for "it." Steaming piles of horse poop were enough to shake any carnal thoughts from anybody's head. Sleeping with Emma might erase the mystery she held, but he realized that then he'd have to contend with the fact that he'd slept with his neighbor. It would make those comings and goings horribly awkward. Especially once she started expecting things from him. Like expensive gifts. The horse poop had made everything clearer. As always.

He looked up just in time to see a hawk swoop down and Emma jumped and yelled, and the dog barked and the cat hissed and Clancy smiled. *Don't smile,* she'd told him. *That's magic.* He'd never had a woman say that to him before. He reminded himself that women would say anything when they wanted something.

The hawk followed Emma all the way back to her house. He knew because he watched. And he realized that she was right. Those jeans did make her butt look awesome and he was happy that she'd been stubborn enough to save them.

Damn woman.

9

Emma did not make it to the UCC church to get the list of singers from Luella on Friday because she just didn't feel like it. Screw it. Her leg was killing her. Not to mention the electric man came and turned her power on just before sunset. When the furnace kicked on, a horrible smell permeated the house and set the fire alarm off. Now, why the fire alarm didn't go off when Emma actually had a fire going, she would never know.

She assessed the whole house for the first time. The beautiful hardwood floors needed some polishing. All the trim around the doors and windows was wood, too. The main floor consisted of the living room, dining room, kitchen, a bath and either a bedroom or an office. She suspected an office, since there were built-in bookcases. The upstairs had three bedrooms and a bathroom. The master bedroom had two enormous windows that let in a ton of sunshine and a spectacular view of a tiny lake. She could see Aurora's house and her group of llamas from her window. Emma vaguely remembered in the description of the house that the property was attached to a small lake and it seemed the two neighbors shared it. Lakefront property in Minnesota was usually expensive.

She guessed that her house was so cheap because the basement was little more than a dirt cellar with a four-foot-high ceiling, there was no modern stove, it had tiny closets, the toilet didn't work, everything needed updating and painting, the porch was falling down and there were so many outbuildings in need of repair that it would take months—and lots of money—to clean it all up. And the economy sucked. And not for the first time, she thought, *I need a job.*

Well, whatever. She liked it. And she was convinced that underneath it all, she had a diamond.

From the front bedroom upstairs, she had a direct view across Lady Slipper Lane and the expanse of fields and corrals and barns and stables that was Stephens Horse Farm. She could see it from her living room window, too, but it was more eye-level and the trees and brush semi-blocked the view. As she thought about what an idiot she'd been yesterday, her cheeks flushed red. Getting kicked by a possessed horse, the whole pants around her ankles thing and then...the whiskey. Then sleeping all night long on their sofa! They must think she was a lush indeed. And Clancy's large hand on her thigh. His strong shoulders holding her up while she tried to fit her rogue feet into his pants. But it wasn't entirely her fault. The man really was gorgeous. But he was kind of a jerk. And now they expected her to go back over there and pet their crazed horse! She really didn't know how she got herself in these situations.

From the kitchen all she could see were tall snow-covered pines. Total wilderness. And it was soothing to look at. Much better to look at the trees than to look at the Stephens farm. It did less weird things to her heartbeat.

Ned Barstow, the former owner of this place, had not taken particularly good care of it. Had he been sick, maybe? Lazy? Old? In the detached garage she'd found oil stains and work benches and thought that he must have worked on cars a lot. Maybe he'd been a mechanic. And either he or the people before him had horses or goats or something, because there was a barn with a stable and a small corral that, of course, needed mending. And every now and then she came upon a box of his belongings. Not neatly packed or anything, just stuff tossed here and there.

And she still needed to fix that toilet.

She was finally able to unpack, even though she didn't have any furniture. She bought cleaning supplies and paint and spent most of Saturday cleaning and disinfecting everything, even though she was in excruciating pain and no amount of Advil really seemed to help. She couldn't remember what Reuben had told her that she needed to do with her leg. Something about corn or rice or some sort of grain? But she did buy a fresh pineapple and ate almost the whole thing for lunch.

Just before six, there was a knock at the door. She opened it to find a pimply faced delivery boy with her pepperoni and double cheese pizza. "Hi," she said.

He blushed and handed her the pizza. "Thirteen-forty-five," he said.

She paid him and gave him a nice tip. Granny had been a waitress for thirty-seven years and one thing Emma knew was that even if a waitress got paid twenty bucks an hour, she'd still be underpaid.

"Is that your cat?" he asked and pointed to the end of the porch. Emma stuck her head out and a fluffy tabby ran right inside her house.

She rolled her eyes and just shrugged at him. "I guess it is now," she said.

She sat on the floor on her sleeping bag eating her pizza with two cats swarming around her, checking out the pizza, while trying to keep an appropriate distance from each other, and Mutt in the corner whining. "Your food is over there," she said, pointing. The black cat looked at her. *Oh really, darling. You cannot possibly expect me to eat that dreadful dog food for one more day. I shan't do it. I just shan't.*

The tabby, however, didn't seem as picky and chowed down. Mutt whined some more. *Oh, look Emma, that big mean orange fur ball is eating my food!*

She checked her Facebook page and noticed that she had numerous notifications on a post that she didn't remember making. She clicked on it and it went to a picture of herself lying on Clancy's couch with her cat molded to her head, Clancy's dog Brandi lying on her feet and Mutt stretched out to the side of her, half off the couch. The status was: *Strange bedfellows times three.*

She pinched the bridge of her nose. *Clancy, you jerk! You hijacked my Facebook page!*

She smiled in spite of herself. She did a search for him and sent him a friend request.

There was another knock at the door, and she knew if she left the pizza on the floor the food would be gone by the time she returned, so she picked up the box and answered the door, box in hand. What greeted her was a filthy man swaying in his boots, reeking of alcohol and badly in need of a bath and a shave. She couldn't make out the color of his eyes because they were so bloodshot that any other color was lost. He removed his Elmer Fudd hat and Emma could see that his hair was blond and stuck out and his hooked-nose almost protruded over his upper lip.

"Ex...shuze me," he said. "But would you by any..." *Burp.* "By any chance be one Emma...?" He pulled a newspaper out of his jacket pocket, burped again and said, "Gordon. Emma Gordon?" Then he looked up at her and smiled. "And do you have any whiskey?"

She banged her head on the door frame and said, "Yes, I'm Emma. No, I have no whiskey."

"I might be your father," he said. "Are you sure you don't have any whiskey?"

"Positive. I have wine."

"Oooh, that'll do."

Emma weighed whether or not she should let him in. She was fairly sure this was the same guy she saw on the street corner with Clancy the other day and he'd said that the guy was harmless. Still. "Are you armed?" she asked.

He held out his two arms. So he was a literal sort of guy.

"Well, I have mace. Just so you know. And I will use it. Take your coat and boots off and leave them on the porch," she said. The coat stunk and if he had a weapon that was probably where he'd hide it. "Please, come in before another cat finds me."

Mutt barked and Emma introduced the animals. "That's Mutt," she said. Then she pointed to the black cat and said, "That's Thing 1, and that one over there is Thing 2. Do you want some pizza?"

"Oh, yes," he said. "I'm starving."

"Figured as much." She went to the kitchen and got the little one-serving plastic bottles of wine that she'd bought out of a bin at the grocery store. Merlot, Pinot Grigio, Cabernet, Moscato. She dumped the bag, probably fifteen bottles in all, on the floor and the man's eyes lit up. "I think the white wines have slightly less alcohol," she said. "Just so you know."

He picked up one of the bottles of red.

They sat down in the floor and she offered him the pizza, which he took. "So, you're my dad, are you?" she asked. She wasn't positive but he might have been wearing a tweed jacket. Honestly, he looked ancient, but she had the feeling that he couldn't have been more than fifty-five. But she seriously rethought why she'd made him take off his boots. His feet were rancid.

"I believe so," he said.

Emma took a bite of pizza and said, "So, what's your story?"

"I'm a drunk."

Well, at least he was honest. "And you're homeless?"

"More or less."

Great.

"I wasn't always like this. Wife left me. Took my kids. And my money."

"And your dignity, apparently," she said.

He narrowed his eyes on her. "Yes, that, too." He ate a bite of pizza. "I used to be a cowboy. I had champion belts and trophies."

That got her attention.

"Met your mother at a rodeo at the fairgrounds in St. Paul," he said. *Hiccup.* "Helen Wishnanewshkiki was a gorgeous woman. But I loved her laugh. She had a laugh that could heal all wounds. After you heard her laugh just once, didn't really matter what she looked like."

Emma's eyes watered. That was a fair description of her mother. She hugged herself because she suddenly realized how much she missed her. Oh, she'd gone months without seeing her mother before, but in the back of her mind she knew she'd still be there. That at some point they'd meet up and do lunch or sit curled-up on the couch and munch popcorn while watching Liam Neeson movies. That was over. It would be hard to have any relationship at all, now that her mother was permanently in Belize. In the future they'd only see each other maybe a week at Christmas time. She felt suddenly very alone.

"I thought about her for months after. Tried to talk her into coming home with me. She wouldn't do it. Said she had other rodeos in her future," he said. "I think it's because of my ugly mug." He turned sideways and pointed to his nose.

Emma cleared her throat. "D-do you have a sister?"

"Did once."

"Was she a gospel singer?"

"Nope."

Emma studied the man. Could he be her father? If Sam Sherman had met her mother at a rodeo that summer it didn't mean that this man couldn't have, too. She could have met them both and slept with both of them. That was so not out of the realm of possibility when it came to her mother. In fact, it would have been just like Helen to sleep her way across one end of the state to the next.

He ate another piece of pizza and Emma just watched him, looking for herself in his face. He had tomato sauce on his chin and she reached out with a paper towel and wiped it off. How could a cowboy end up like this? How could a person completely fall apart because one person left? Emma had never had that kind of love before. Anytime she'd ever been dumped, life went on. Sure there were tears and binges of ice-cream and a photo-deleting ceremony, but she still got out of bed the next day and carried on. In fact, after a week or two, she actually welcomed the challenge of what lay ahead. What was next? She'd never belonged to somebody so entirely that his leaving would destroy her. What had happened to this man?

They stared at each other with a fire blazing behind them. Emma had realized that even with the furnace, without furniture in the house, it was drafty and cold and there was something comforting about the fire, so she'd built one anyway.

"I don't want nothing from you," he said and guzzled the wine. "I just wanted to see you. You're awfully pretty. And I wanted...just thought you'd like to know the truth of it."

She smiled at him and she poured all the compassion and understanding that she could into it.

And then his brow relaxed, and he smiled back, and for a split second, there was a genuine connection between them. Emma had pointedly, mentally, sent him compassion and he had felt it.

"Oh, and I wanted to give you this," he said after a moment. He pulled a rodeo champion belt buckle out of his pocket. "One of the few things I got left."

"Oh, no," she said. "You keep that."

"No, no. I got nothing to offer you but this and I want you to have something to remember me by." If he was her father, she didn't really need anything to remember him by. She had her life. That was the greatest thing he could have given her. *If* he was her father. But it seemed so important to him that she take it, so she did.

She cleared her throat of the knot that had formed there. "Well, okay. Thank you," she said. "Would you like to take a shower and clean up?"

"Oh, no. I can't impose on you like that."

"Look, somebody offered me the use of her shower when I needed it and it darn near saved my sanity," she said.

He looked long and hard at her, unflinching and surprisingly steady. "Well, all right, then."

"There's just one thing. If you're going to use my shower, I need to know your name."

"Martin Pepper," he said. "Most people call me Marty."

"Well, it's nice to meet you, Marty."

She reached out then and squeezed his hand and Marty looked like he might cry. When was the last time anybody had touched him voluntarily? When was the last time he'd had a hug and was told that everything would be okay? When was the last time this man mattered at all? She smiled at him and he willingly returned it.

Then Thing 1 pounced on Thing 2, and Thing 2 skidded against the wall, jumped up on the ledge of the fireplace, singed his tail and ran down the hall.

10

Early Sunday morning Clancy was outside in the front yard building a snow family with Caitlin. Not just a snowman. No, his achingly adorable and terrifyingly manipulative niece wanted an entire family of snow people. So, of course, that meant Clancy had to do it. Caitlin had Clancy wrapped around both of her pinkies with no effort whatsoever. The first time she'd looked up at him from beneath her pink knitted hat on the day she was born, Clancy knew that there was nothing he wouldn't do for her. It was if she'd instinctively felt it. *This one is weak. I'll make him my plaything. Mwa ha ha ha haaaaa.*

They'd finished the Papa Snowman and were on to the Mama Snowman when his sister came outside and handed him a mug of hot coffee. His dad was inside making breakfast and Clancy's stomach growled in anticipation. After all, his dad was making his world-famous waffles and omelets. "She got her way, huh?" Peri asked.

"Well, it's not as if there's not enough snow for it," Clancy said and shrugged.

"Sucker," she said.

Clancy took a drink of his coffee and handed it back to her. "I have to roll the body for the Baby Snowman, while Caitlin decorates Mama."

Peri laughed. "So, the new neighbor," she hedged.

"What about her?" Clancy asked.

"She's really attractive," Peri said.

"Uh-huh." He rolled the snow around making the ball bigger. "I suppose."

"What do you think of her?"

He stopped and took another drink from the mug she held and then handed it back again. "Hadn't given her a whole lot of thought, period." Until she'd gotten in the pen with Zeus and rubbed his neck. He'd been so angry. So covetous. So...enchanted by it.

It was Peri's turn to say, "Uh-huh."

He stared at his sister. She was a few years younger than he was and he hadn't really started to like her until she was about twelve. Prior to that she'd been a pain in his side. It was amazing how she could return right back to being that pain in an instant. She took a drink of her own coffee and smiled at him.

"What?" he asked.

"Okay," she said. "She's not just attractive, she's sexy. I can't believe you didn't notice. I mean, I'm straight and I noticed."

"I don't pay attention to that kind of thing anymore, Peri," he said. *Although her skin was so smooth, and her thighs were perfect.* "The price is too high."

"Right," she said. "It might not be any of my business, but I kind of think it is my business since you and seven of your best buddies stalked my boyfriend when I was eighteen. So, I'm going to give you my opinion."

"That stalking thing was for your own well-being," he said. "The guy could have been a criminal. A total loser."

"Uh-huh, well, since you can invade my privacy like that, I can give you unsolicited advice."

"I'm not dating my next-door neighbor, Peri."

"Well, good grief, Clancy. Date *somebody*, then."

"Peri."

"Look, you are attractive. You're smart. You're good with kids and animals. You're financially sound. You could have any woman you wanted. But you're going to have to go looking," she said. "You've scared everybody off!"

"You don't get it," he said.

"What?"

"I haven't met a woman yet that actually wants *me*."

Peri blinked. "You sound like a woman. 'All men want me for is my body.'"

"They want the financial soundness, as you put it," he said. He placed the bottom snowball of the Baby Snowman next to its mother. "And that's being kind about it."

"Is this about Diane?" she asked and rolled her eyes.

"Of course it's about Diane," he said. "And it's about Tanya and Angie too. They were more excited about getting their claws into this farm than they were about me. When I meet somebody who doesn't care about the farm and wants me regardless, I'll think about it."

"Well, how are you going to find out if you don't at least *date* somebody?" she asked, raising her voice.

"It's so much work," he said.

"What?" she asked.

"Dating is work. And the payoff is not that high."

She blinked at him.

"Seriously. I'm pretty content."

"No, you're not," she said. "You're stuck in a rut and you just don't know the difference."

"Can we drop this?" he asked.

"Sure," she said. Clancy made the rest of the body and the head for the Baby, while Caitlin stuck two dark-colored rocks on Mama's face for eyes. She gave him her brightest smile and Clancy flushed with avuncular pride. She was so precious.

"All finished?" Peri asked.

"No, no," Caitlin said. "I think they should have twins, too."

"*Three* snow babies?" he asked, and Caitlin nodded.

"And maybe a horse," she said.

"I don't know how to make a snow horse," Clancy said.

"Sure you do," Caitlin said. "You can do anything."

His heart swelled, even though he was fairly sure he was being played.

"Did I tell you that I saw Diane the other day?" Peri said.

Clancy stopped. He liked to forget that Diane existed. In his mind when they'd broken up, she went off to some other planet, not two towns over. Two towns over meant that he could, theoretically, run into her occasionally. And it wasn't as though he had feelings for her. He wasn't worried that if he saw Diane that he'd break down or get jealous. He was more concerned that if he saw her, he'd light her on fire or commit some equally jail-worthy behavior. Not only did he not want to go to jail and have Caitlin think he was an awful person, but he didn't want Diane to know that her deception cut him that deeply. And well, if he set her on fire, she'd probably realize it.

"What do I care?" he said.

Peri shrugged. "Apparently she's moved on. Saw her on the arm of that real-estate guy, Hudspeth. Had a ring on her finger the size of a turtle."

"I'll say a prayer for him," he said. *How do I build a snow horse?*

"My point is, Clancy," she said. "If you don't move on and find happiness and she does then she wins."

"Peri, I'm going to say this one more time and then we're going to drop it. Okay? Because you're starting to make me feel like you did when you were five."

"Bossy with unrealistic expectations?"

"Irritated," he said. "I don't have to have a wife, girlfriend or lover to be happy. I can be perfectly happy with Dad, the horses, you, Caitlin and my friends."

"So, you're what, celibate?"

"Celebrate, celebrate!" Caitlin chanted.

"I'm saying I don't need a meaningful relationship with a female to make me a happy camper. Okay? So, drop it. I don't give a damn if Diane wins. She can't win if I'm not even playing the game."

"So, you are celibate." Peri stated.

"I'm not celibate. Not that it's any of your business. But I just can't do meaningless 'physical contact,'" he said. "I've tried."

"And you're too stupid to find something meaningful," she said from behind her cup. He got ready to say something, but she held up a hand. "Okay, okay, Mister Grumpypants. I'll shut up now."

She hadn't called him Mister Grumpypants in years.

Clancy looked down at Caitlin's red chafed cheeks and dark eyes and a pang hit him in the gut. *I'm going to break her heart because I have no idea how to make a snow horse.*

Emma went to church on Sunday morning at the church Luella sang for and that most of the townspeople attended. At least it seemed like most of the townsfolk. The place was packed. And aside from the fact that Emma, having attended Catholic school her whole life, kept wanting to stand or kneel every time the minister paused, she rather enjoyed the experience.

Especially the choir. They sang several songs that Emma didn't recognize but that didn't matter because they moved her just the same. Luella was the soloist, and her voice was infused with an emotion that was primal and brutal and Emma couldn't remember a time that she'd heard anything that made her want to sob and shout for joy all at the same time. There was a timbre to Luella's voice that spoke of sorrow and suffering, and Emma hoped that Luella had just been born that way because to think that Luella had suffered enough to sound like that made Emma overwhelmingly sad.

They did a song called "Lord Don't Move My Mountain," and at that moment the world seemed to fade away for Emma. The only thing she was aware of was that voice, that song, and those words. And when it was all over she felt as though she'd just been thrown from a warm sauna into the frozen tundra. She'd lost herself so completely that she wasn't even aware when she shouted out, "Damn, girl! You can sing!"

The silence that followed was abrupt and all encompassing. Even the babies stopped crying. After a moment of being stared at, Emma added, "Well, she can." And her face burned with embarrassment.

"Thank you," Luella said into the microphone and then the minister picked up the cue and finished services.

Afterward Emma found Luella and said, "Sorry about that. I've just never heard anything like it."

Luella smiled and said, "That's the highest compliment you can give me. It means I reached you."

"Oh, you reached me all right."

"Do you sing?" Luella asked.

"I used to in school. Now I just sing in the shower."

"You still need that list of choir members?" Luella asked.

"I do. That was the real reason I came today. Things have just been crazy out at my house."

Luella motioned her back toward the offices of the church. She entered one that had a sign on it that read CHOIR. There was somebody waiting in the office already. A tall and slender woman of about forty stood and said, "Hello. You must be Emma."

Emma nodded.

"I'm Zoe," she said. The woman had expressive eyes and short dishwater-blonde hair. She had a faint scar that ran from the corner of her mouth to her chin. "I run the animal shelter."

"Oh, nice to meet you," Emma said.

"I finished downloading those music files for you," Zoe said to Luella.

Luella smiled and said to Emma, "I hate computers. And they hate me. I get Zoe to do anything electronic." Luella rummaged through the papers on her desk and handed a folder to Emma. "That's a list of the choir members from 1986. I don't know how much it will help. I've crossed off the members who've died and underlined the ones that I don't know. I grew up here, moved away and then I didn't move back until 1998, so if there is anybody on that list who moved or quit coming to the church or whatever, between '86 and '98 I won't know anything about them."

"Wow," Emma said. "That's incredibly nice of you. I don't know what to say."

"Can I get a favor in return?" Luella asked.

"If I can," Emma said.

"You moved into Ned Barstow's old place, right?"

"Yes," Emma said.

"He's my brother."

"Really? I bought your brother's house?"

"Well, my half-brother. We have the same dad, different moms."

"I keep finding boxes of his stuff laying around, do you want it?" Emma asked.

"Not really. He moved a few years ago. Just decided to put the house up on the market this past fall. I think most of whatever he left behind he could live without, so, I can too. But anyway, my point is that you have a neighbor then, Aurora," she said. "That woman's got to be ninety."

"At least," Zoe said. "I think she's older."

"Would you just pop in on her every once in a while and make sure she's okay? Maybe give her a call when bad weather is supposed to hit?"

The image of Aurora riding the snowmobile came to mind and Emma didn't really think Aurora needed any help with anything, but there was no reason she couldn't be concerned in the guise of neighborliness. "Sure," Emma said.

"Ned used to make sure she had plenty of wood, but since he moved, I'm not sure who's been doing it for her," Luella said.

"Probably Clancy," Emma said.

Luella shrugged. "Maybe."

"But for God's sake," Zoe said. "Do not tell her that you're there to check on her."

"No," Luella said. "Don't even say anything like, 'Do you need anything?' Because she will shoo you out that front door in nothing flat."

"You have to pretend *you* need something," Zoe said.

"Like, go and ask her for firewood and then offer to chop it while you're there. Of course, chopping more than you need and leaving her a big pile of it," Luella said.

"And whatever you do, don't smoke anything she offers you," Zoe said. "She's got some major wacky weed that she uses for ceremonies."

Emma laughed. "I can handle her." She was used to spirited old ladies. They made her happy.

I I

When Emma arrived home, she was surprised to find a couch on her porch. It was non-descript brown, but clean. In fact, it barely looked used at all. The note said: *Emma: I have a friend whose grandmother moved to a nursing home and was going to give this couch away. It's practically new. It might smell like old-lady perfume. – Sam P.S. Please come out to my bar tonight. We're having live music. I'll buy you a beer.*

Once inside, she noticed that Marty, who'd spent the night on the floor of the kitchen next to the stove, was gone. Not that she'd invited him to stay. That was just where he'd ended up. Well, at least he was clean when he left. She'd given him a pair of her socks and burned his. It made her cringe to think that he put those disgusting clothes back on after taking a shower, but she wasn't a miracle worker. She had no clothes to replace his. Not that he would have taken them, anyway. He'd fought her over the socks, even.

Emma dragged the couch into her house and situated it in front of the fireplace so that she could feel the warmth of the fire, and yet still see out her windows. All the animals had scattered when they heard the couch scrape across the floor, but now they peeked their heads into the living room, one by one. She went to the fridge and made herself a sandwich, and when she returned, both cats and the dog were on the couch. Thing 1 and Thing 2 were, of course, on opposite ends with the dog in the middle. Mutt seemed to register the fact that he was in the middle of them and jumped down to the floor.

Note to self: Take cats to vet. Get them fixed? And Mutt. She glanced over at the dog who dragged his butt across the floor. *Check for worms.*

She spent the rest of the afternoon painting the living room and swallowing more Advil and inspecting her thigh with fascination. The colors reminded her of a Monet painting except a painting didn't hurt. Around five, she propped her leg up on the arm of the couch and fell asleep. She awoke a few hours later with Thing 2 sprawled out along her torso, purring, and Thing 1 wrapped around her head, while Mutt lay on her foot. She'd never be cold again.

She grabbed her phone, snapped a picture of Thing 2 and posted it to Facebook with the status: *My newest sleeping partner.*

There was a text from Clancy's cousin, Brandon. They texted back and forth on what work needed to be done, how much he charged, and what she was willing to pay, and set up a date for him to start.

She decided to go out to Sam's and take him up on his offer of a beer, but only one because she was driving. The problem was she didn't know how to dress. What if she had to walk somewhere that there was snow? Or what if she broke down? Should she just throw her boots in the backseat for safe measure? Should she dress like an Eskimo since she was going out after dark and it was four degrees?

Finally, she decided on a nice pair of jeans, a black form-fitting sweater and very impractical spike-heeled black boots that came up to her knees. *Another note to self: Buy a pair of cowboy boots.* They looked good with jeans and were somewhat weatherproof.

She stopped and asked somebody at the gas station for directions to Sam's. Turned out it was called "Sam's Waterfront Saloon and Grill" and was located right at the edge of Odin Lake, which was frozen solid. She gazed out at the frozen lake in darkness and the quarter moon illuminated little huts nestled on the surface. Those must be ice-fishing huts! She'd heard about that peculiar custom.

Sam caught sight of her as she entered the bar and came down to her end. "Hey," he said. He looked very different, although just as woolly. He was clean—no fish smell—and he wore a blue flannel shirt to match his eyes and a pair of Wranglers.

"Hi," she said. "Thank you, so much, for the couch. It was my intention to go shopping for furniture tomorrow. So that's one thing to strike off my list. And it's neutral so it'll go with whatever else I buy."

"Good," he said. "Glad you could use it. What kind of beer you drinking?"

She started to answer and then he said, "No, no, let me pick for you." He popped the cap off a bottle and poured it into a glass. It was a dark beer, so most likely a porter or a stout. "This one is brewed up north in Duluth. I think you'll like it."

She took a drink. "Mmmmm...a hint of vanilla, with lots of coffee and cocoa flavors."

Sam smiled. "A connoisseur."

"What kind of music do you have lined up for tonight?" she asked.

"A local blues band."

As the band set up, they continued to talk. She must have rambled for half an hour. She told him some of the crazy stuff she'd done in her life and how she really missed her Granny and now her mom. She told him these things because he asked. And because he seemed genuinely interested.

"So, what did you study in college?" he asked.

Emma shrugged. "I got a degree in business. Which has clearly gotten me nowhere. It took me five years to get a four-year degree because I took two semesters off."

"Why?" he asked. His chin rested in his hand and his eyes never left her face.

"Well, one semester I took a road trip with my Granny. We went back to Maine where she's from originally, to see the last of her people. She wanted to see a couple of her cousins before they died, but she couldn't go alone. We were gone almost eight weeks. Just driving down those winding roads, stopping at this relative's house for a few days and that relative's house for a few days. And you know what? That trip was mostly uneventful except we were at this expensive seafood restaurant and she choked on a fish bone and some guy at the next table performed the Heimlich on her. She threw up everywhere and then I passed out. I hate vomit. I got a scar from when my head hit the table. Look," she said and raised her mass of curls to reveal the white scar right at her hairline. "But, anyway, oh, and the only other thing that happened was we got lost in a cemetery. Like, a huge cemetery and it was getting dark, and we couldn't find the car and then Granny started crying..."

Emma teared up and Sam straightened. "What?" he asked.

"Granny started crying because she said she was having so much fun with me and that her time was short and that she was going to miss me when she was gone." Emma started to cry. "All because we couldn't find the freakin' car."

"Oh," Sam said, not sure what to do. "I'm...well...it'll be okay."

She dabbed at her eyes and he handed her a paper napkin. "We didn't make that trip to see her cousins before they died, we made that trip to see her cousins before *she* died. She knew it was coming. She passed in her sleep the night we got home from that road trip. That was almost three years ago."

Sam was quiet.

"She was my one true constant," Emma said. "My north hand on the compass of life."

"She sounds wonderful," he said.

"That woman knew everything about serial killers. I mean everything."

Sam smiled. "And the other semester? Why'd you take it off?"

"Oh, my cousin Suzanne, her little girl got meningitis and went deaf from it, so I took off a semester to learn sign language and help with the transition. I mean, can you imagine being six and suddenly you just can't hear? She was terrified."

Sam studied her. "Jimmy Hollingsworth's son is deaf. He's a car salesman here in town."

"Well, I hope his family learned how to sign because, I can tell you, Janelle was terrified and lonely."

"So you got a degree in business and now you're not qualified to do a damn thing," Sam said.

"Exactly. And what about you?"

Sam looked past her and nodded at a patron and Emma turned around to see who it was. Clancy Stephens sauntered in wearing one of those studly tight-fitting rodeo shirts, jeans and his cowboy hat. The reason those shirts were so dangerous was because they were contoured and fitted, and if a person—like Clancy Stephens, for example—had more muscles than he ought to... *And holy shit, he'd shaved his face!* Hadn't cut his hair, which she was glad of, but he'd shaved all that beard. She studied him and his swagger for a minute and wondered if he really was swaggering or if she just imagined it because she thought he *ought* to have a swagger. He was a right and good, square-jawed specimen of testosterone, but she preferred him when he wore his mechanics coveralls. He was more manageable like that. Less...defined.

Emma rolled her eyes, pretending that his freshly shaven face hadn't almost sent her into cardiac arrest.

"You don't like your neighbor?" Sam asked.

"He's kind of a jerk," Emma said. A gorgeous jerk, but a jerk all the same.

"I heard what you did," Sam said. "With Zeus. All I can say is that took some balls."

"Balls?" she said. "I thought he was a perfectly nice, sweet horse. I had no idea what I was getting into. So, anyway...about you." They had discussed Sam's childhood and his parents quite a bit during that first two-hour visit, but he'd been pretty vague once they got past 1986.

"Not much to tell," he said. "I grew up here, did a tour in Kuwait, got married, got divorced, and lost my son."

"Lost him? What do you mean *lost*? I thought you told me before that he was in Texas?"

"He had very different ideas than I did about what it means to be a man."

"Is he gay?" she asked because some people took issue with that.

"No, he's not gay. Well, I don't really know, he could be. But, no I don't think so." Sam wiped down the bar and quit talking.

"Drugs?" she asked in a calm and sympathetic voice.

Sam stopped rubbing the counter and looked at her. He nodded and the pain showed all over his face. "Probably dead in a ditch by now."

"Good intentions and a strong will aren't always enough," she said.

"Meaning?"

"Meaning you should think of him as having something like diabetes. If a diabetic gets insulin it regulates blood sugar and he's fine. If he doesn't get the insulin, his body reacts. Sweats, dizziness, thirst. If an addict doesn't get his drug, his body reacts in a similar way. They will do anything to stop that because it feels like they're dying. I knew a kid in high school who had diabetes and he told me one time that when his blood sugar dropped below sixty that he'd run over a little old lady with a lawnmower to get sugar."

Sam's eyes grew cold. "Then I guess my son shouldn't have started using in the first place, huh?"

Emma was about to say something but she felt a presence behind her. Standing almost close enough to touch her. "How's your leg, Emma?" Clancy said.

She turned around to him and said, "It's black and blue today, thank you very much."

"Whoa, what's with the attitude? I never told you to go in that corral. You did that all on your own."

She opened her mouth to say something and then didn't. He had a point.

"Dad wants to know if you'll come over tomorrow? Yeah?"

Emma thought about it. She really didn't want to get kicked in the head by that horse. But she instinctively knew that he wouldn't hurt her. He'd been fine when it was just the two of them. It wasn't until Reuben had stepped into the pen that things went south. "Just keep your dad out of the pen," she said.

"We'll all stay out," Clancy said. "We're taking no chances. Heck, if you just want to approach him from the outside of the fence, that's fine with me. If he lets you near him that would be something."

She studied his face. He seemed genuinely excited about any help that she could give, even though she doubted that she could do anything. Yesterday had been a fluke. Yesterday had worked because she hadn't known she should be afraid of Zeus. She just ambled into Satan's paddock without knowing it was Satan. Clancy worked his jaw, probably a nervous habit when he thought about things that upset him and she said, "Why aren't you married?" Seriously. How did a guy who looked like that and owned a successful ranch—at least it seemed successful—not come with a gorgeous wife on his arm?

He looked down at her and swigged his beer. "To be as honest as I can be, I don't like women much."

"Wow," she said. She didn't understand that kind of broad generalizing. Unless it was about ticks because ticks only had one purpose in life and that was to suck the blood from another living creature. But people? How could he just declare something about an entire group based on the tiny percentage of women he'd encountered? "But surely there are women you like. Your mother?"

He glared at her.

She raised her hands in surrender. Okay, he had mommy issues.

"Your sister? Caitlin?"

"Peri and Caitlin are the exceptions to the rule," he said.

"Ahh, because those are the two women whose behavior you can predict," she said. "You know they adore you. There's no guesswork and no effort."

The band started playing and he said, "Change the subject."

"Well, go somewhere else if you don't like what I'm talking about. Nobody's forcing you to stand here next to me."

It was his turn to open his mouth and then shut it before words came out. And just why was he standing here talking to her, anyway?

"So how long are you staying?" he asked.

"Staying? Where?"

"Here in town."

"I bought a house," she said. "I plan on staying awhile. Why? You in a hurry to see me leave?"

He shrugged and studied the head on his beer. "You just don't seem like the type to stay in one place very long."

"People change," she said.

"People don't change," he declared.

"They do so."

He gave her a condescending look. It felt like he'd just patted her on the head.

"You stopped sucking your thumb, didn't you? You stopped messing your pants, right? We all move on, change, and come to different stages of our life. We change for the thing worth changing for," she said.

"And that fifteen acres across the road is worth changing for? You could have bought fifteen acres anywhere," he said.

"But my father is from here. Seemed like just as good a place as any."

He nodded. "About your father. If you find him, then everything will be all right? The fairy tale ending?"

She shrugged. "It's a start."

She drank a little more of her beer and suddenly there were deep-fried mushrooms and pickles on a plate in front of her. Her mouth instantly watered. "Did you order these?" she asked.

"No," he said and snatched a mushroom. He rolled it around in his mouth because it was super hot.

She glanced up and Sam nodded to her from the other end of the bar. "On the house," he shouted above the band.

Clancy looked from Sam to Emma and back to Sam and then a knowing expression crossed his face. "Oh, wow, that was fast."

"What?" she said.

"You two an item already? You've been here what, a week?" he said. "He's a bit old for you, though."

She stared him right in the eye and said, "Does it make you feel good to pick apart what I do?"

"Well, no...I..."

"You what?" she said. "If you must know, Sam and I are friends. He might be my dad."

Clancy glanced up at Sam quickly. "No kidding?" he said quietly. As if it was something to be ashamed of.

Emma shrugged. "He knew my mother. Whether or not it was his dart that hit the bullseye, we're not sure. He's agreed to a DNA test."

100 of Rett MacPherson

"Oh..." Clancy said. "I didn't realize..."

"Probably because you're too busy judging me."

His shoulders rolled forward as if he realized he'd behaved like a slug. He held his hands up in surrender and said, "Okay, yeah. You're right. I was judging you. Just trying to find your angle."

She studied him as he stole another one of her mushrooms. He moved to the music, and she wondered what his story was. What had made him so judgmental? Especially of women. Well, usually a sour relationship with a woman would make you judgmental of other women. That was a no brainer. But, it felt like more.

"Angle? You assume I have an angle? I can't just...*be?*" she asked.

"Everybody's after something," he said and took a drink.

"Everybody's *looking* for something," she said. "There's a difference."

"Well, what are you looking for?" he asked.

"Why should I tell you?" she asked. "So you can poke fun at me again? Were you a bully in school?"

"Just making conversation," he said and tipped his hat to her. That stupid hat with that stupid beaded flower on it.

"Well, if it's conversation you're after, why don't you tell me what *you're* looking for?" she asked.

"Peace and quiet," he said and turned all the way to face her. "I just want to ride my horses, watch my niece grow up, maybe do some fishing on the weekends."

"Malarky," she said.

Why did he have to look so incredibly sexy while being a condescending, antagonistic jerk?

The music slowed way down, and Clancy said, "They're playing Eddie Boyd's 'Third Degree.' You want to dance?"

She almost choked on her beer. "You just belittled me and insulted my entire sex" she asked. "Why should I dance with you?"

"It's just a dance. In a bar. It's what people do. What do you say?" he asked and leaned in close to her. She could smell man soap and a mild aftershave and the faintest scent of sawdust. "Want to move your hips?"

She glanced at the plate on the bar. Fried pickles were her absolute favorite. "Granny, you got an opinion on this?" she asked and looked heavenward.

Clancy's eyes darted around. "Who are you talking to?"

"Nobody," she said.

Clancy moved a few feet away from her and put one hand on his abdomen and began to sway his hips. He did the little "come here" motion with his other hand. His smile was positively devilish. Emma laughed and rolled her eyes, and thought, *you don't want to be left alone. You're looking for human contact, whether you know it or not.*

"Come on. You hear that music? How can you stand still?"

And then she did what Emma always did. She went for it. Why not? She'd always had that motto of regretting the things she never did more than regretting the things she *did* do. She'd seen that on one of those Facebook meme things with the words superimposed on a picture of a beach sunset. Of course, she did regret some things that she'd done. Like that whole city block burning down, but she couldn't live in fear of the next pyrotechnic indiscretion.

On stage, the singer threw his whole heart and soul into "The Third Degree." He sang about how bad love was killing him and he couldn't stand no more of the third degree and the guy on the left started wailing on the guitar and the sensual rhythm of the bass line made her want to move. Clancy took Emma by the hand and pulled her straight to him. Chest to chest. No room between them. She was fairly sure she'd stopped breathing. His warm, hard body was pressed against her and the sultry licks on the guitar just ground on.

He swayed left to right and then back the other way and he swayed her along with him. He pulled her right hand close into his chest and his other hand settled lightly on her left hip. She gazed into his eyes and determined, without any hesitation, that he was horny as hell. At that moment, he wanted her. It was unmistakable, even if he wouldn't admit it. He might not like women, but he definitely *liked* women. She met his gaze just like she met his movements. He wedged his right leg between hers and moved his hand up to the middle of her back and pulled her as close as he could without grafting her to him.

They said absolutely nothing at all to each other because what was the point? Small talk would have been ridiculous. And besides, she was fairly certain that he'd scold her for ruining the song, anyway. So, she closed her eyes and lost herself in that guitar and that raspy baritone singing about bad love and the feel of Clancy's hand on her back, holding her there like she'd slip away at any moment. His thigh worked slightly upward between her legs and she thought, *he's done this before. And he's damned good at it.*

When the song stopped, she jolted back to reality. He stared deep into her eyes and she stared right back. The song had been over for a while, the band had moved on to a faster number, but Clancy and Emma couldn't seem to separate. Finally, she mumbled, "I'm gonna go eat my pickles now."

Clancy smiled and said, "Thanks for the dance."

12

She made her way back to her barstool, sat down, and tried to catch her breath. That was one hot dance. Clancy moved on to a table of people that he knew, which was probably wise. *Wow, damn.* That was the second time in less than twelve hours that a musical experience had shaken her to the very core. For two vastly different reasons, but they were both equally rapturous. She chowed down on her pickles and talked to Sam some more. She denied any and all accusations about a liaison between her and Clancy and Sam just winked at her. Uh-huh, sure right. *No seriously, the guy hates me,* she tried to argue. But Sam would have none of it.

She ordered a glass of water and listened to the band some more and watched Sam work the bar and mingle with his people. It struck her that Sam enjoyed his work. He may have felt like a failure in certain areas, and he might downplay his life as not much to talk about, but he seemed really happy. And in her experience that was a lot to talk about. Fifteen different stuffed fish hung on the brown paneled wall behind the bar and white Christmas lights twinkled all about the whole place. They'd even been strung along the outside deck. She could stay here all evening and listen to this band and eat this food and dance with hot horsemen and be quite content.

She talked Sam into letting her take a selfie of the two of them with her phone. Then she posted it to Facebook with the status:

What do you guys think? He says he's my father. So excited to be here and to get to know him.

About half an hour later, Clancy got up and said good night to his friends—Emma noticed because she'd been stealing glances at him the whole time—and as he headed for the door, he threw his hand up and said, "Later, Sam." And Sam nodded. Then Clancy looked at her, touched the brim of his hat and walked outside.

She was deep in thought, replaying their dance together, when he rushed back in the door and said to her, "Come here. You've got to see this."

"What?" she said. She worried that by the look on her face, Clancy would know she'd been thinking about him. And that dance. And his hips. And *her* hips matching his.

He motioned for her. "Just come on. I bet you've never seen this before."

She told Sam she'd be back and ran outside to see what Clancy wanted. When she emerged from the bar, she noticed that the sky had an odd cast to it. He took her hand and guided her around the back of the building where the deck hung out over the lake. And there, above the horizon, were the northern lights. Aurora borealis.

She sucked in her breath. "Oh my God," she said.

Streams of green light danced across the sky, flowing and ebbing like a silk ribbon. Along the bottom edge of the lights were pinkish red bursts that twinkled and rippled until it had all worked its way off into the western part of the sky. Then another burst came from the eastern side, this time five or six fingers of light spread above the whole frozen lake with a mauve dusting right in the center. It was as if the lake was a witch's cauldron and it released the electric green smoke, illuminating the entire night sky.

Clancy still held her hand.

"Amazing, isn't it?" he asked.

"I...I...I'm completely speechless."

They watched in silence a bit longer, hearing only the muffled sound of the music coming from within the bar. Somebody in one of the fishing huts out on the lake stepped out and shouted, "Oh jeez! Will you look at that?"

Emma giggled, but she was afraid to look away from the sky for too long. Afraid she'd miss something.

"It's caused by a coronal mass eruption," he said. "Can you imagine what ancient man must have thought when he looked up and saw this?"

No. She couldn't. She couldn't think of anything. Her mind was empty. It was simply in awe of what she was seeing.

"He must have thought it was the end of the world," Clancy said.

"Or the beginning," Emma said.

Clancy turned her slightly toward him and then bent down and kissed her. Slow and firm. She leaned in and kissed him back. His tongue found hers and she welcomed it and he leaned her up against the railing of the deck and she arched her back and he kissed her deeper, longer, as her hands pulled him closer. Her fingers went to the hair that curled on his collar. His hands caressed her shoulders and up to her neck and to her jaw and then...

"Will you look at those lights, Norbert?" somebody said as the door to the bar opened and a flood of people came out to huddle on the deck and gawk up at the sky.

Emma shivered because she was outside without a coat, and Clancy pulled her closer and rubbed her arms. They stood there like that until the lights were finished and then she said, "It's late. I have to let the dog out."

He smiled at her and said, "You coming over tomorrow?"

"Yes," she said. "But not until after I go buy some furniture."

"Fair enough."

She went back in after her coat and hugged Sam good night. "Thanks again for the couch," she said.

"My pleasure. You come back," Sam said. "Anytime."

"I will," she said.

As she headed out to her car, Clancy stood next to his truck, watching her. She fumbled with the keys—which had nothing to do with the cold and everything to do with the blood rushing through all the parts of her body—and finally got her car started.

"Just a dance, my butt. Stupid cowboy hats," she said to herself.

She'd completely forgotten to get video footage of the northern lights!

13

Clancy was at the local feed and tack store the next morning, picking up supplies for the horses, when he saw Zoe Williams in the vitamin and supplement aisle. She ran the animal shelter out by the river and was one of the nicest people he'd ever met. What he'd said to Emma the night before about not liking women was a defense. A deflection, so she'd change the subject. It was what he always said in response to questions about marriage, but he hadn't had to use it in a while. Most people in Quail Bottom had quit asking. They knew why he wasn't married. They knew about Diane.

"Clancy!" Zoe said. She held her basket in one hand and a box of flea shampoo in the other.

Zoe's animal shelter survived on a government grant and donations, and she worked tirelessly with no benefits, other than a paycheck, day and night. She was a veterinarian by trade and could have easily had a private practice—with benefits—but she'd told him on more than one occasion that Rover was not the animal she needed to help. Any veterinarian could help Rover. She was in a unique position to be able to help the animals that would otherwise die if not for crossing her path. Mostly wild animals, but also domesticated animals that were in danger from abuse or neglect.

"How's it going?" he asked.

"Some asshole shot a bald eagle last week."

Clancy shook his head. "Federal crime."

"A bald eagle. Why would anybody do something like that?"

"To be able to thump his chest and say he did so," Clancy answered.

"Bragging rights? Disgusting," she said.

"Did the eagle make it?"

"Barely," she said. "He'll probably never fly again, though."

"You keepin' him or are you shipping him out?" Clancy asked. Zoe had room at her shelter to keep some rehabbed animals that couldn't be integrated back into the wild. But the sheer lack of space meant she couldn't keep all of them. Some went off to zoos. Some went to sanctuaries. If the eagle couldn't fly again, he couldn't be released.

"I put out feelers to see if any of the long-term shelters had room," she said.

"You let us know if there's anything we can do," he said. Aside from giving her more money there wasn't much he could do, since it was against the law in Minnesota to keep a wild animal more than twenty-four hours without a rehab permit from the DNR. Clancy didn't have one of those.

"Your monthly donation is enough," she said. "And the use of your trailers, on occasion. I'd like to get a trailer of my own, though, so I don't have to keep asking you and the Keeners."

"Maybe we could have a charity rodeo or something and raise money toward a trailer."

She smiled. "That would be awesome," she said. "If you're serious, we can discuss it later."

"Oh, I'm totally serious," he said. "Whatever we can do."

"Thanks," she said.

"I should get going," he said. "I still have to finish repairing that shelter."

"So, I hear your neighbor has a way with horses," Zoe said as he was about to leave.

"Well, with Zeus, anyway," he said. And Roy, for some reason. His mind flashed to that kiss last night. And the dance, which had been more erotic than the kiss. He'd asked her to dance on the spur of the moment. He hadn't planned it. In fact, he'd been ready to walk away but then the band started playing that song and she looked so fabulous sitting there. Maybe it had been that mass of wild curls and that black sweater that clung to all the right places. Maybe it was because he'd just accused her of having a thing with Sam—a thought that had irritated him far more than it should have—and he didn't want her to leave thinking he was an ass with a capital "A." Which he was. Or at least, he had been at that moment. He liked to think that he wasn't a jerk all of the time. So he insulted her, accused her, danced with her, kissed her and left. Right, she'd think he was a regular Prince Charming for sure. But why did he care what she thought? That had been bothering him all morning. His thoughts were all scrambled.

And she'd met his gaze without flinching and her eyes had been as lust-filled as his. That was new. Finding a woman whose thoughts seemed to pour right out of her eyes.

"Clancy?" Zoe said.

He snapped out of his reverie and said, "She's coming out today to see if the first time was just a fluke."

"I'd like to watch," Zoe said.

Clancy looked at her quizzically.

"If she's got a nice touch, Clancy, I could offer her a job. I can't keep doing this by myself," she said.

He shrugged. "I get the feeling she's not going to stay long," he said.

"Really? Why not?" she asked. "She seems happy to be here."

Maybe it was more like he was hoping she wouldn't stay. *Then why did you dance with her? Why did you kiss her? Why did you rush back into that bar and yank her outside to see the northern lights?* Because he knew she'd think it was awesome and he'd wanted to share it with her. Holy Christ.

The woman had to move.

"I don't know," he said. "Just a feeling I got. Once she gets what she wants I think she'll move on. She doesn't seem to have had a very permanent sort of past. Putting down roots doesn't seem like her thing."

"Well, maybe she hasn't found what she's looking for yet," Zoe said. "Everybody's got to find the right pasture, you know."

Clancy shrugged again. "She'll be out later today. Can you come out then?"

"Text me when she gets there."

"You betcha," Clancy said.

Emma stood at the edge of the corral, heart beating and palms sweating even though it was twenty-five degrees today. From what she understood, though, that was a minor heatwave for the end of January. Zeus stood over in his corner of the pen, flicking his tail, and watched the world cautiously.

"Just do whatever you did the other day," Reuben said. "If his ears flick back and he levels his head at you, get out of there."

"Just try not to run," Clancy said.

"Horses sense everything you feel," Zoe said. "So, if you go in there scared, he'll know it."

"Right," Emma said. Why did she feel like she needed a hockey helmet and a baseball bat? "You guys just stay back. Like, go over there and do something. Pretend you're not watching."

The three of them walked over to the water pump and discussed the cleanliness of the buckets, while Emma raised one leg and stood on the bottom rung of the fence railing. Zeus didn't move. She was right in his line of vision, so he had to have seen her. After a few moments she threw one leg over the top rung and then brought the other leg over and then sat there. Zeus blinked and fluttered his nostrils.

She looked off toward the pasture and then studied her nails. Zeus tossed his head about.

After sitting there awhile, she got down and took a few steps, using the fence as her guide. She wasn't about to step into the middle of the corral. Not yet. When she was about ten feet from where Zeus was cornered, she climbed back up onto the fence and sat there.

The horse flicked his nostrils. She had sugar cubes in her pocket, but she wanted to see if he would come to her without the bribe. Ten minutes went by and nothing. She glanced over her shoulder and her three guardians stood by the water pump scratching their heads. Emma sat there another ten minutes, determined to out-wait the horse. Another fifteen minutes went by and her butt hurt, and her legs were losing the feeling in them and finally, Zeus took one step toward her.

Her heart beat a little faster and he stopped.

Deep breath, Emma. Deep breath.

She decided to throw caution to the wind and talk to him. The only thing she'd done the other day that was different from what everyone else had done was walk into his territory completely oblivious to the threat. She hadn't been the least bit afraid because she hadn't known she was supposed to be. Everybody else—from Reuben to Clancy to his vet to his dentist and on down the line— was afraid of him. She was on the fence, if he decided to attack, all she had to do was swing her legs over.

"Hey Zeus," she said. "Remember me?"

He took two more steps.

"That's it, big fella."

He took a few more steps and a few more until he stood right in front of her. Emma smiled to herself. This was a good start. He extended his nose as far as he could without getting any nearer and sniffed her coat. Then her pocket. His lips quivered. He wanted the sugar cubes.

She raised her hand cautiously and said, "I'm going to have to put my hand in my pocket. Okay?"

Slowly, she reached in and brought out the sugar cubes and held them out, palm up. Zeus took the cubes with his lips, leaving her palm wet with saliva. She made no move to pet him but just sat in his presence. Her body relaxed even more and she smiled. He stepped over closer and nudged her hand with his nose. She heard Reuben say something to Clancy, but she couldn't make out what it was.

The horse raised his head and moved even closer. Emma petted the side of his face and stroked his nose. His forelock was matted and tangled, but she didn't dare touch it. He moved in as close as he could without shoving her off the fence and rested his head on her shoulder. Did he want her to hug him? She briefly thought of his teeth gnashing into her flesh, but she wore a thick coat, and she didn't think he could do much damage. It wasn't like he was a carnivore with big fangs. She reached up with both arms, laid her head against his and gave him a hug. "It's okay," she said. She stroked the side of his neck for several minutes and then thought she should probably quit for the day. She didn't want to overtax him, but she wasn't sure how to initiate the separation without startling him.

"I've got to go now, okay?"

All of her movements were like she was swimming in molasses. Very deliberate and slow. She raised one leg over the top of the fence and Zeus whinnied. Emma stopped, waited ten seconds, and then continued when she realized he wasn't going to attack. When she thought it was safe, she pulled the other leg over and instead of jumping down, she turned and took each rung deliberately.

When she approached Reuben, Clancy and Zoe, she was smiling from ear to ear. Zoe and Clancy were astonished, but Reuben, well, Reuben swiped at tears.

"Same time tomorrow?" she said to them.

"Right," Clancy said.

When she got home there was a man standing on her front porch, which didn't seem all that unusual for her as of late. He scratched his head, paced from one end of the porch to the other, and when he saw her approach, his back stiffened. It was as if he'd been practicing a speech and now suddenly had to deliver it. "You Emma Gordon?" he asked.

"That's me," she said.

"I'm James Hollingsworth, you can call me Jim."

"Hi Jim, what can I do for you?"

"I'm answering your ad," he said. "I think I might be your father."

"You don't say?" she said. How did these people keep getting her home address? She had specifically listed her cell phone number in the ad, and yet all three of them had bypassed the phone altogether and come straight to her house.

"I own the used car lot in town," he said.

"Oh, Sam mentioned you. You've got the boy who's deaf," she said.

"Why yes," he said.

"I'd like to meet him sometime. What are his interests?"

James blinked. "Um, comic books. Especially the Avengers."

"Oh," she said. "I ought to be able to handle that."

"He's not real great at lip reading yet."

"Oh, I sign."

"You do?" he asked.

"Yeah," she said. "Won't you come in? All I have is a couch right now. My bedroom furniture is being delivered tomorrow, but the rest of my living room stuff won't be delivered for a couple of days. I figure I don't really need a dining room set just yet. Maybe I'll hit some garage sales this spring. Are garage sales big up here?"

She unlocked the door and they went inside just as all three animals barreled out the front door. "Sorry about them," she said. "Have a seat."

He sat down and said, "This is...this is weird for me. My wife, well, she didn't want me to come out here."

"Oh," Emma said. "Why not?"

"Well, until I saw your ad, she was blissfully happy as the only woman who'd borne me children. You're a threat," he said.

James had dark hair and hazel eyes and was almost rounder than he was tall. His cheeks were ruddy. High blood pressure, she thought. He was by far the youngest of the three paternal candidates, with Marty being the oldest. In fact, he didn't look much past forty, but he had to be. Jim sat with both feet on the floor looking straight ahead, while Emma faced him with one leg bent under the other.

"How many children do you have?" she said.

"Not counting you, two. My wife is ten years younger than me, so I got a late start at this parenting thing. My boy is ten and my daughter is four."

"So, what makes you think you're my father?" she asked.

He cleared his throat. "It was the summer I turned eighteen," he said.

Oh, for Pete's sake. Her mother had robbed the cradle on this one.

"I wasn't always heavy like this," he said. "At one time I was a regular stud. That summer I rode my neighbor's horse...barrel racing. I still hold one of the records for the state. I bought my own horse a few years later, moved to South Dakota, but by the time I was twenty-eight I'd sold him and given up the horse life and moved to Minneapolis."

"Why?"

"Took on lots of other responsibilities. When I met my wife I thought I should come home to Quail Bottom. This is a great place to raise a family. But anyway, that summer I met your mother, I was like a wild mustang, let me tell you. She took to me and she showed me the ways of..."

"I don't need those kinds of details," she said.

"Well, she was my first," he said. "I could never forget her. Helen Wisniewski. For years I just remembered her as Helen Polish, because I couldn't remember how to spell her last name. I have a picture of the two of us."

"You do?" she said, perking up.

"Yes ma'am." He pulled a photograph out of his pocket and sure enough, there was Helen. The picture looked like it had been taken by a journalist. The two of them faced each other over the top of a corral. He was inside the ring in his sky-blue shirt and cowboy hat and her mom stood outside. The real focus of the picture was the horse in front. It appeared as though her mom and James just happened to be in the picture. Still, it touched her that he'd kept it.

She couldn't tell by looking whether or not he was the same man in the photograph her mother had given her. She glanced up at him and smiled. "There are two other men who've answered my ad. My mom got around that summer."

"She was a wild one," he said with a wistful expression.

"Would you be willing to take a DNA test? My mother never told me my dad's name."

"Well sure," he said. "I guess that would be all right."

Emma handed him back the picture.

"No, you keep it," he said. "I'm afraid my wife would rip it up."

14

The next day Emma's bedroom furniture was delivered and her packages from her cousin arrived, too. The boxes from her cousin were a godsend because they had sheets and quilts, towels and some books. So as soon as her bed arrived she was able to put sheets on it and the thoughts of getting to sleep in her own bed made her so giddy that she felt like dancing.

Now if she could just get her toilet fixed so that she wouldn't have to use the outhouse or drive into town every time the urge hit her, she might start to feel like a bona fide human being. She'd always wondered when having a bladder built like an iron-side ship would come in handy and it finally had. She'd called several plumbers and none of them could fit her in the schedule for another week, and Brandon, who was due out sometime next week, had no plumbing experience.

In one of the sheds outside she found some old wooden chairs that she put on the front porch with the intention of painting them come spring. She also found two old side tables that she put in the bedroom, since all she'd bought for that room was the bed and the dresser and curtains and a big pink rug with mauve roses on it.

The next few days were a blur. She took the animals to the vet and got everybody fixed and dewormed just in time to arrive home and find a three-legged terrier sitting on her front porch. *Another trip to the vet.* She had dinner with Sam, who taught her the finer points of gin rummy, and lunch with Aurora, who told her as much gossip about the town as she could take in. Zoe offered her a job four days a week at the animal shelter, and Emma jumped at the chance. She'd start in a few weeks once she got her house in some sort of order.

She'd been over to the Stephens farm every day working on Zeus. Reuben insisted Emma stay for dinner most nights, which at first seemed awkward considering the dance and the kiss that she'd shared with Clancy. He acted like it had never happened, but Emma replayed it in her head over and over. But by the second night she had them both laughing with stories of her adventures in Arizona, and it was like the three of them had been doing this for years. Neither Reuben nor Clancy batted an eye when she told them that she'd stolen a stolen car.

On Thursday, Reuben made some sort of sausage, pepper and potato dish that he fried in a cast iron skillet. He cooked some green beans and baked bread in one of those machines. She was in heaven. "Dad's a really good cook," Clancy said. "Always has been."

Reuben shrugged. "Gotta eat. May as well make it something that tastes good."

"Can't argue with that logic," Emma said. She accidentally dropped her fork and got up to get another one, going right to the drawer where the utensils were kept. While she was up, Reuben asked for the paper towels, which she grabbed from under the sink. She noticed that Clancy didn't have a glass, so she snatched that, too, along with the milk out of the fridge. They both mumbled thanks and it didn't seem odd to any of them that Emma not only knew her way around their kitchen but helped herself.

As she sat back down, she said, "My mom wasn't much of a cook."

"Neither was mine," Clancy said, shoveling in food. "It was beneath her."

Emma ignored his comment because she wasn't sure where it would lead. "My mom had a handful of recipes that she was really good at, but overall, I ate boxed macaroni and cheese with white bread and margarine as a garnish. I tell ya, half the time I told her not to even bother with dinner and I just ate cereal. But when she cooked her famous fried chicken and mashed potatoes...or her vegetable beef soup...uh. Heaven. Just didn't happen that often."

"I'm headed out to the north side of the lake tomorrow," Reuben said, changing the subject. "I'm taking the team with me. I've got some logging to do. Couple of felled trees that need clearing. So, I won't be here. Feel free to come on over though, Emma. Work with Zeus if you can. It's a miracle, what you're doing."

He said that every time.

But this time, he really meant it, because Zeus had come out of his corner and into the middle of the corral.

After dinner, Clancy and Emma cleaned up. She washed, he dried. He sang "Tumbling Tumbleweed" to her and Emma hummed the harmony because she didn't know the lyrics well enough to sing it. This had become part of the ritual of the day. She came over and worked with Zeus. Reuben cooked and fed her. She and Clancy did dishes. Then she walked home with Roy as her escort. Doing dishes became sort of a dance with Clancy. She'd set a dish in the drain and he'd stand on the opposite side of her so he'd have to reach across to get it, when he could have just stood on that side of the sink in the first place. He'd pass behind her dozens of times to put each dish away, brushing against her just lightly enough that it didn't seem intentional. Except Emma would have bet money that it was intentional and by the time they were finished her skin tingled and every nerve she had was ready to spark. Doing dishes had never been so erotic. She went home frustrated.

Also that week, Emma had talked to her mother on the phone, albeit briefly. Her mom seemed completely disinterested in the fact that she'd moved to Minnesota but perked up a bit when Emma mentioned the horses. "Were any of the guys you met that summer named, Jim, Sam or Marty?" Emma had asked. Her mother had said, "Maybe." After fifteen minutes Emma had hung up feeling as though her mother was more of a stranger now than she'd ever been. She was even more convinced that her mother remembered nothing about that summer. Other than the fact she'd had "a blast."

Marty showed up every night at ten o'clock and slept in the sleeping bag on her floor in front of the fire. He took another bath, and he was noticeably less drunk than he had been before, although still under the influence. Emma fed him, and she began to see that gray skin-tone replaced by healthier pink tone. He brought her a parrot, which he had no cage for, so Emma kept it in one of the bedrooms away from the cats, until she could get one. She finally finished painting the rooms on the main floor and was ready to start on the second floor.

James invited her to his house to meet his family on Sunday, and with an anxious heart, she accepted. What if his wife really hated her? What if his kids didn't want a sister that was twenty years older than they were? Of the three men who'd answered her ad, James was the only one who had physical proof that he'd known her mother. But she still wasn't convinced that he was the one. She went online and ordered three DNA tests for them and one for herself.

On Friday, Clancy showed up at her house with a toolbox.

"I'm here to fix your toilet," he said. "Or try to, anyway."

"Oh," she said. "I could kiss you!" And then she realized what she'd said and started shooing animals in every direction so he could make his way to the bathroom and to distract him from the words coming out of her mouth.

"Okay, those three I've met, who's this?" he asked, pointing to the three-legged dog.

"That's Tricephus. She just showed up one day, like the rest of them. She is a sweetheart, though. Very calm."

"Tricephus is a boy's name," he said.

Emma laughed. "Tricephus is a made-up name and I don't think she'll care."

Clancy smiled at her and she could see the wheels in his mind working. She had no idea what he was thinking, but he was definitely thinking something. "Oh, and there's a parrot in one of the upstairs bedrooms, so don't open any doors unless you ask first. I haven't named it yet. I don't know if it's a him or a her."

"Where'd you get the parrot?" he asked and set his toolbox down.

"Marty brought it," she said. "He said he found it flying loose around some hardware store. The owner said it had showed up in the fall and nobody had claimed it. So, he's been feeding it."

"Wait, Marty? The homeless guy Marty?"

She nodded. "He answered my ad."

"Wow," Clancy said. "How many guys have answered?"

"Three."

"I don't understand."

"Me neither. Apparently, my mother slept with three different guys in the summer of 1986 who all just happened to be from Quail Bottom," she said. "Three that I know of. I guess there could be more. What are the odds of that?"

Clancy thought a minute and then he said, "Well, there used to be a Quail Bottom saddle club, a...a riding club, back in the eighties and nineties, that a lot of men and women belonged to. And they'd do the circuit."

"What do you mean?"

"They'd start the end of May and go until Labor Day. They'd travel like a wagon train from one rodeo and horse show to the next. It makes sense that if your mother was traveling the same circuit, she could, theoretically, hook up with more than one guy from the same town."

"Really?" Emma asked, her heart beating faster. "So, is there a way I could get a list of who belonged to the saddle club? I could send it to her and maybe she'd recognize a name." And she could cross reference it with the list of names of church members that Luella had given her, because Luella's list alone had turned out to be impossible to use. She had no frame of reference for any of those names unless she just started making cold calls.

"Well, yeah, I guess. Aurora was the president for nearly two decades. I think she has all of the pictures and old records in her basement. It's like a horse historical society down there."

Emma smiled. "That's fabulous!" She could barely contain her excitement. "God, I wonder how many guys she was with from *other* towns?"

"Only your mother knows for sure," he said. "I guess she was a...a player?"

Emma laughed so hard that she made the dogs bark. "When I was growing up, she had seventeen different live-in boyfriends."

"That's one per year?"

"Oh, no, Lionel lasted three years, while Butch and Emilio only lasted a couple of months each," she said. Then almost as an afterthought she said, "Butch was a bastard."

They stood there uncomfortably for a minute and finally he said, "So, the toilet? I really don't like using the outhouse."

"Oh, yeah."

The bathroom was too small. At least for the both of them. She'd gone in first to point at the commode. To say, "this is it" except he wasn't that stupid and he knew what a commode looked like. She should have just stayed out in the hallway and let him go in on his own, but she hadn't, and she realized her mistake too late. She was suddenly very aware of the fact she'd have to squeeze by him to get out. Unless of course, he'd be a gentleman and step out on his own.

He wasn't going to be a gentleman.

She scooted by him, her hips brushing against his crotch and there was a tightening in her groin, a warmth that spread throughout her chest, and she heard him take a swift intake of breath. When she made it safely to the door, she glanced back at him and his eyes were glazed over. He reached for the sink to steady himself. *So, he'd felt it, too.* She could not remember having such an instantaneous and strong reaction to fully clothed physical contact before.

"Emma?" he said. His voice was different now, thick with lust.

"Yes?" she said from the safety of the doorway.

"Look, about the other night at Sam's," he said. "I was being a real jerk. The part before the dance."

She smiled and he smiled back lazily. "Yes, you were," she said.

He shrugged. "Truce?"

She stepped inside the bathroom, held out her hand and said, "Truce."

She hadn't meant to give that little sigh when he shook her hand, but she couldn't help it. He was touching her again. And she became fully aware of the fact that she'd wanted him to touch her all week long, no matter how much she'd denied it. She'd psychoanalyze why she wanted a jerk to touch her later. Maybe it was because down deep she knew he wasn't a jerk. *Later, Emma. L-a-t-e-r.*

"I..." he said.

"What?" she asked.

"Would really like to kiss you again."

"Sure," she said like a silly girl. "Any time."

The words had barely left her lips when he'd grabbed her by the waist and yanked her to him. He kissed her passionately, hands roaming along her back. She wrapped her arms around him and

kissed him back, matching his urgency and desire. His lips broke
from hers and he trailed kisses down her throat and back up the
other side, finding her ear and then her temple. He kissed her
again, moaning into her mouth, and her heart beat so hard she was
dizzy. He grabbed her upper thighs and hoisted her up onto the
vanity and leaned into her and he felt hot and right and firm
and...she couldn't think anymore. Her fingers dug into his
shoulders and her legs wrapped around his waist. She wanted him
and she wanted him right now.

Well, maybe not in the bathroom, but if that's what he wanted,
she was game. She'd do anything he asked right now. They'd been
having foreplay in the kitchen all week. She moaned and Clancy's
body reacted to it. He shivered and kissed her deeper if that were
possible. He leaned her back and her head hit the mirror, but she
didn't mind.

She pulled his shirt up so she could feel the warm skin on his
broad back.

"I want you," he said.

"I know," she said. "Shut up and work faster."

He slipped a hand under her shirt and cupped her breast. Her
mind went blank, buzzing with desire and need. He kissed her
again and again and no matter what his hands did, he kept kissing
her.

For the love of God, don't stop.

She reached for his belt buckle and ripped it open.

Must get pants off faster.

His hand slipped inside her pants.

Oh, oh, oh!

She pulled his shirt over his head, breaking skin contact for a
just a moment, and it was a moment too long. She pawed at him to
bring him back to her. He kissed her again and buried his hand
back in her pants and his head in her neck, kissing and sucking
along the curve.

Want. Him. Now. Her hands fumbled around his crotch. *Zipper! Where the heck is his zipper? What? Button-fly? He's torturing me! Freakin' sadist!*

Inside her pants his fingers found the magic spot and she gasped.

He doesn't need instructions! No, no, no, but we need a condom. What did I do with those condoms?

She opened her eyes because she wanted to see him. She wanted to see his body and his face and...

She screamed bloody murder.

Marty stood in the bathroom doorway, swaying back and forth, with a confused expression on his face. Clancy stumbled back and tripped over the door track and fell right into the shower stall with his belt buckle open and some of the buttons on his jeans undone. There was only one button left fastened. *One button! I only needed one more button!*

"Oh, my God," Emma said, breathing heavy. "Are you all right?"

Clancy growled.

Marty hiccupped. "Did you get the toilet fixed?" he asked. "I hate that outhouse."

15

"So you found your dad?" Jackie said. Her voice sounded thin over the phone but still comforting, as always.

"I don't know, Jackie. There've been three guys who answered the ad," Emma said.

"Well, honey, no offense, but your mother was a slut," she said.

Emma wasn't offended by Jackie's words. They'd had this conversation before.

"So are you taking bets on who it is?" Jackie asked. "No. I do keep trying out their last names, though. Like, whichever one sounds the best is the one. Let's see, I'd be Emma Sherman if it's Sam. Emma Pepper if it's Marty. And Emma Hollingsworth, if it's Jim."

"Emma Sherman doesn't sound right. Emma Hollingsworth makes you sound like some society dame. I like Emma Pepper. It's cute. And it so fits you. All spicy," Jackie said.

Jackie had a grown daughter, Willa, who had just turned eighteen, and Suzanne had the two kids, Janelle and Scotty. Those five people, along with her cousins' husbands, and Jackie and Suzanne's parents, were Emma's only family. Seven people plus two in-laws. It was good to hear Jackie's voice, and Emma was grateful that Jackie and Suzanne had never treated her like anything but a baby sister.

Emma was quiet.

"Emmie, what's going on? You don't sound normal. And even when you called me from San Diego...you know, right after Juan had run out on you for that Russian ballerina? You were heartbroken, but you were still you. You sound..."

"I don't know," Emma said, petting Mutt until his eyes rolled back in his head from sheer pleasure. "I feel like that one conqueror who wept when he realized he had no more worlds to conquer."

"Was that in a 'Star Trek' movie?"

"Yeah, but I'm pretty sure it was based on a real guy," Emma said. Tricephus stood next to the couch and wagged her tail. Emma bent forward and picked her up, accidentally squishing Mutt's head between her thigh and her breast. "Oh, sorry Mutt."

"Who's Mutt?" Jackie asked.

"A stray dog that I found."

"Oh yeah, I saw that on Facebook," Jackie said. "That's so sweet. Somebody to keep you warm at night."

"Yeah."

"So, back to the conqueror thing."

"I just feel like this has been the one big question mark of my whole life. Like all roads would lead to here eventually. And now that it's here...when the DNA test comes back, and I find out who my father is...what do I do then?"

"Well, I told Suzanne that this moving to Minnesota and buying a house, was by far the craziest thing you've ever done. Even crazier than when you snuck backstage at that Green Day concert and got Billie Joe Armstrong to sign your boob," Jackie said.

Emma smiled. She hadn't washed her boob for a week.

"You used to give me a heart attack when you were little. You always had to swing the highest, swim out the farthest, push every envelope there ever was. As a teenager? The whole reason I was on Xanax was because of you."

Jackie was ten years older than Emma and so she could attest to Emma's craziness. Her craving for what was next. What was out there that she hadn't seen? She hadn't done? She'd zip lined through a jungle in Belize—but the scariest part about that was that she'd been in the country illegally. She'd hitched a ride on a yacht leaving Miami with a guy she knew from college. She didn't even have a passport. She'd watched Mexican free-tailed bats fly out from under the Congress Avenue Bridge in Texas, and then for a week she'd had nightmares that they were chasing her. She'd seen whales off the coast of Alaska. She'd leaned too far out to get a picture, lost her footing and her camera went into the ocean. She'd watched the sun rise in Boothbay Harbor, Maine, with her grandma while finishing off the champagne that they'd nicked from the restaurant.

And all of it was the desperate effort of a lonely girl trying to get her mother's attention, failing to do so, and filling that void with bad decisions and crazy adventures. She was glad for the crazy adventures, though. No matter how they turned out, they were the fabric of her life. They made her what she was, and she wouldn't trade them for anything. Emma said no to drugs. She said no to sex with total strangers. She balked when it came to breaking the law, well, at least the *big* laws. She could not physically hurt another being—except ticks. And fleas. But she'd felt guilty as a person could feel over those fleas. But she said no to very little else. And the rest of her family had to just watch from the sidelines or get caught up in the tidal wave.

Emma believed to the very core of her being that life was about experiences. Not possessions or accomplishments. But in retrospect, it felt like her life had been spent grasping at something unseen and that she'd not been on *her* path, but that she'd just been tumbling along, crash landing on other people's paths. She'd been freefalling through life. So what did a woman do when she finally landed on her own path?

"I told you that you might just want to rent a house instead of buying one," Jackie said. "I can't see you staying long."

"But I *want* to, Jackie. That's just it. I'll be twenty-nine in March. I need to rein it all in." The thought occurred to her that maybe this was just her biological clock getting ready to explode. Maybe it was hormonal. This need to put down roots. Maybe all women went through this when they were approaching thirty. And maybe her mother going to Belize just magnified it.

"You don't have to," Jackie said. "Maybe the staying-in-one-place kind of life just isn't for you. Girl, you're out there searching for a treasure and you don't even know what it is. How are you going to know when you find it?"

Emma shrugged even though Jackie couldn't see it. She scratched Tricephus behind the ears and the dog licked her hand. "I guess I thought..."

"What?"

"I guess I thought I'd be more excited when I found my dad. I mean, I am excited. But I thought when I found him...it'd bring me some sort of peace. That the restlessness would stop."

"Well, maybe it's because you haven't found him for sure. Wait for the DNA results. I'll bet you're super excited then, when you know for sure. And for Pete's sake, don't deny who you really are. If you don't want to settle, don't. Stop thinking you have to settle down because that's what the world expects. In the meantime, is there anything I can do?"

"Nope," Emma said. "I'm going to fly down to see you guys this summer, though."

"Can't wait," Jackie said.

"Oh, but there's this guy..."

"Yeah?" Jackie asked.

"But he's really uptight about women. Like, he's definitely straight..." her mind wandered to what had happened yesterday in her bathroom. She would seriously never look at that vanity the same again. "But other than sex, I think don't really think he cares."

"About you or about women in general?"

"Women in general."

"Sounds like he had a run-in with a she-wolf in the past."

"Yeah, but it's more than that. I think it might have something to do with his mother."

"Oh, God. Never get in a land war with Asia and never, ever, get mixed up with a guy who confuses you with his mother."

"I love you, Jackie."

"I love you, too, Emmie."

Emma hung up and now that she had both hands free, she scratched both dogs.

Sunday, Emma went to church again just to hear Luella sing. The woman didn't disappoint. Afterward, Luella invited her back to the diner where she served Emma the best burger she'd ever eaten in her whole life, cheese fries and a hot-fudge sundae. Luella ate the same thing right along with her, sitting opposite her in a booth by the window.

"So, I hear that you're going to go to work with Zoe," Luella said.

"Yes, and I'm very excited about it. I'm not much good with desk jobs and the usual 9-5 stuff. I get this panicked feeling thinking about a cubicle. And I like the idea of making a difference."

"Then you oughta love this. I've seen Zoe take an animal that I thought for sure was on death's door and bring them back," she said.

"Are you two good friends?" she asked.

"She's one of my best friends," Luella said. "Her son went off to college last year and I thought she was going to die from heart break. He went all the way to England."

"Is she married?"

"Recently divorced."

"So where'd you learn to sing like that?" Emma asked and took a bite of her cheese fries. God, how she loved salty fried cheesy stuff.

Luella shrugged. "I could always sing, always loved to sing, as long as I can remember. But when I got to high school, I had a choir teacher who took special interest in me."

"Did I remember you saying you weren't from Quail Bottom?"

"Oh, I'm from here originally," she said. "But I had moved away."

"How many siblings do you have?" Emma asked.

"Lots. I've got whole ones and half ones and step ones and step half ones...it's convoluted," she said. "Thirteen in all."

"Do they all live in town?"

"Nope. Only two or three."

Emma took a drink of her tea to wash down the last of her burger.

"Can I ask you a question?" Emma said. Luella nodded.

"What happened with Zeus? I figure I've got a right to know since I'm putting my life on the line every time I step in the corral with him," she said, even though she didn't believe that. If there was one thing she knew without a doubt it was that Zeus trusted her. He liked her. He wanted to do what she asked of him, but he just couldn't bring himself to do it. But she never once got the feeling that he'd hurt her. Maybe if she came in sounding a trumpet he might attack, but even then, she thought he'd run instead. Fight or flight. He only picked flight with Emma. It was with everybody else he picked fight. "I mean, I've hinted at the question around Reuben and Clancy but they don't seem to want to answer."

"Well, girl, in order to answer that question, you have to know the history of that family. And I'm not sure how much to tell and how much not to tell, but June Stephens was a snotty, haughty, hateful, selfish woman. I lost track of how many times she up and left that family."

"But she always came back?"

"Uh-huh."

"Why did Reuben let her come back?"

Luella shrugged. "Why do people do the things they do? I think it's because of Clancy and Peri. I think June thought the kids would go with her when she left, but they never did. They always stayed with their dad. They knew who really loved them. Don't get me wrong, I think June loved her kids. I just don't think she loved them as much as she shoulda. But she loved them enough that she kept coming back. And Reuben...well, Reuben was like a rock. Early on in that marriage—so I've been told—he was a lot more volatile. He'd do awful things to get revenge on her for leaving. But then after Peri was born he just couldn't bring himself to do it anymore. He decided that he would just take June's shenanigans."

"Really?"

The hot fudge sundaes arrived and Emma's heart leapt. *Sugar!*

"It's almost like he thought he deserved it. Like it was his sentence. I know it sounds like I'm speculating, but we all saw it. We'd all seen the public arguments. We'd all heard things said to neighbors and family. He was atoning for something. So he just kept taking her abuse, and her spending, and her pushing, and her never being satisfied."

Emma swallowed the mixture of cold vanilla ice-cream and warm chocolate fudge. It almost seemed like a sin to actually eat the stuff.

"So, one day back in November, they'd had a big fight."

"Wow, you'd think at their age they would have mellowed. I mean, how old are they?"

"Mid-fifties," Luella said. "Girl, I know it. You're not telling me anything. So, they had a big fight, and it was during an awful snowstorm. An early storm for this area."

"What was the fight about?" Emma asked.

Luella shrugged. "Reuben probably wouldn't buy her a new car or something. None of us really know. But she was determined to leave, because she always knew that the leaving part hurt everybody more than anything else she could do, only the truck was stuck in the snow and the other cars were trapped by the truck, so she took off on the snowmobile because in weather like that there ain't much else that's gonna get you around."

Note to self: See about buying a snowmobile. They seem to be invaluable up here.

Luella took a couple of bites of her sundae. "Now this is the tragic part. She lit outta there on that snowmobile and come dark nobody had seen her. Well, she'd left her purse behind so it wasn't like she could go to a hotel or go shopping. Reuben called all her friends and family...nobody had seen her. So Reuben took Zeus out to find her."

"Why Zeus? Why not Roy? Or one of the Belgians?"

"Zeus was by far the most experienced, trusted horse that they had. The Belgians had been out earlier in the day clearing logs, and Reuben wanted a fresh horse and one that was agile. The Belgians, from what I understand, are hardy work horses, but they're not very fast or agile."

Emma was so engrossed in Luella's story that she'd forgotten about the sundae and the ice-cream dripped off of her spoon. "And what happened?"

"Zeus stepped into a ravine the wrong way, tumbled down the side of the hill and threw Reuben clear. Reuben said he must have tumbled five or six times. When Reuben got to him, Zeus had somehow gotten wedged between a fallen tree and the frozen creek and he had a small tree branch stuck in his skull. Said he was going crazy trying to get up. Reuben managed to lift the dead trunk enough that Zeus scrambled out and ran off."

"Oh my God," Emma said.

"He wandered around for a day and a half before anybody could find him. When they did find him, they had to bring him down with a tranquilizer dart. His hind leg was all cut up, and he had torn up his bum and broke a couple of teeth. He's not been the same since. Neither has anybody in that house. The branch that was stuck in his head had missed his brain by a centimeter or two. He was lucky. Or at least that's what we thought. But now...kinda makes you wonder if he'd been better off dying."

"So, what happened to June Stephens?"

"They found her body in the highway median. Most people think she was going to the nearest town by following along the outside edge of the road. Witnesses said that when she came over the hill right there south of the turn off, she was going too fast, lost control and slammed into the railing. Threw her body like a rag doll across the highway into the median."

Emma's hands flew to her mouth as she sucked in a breath. "Jesus," she said.

"The truly sad part is not a one of those Stephenses—not Clancy, Reuben, Peri or Caitlin—grieved for June like they've grieved for that horse."

Emma blinked, horrified at the story.

"I don't even know what to say," Emma said and then shoved a spoonful of partially melted sundae into her mouth.

Luella made a "what are you gonna do?" motion and then scraped the chocolate out of the bottom of the bowl with her spoon. "That horse hasn't warmed to another person since that happened in November. Until you. Now you know why it's so important to Reuben and Clancy that you keep doing what you're doing."

Emma blinked, holding back tears. "Of course," she said. "I'll go over there for as long as it takes."

"So, enough of that," Luella said. "What are you doing tonight?"

"I'm having dinner with Jim Hollingsworth and his family," she said.

Luella raised her eyebrows. "Another candidate for dad?"

"Yes," she said. "After that, nothing. Why?"

"You want to meet me out at Sam's? It's karaoke night," she said and grinned from ear to ear.

Emma laughed and said, "I'll be there."

16

The Hollingsworths lived in a two-story cookie-cutter house in a cookie-cutter subdivision that was situated on the outskirts of Quail Bottom. All the houses in this "luxury living" neighborhood looked exactly the same, with postage-stamp-sized yards and matching garages. The subdivision itself was in the middle of what was once a cornfield. Everything was neat and orderly. Emma nearly had a panic attack imagining a life that structured.

She found their house and rang the doorbell and James answered, wearing a freshly pressed sky-blue shirt and his hair slicked back. Waiting just inside the door were his two children and his wife. Emma waved and James introduced her.

"This is my wife, Heather," he said.

Heather was an attractive woman, noticeably younger than James, with dishwater blond hair cut in one of those long-in-the-front-and-short-in-the-back haircuts. She had kind brown eyes and wore jeans and a pink sweater. "Nice to meet you," Heather said. The woman studied Emma closely and Emma knew that she was looking to see if there was any resemblance to her husband.

"We made pot roast, I hope that's okay," Heather said.

"Oh, of course," Emma said. "I love pot roast."

"This is my daughter Jamie," Jim said pointing to a four-year-old who was cuter than any child had a right to be, with reddish blond hair and expressive hazel eyes. She even had a dash of freckles across the bridge of her nose. She waved and sashayed side to side like Emma had often seen little girls do when they were embarrassed or uncomfortable.

"And this is Micah," he said. Micah, if she remembered right, was ten. He had his mother's dishwater hair and his father's eyes, and he was trapped in that horrible stage that boys often go through where their teeth look too big for their heads. He was skinny, and he only made eye contact briefly.

His mother tapped him on the shoulder. Emma knew that tap meant; *you're being rude.*

Micah glanced back up at her and Emma signed that it was nice to meet him. His eyes lit up when he realized she could communicate with him.

Emma had brought him some comic books, but she hadn't wanted to leave Jamie out, so she'd stopped and bought her some cute barrettes with Elsa ribbons from that Disney movie. When she handed them to her, the girl almost jumped, she was so excited. Emma bent down and signed to Micah that she'd brought him Avengers comic books. He took them from her and went to the couch to read them.

Emma followed the adults into the kitchen and Heather said, "So..."

Emma smiled and said, "Oh, my gosh! My grandma had an owl clock just like that!" She pointed to the wall above the refrigerator. "I loved that thing. Does yours hoot?"

Heather nodded. They all sat down to dinner a few minutes later and Jamie asked all sorts of questions, but nothing about whether or not they were related. It was Emma's opinion that Jim had probably not told either of his children the possibility that Emma was his daughter. He wouldn't, she hoped, until he'd taken the DNA test. Heather was polite, but cautious, and Emma was okay with that. What would she think if the shoe was on the other foot?

Once they started eating Emma began telling stories. But the whole time she talked, she also signed so that Micah did not miss a single word that was being spoken. Some people would only sign to a deaf person when they were talking directly to them, so the deaf person missed out on much of the conversation. It isolated them in a way that people who could hear couldn't fathom. So, if Micah was present, Emma would not speak one word without signing it, too.

"So there was my Granny," Emma said and signed. "Running alongside the car because her dress was caught in the door and she'd saved up her money for months to buy that dress and she refused to rip it. So she's banging on the window and finally my Grandpa stopped the car, opened the door and caught her in his arms as she broke the heel on her shoe. That was the end of their first date and my Grandpa proposed right then and there."

The kids laughed. Even Micah.

"He said he'd never met a woman with more spunk than my Granny and he couldn't let her get away."

Micah asked with his hands, "She said yes? That soon?"

"My Granny told him that she'd think about it. She told him that it depended on what he got her for Valentine's Day."

Micah signed, "What did he get her?"

Emma smiled. "He didn't buy her anything like chocolate or flowers or even jewelry. He'd spent the entire autumn planting trees in a local park in her name. He planted forty trees and each one had a plaque that said, 'For my darling Barbara. My love for you will last as long as these trees shall live.' Forty trees. One for every week between the time he proposed and Valentine's Day." Emma got choked up thinking about it like she always did. She swiped at a tear.

Micah signed, "So then he still loves her?"

Granny and Grandpa were both gone now. But those trees still lived, giving shelter to birds and squirrels, and oxygen to the earth. All in the name of Barbara, her Granny. "He still loves her."

"That is the most romantic thing I've ever heard," Heather said, clearly moved.

"Yeah, my grandpa was a regular Romeo."

A contemplative silence filled the room. It only lasted a few seconds.

"So," Emma said. "There was this one time I was on a plane going to Seattle. Just as we got over the mountains the captain comes on the overhead speaker and says, 'We're experiencing a little trouble with the right engine.' Only I look out the window and the darn thing is on fire! Fire is a lot more than a 'little trouble'!"

Micah's eyes were huge.

"What's an engine?" Jamie asked.

"It's the thing that makes a car go," Jim said. "Or a plane."

"And I hear my Granny's voice—because I always hear Granny when I'm doing something stupid or I'm about to die—and she told me to stay calm, that I wasn't going to die. Now, I've had Granny warn me about serial killers before, but I've never heard her tell me to calm down."

"What's a serial killer?" Jamie asked.

Emma grimaced.

"Somebody who finishes off a bowl of cereal in under a minute," Heather said.

Emma laughed and she made the "I'm sorry" face to Heather who just waved her off. No damage done.

But then Jamie said, "Oh, I'm a serial killer!"

"No you're not, honey," Heather said.

Micah pounded the table. Then he signed, "What happened?!"

"Granny said that there was a flat field in the next valley where they could land the plane and so I stopped one of the flight attendants and told him we needed to make an emergency landing. Now, the flight attendant was a little tiny pip-squeak of a guy and he had a voice way *up here like Mickey Mouse...*"

The kids laughed, even though Micah had no reference for what a high-pitched voice would sound like.

"And he said, *'Ma'am, we're in the mountains!'*"

"And I said, 'no, no, there's a valley coming up. I swear.' So he disappears for a few seconds then all of a sudden I hear the captain say, 'Folks, this is your Captain. We're going to make an emergency landing. Please follow the instructions of your flight attendant.' Sure enough, he lands the plane in the valley—took out some poor guy's hunting shack in the process—and everybody survived. I broke my tibia. But that wasn't nearly as frightening as the flight I took to London! I just happened to be sitting on the toilet when we hit air turbulence—right over the Atlantic ocean!—so bad that I rose up off of that seat by a foot, slammed back down, then I was knocked forward into the door, had a big ol' bump on my head and started crawling back to my seat—because there was no way that I could stand up—only I forgot that I hadn't pulled my pants up yet."

The kids belly laughed at that vision.

"Hey," Emma said and signed. "You have to forgive me. I was twelve and I was scared to death. You'd forget your pants, too! So, I got back to my seat and we made it through the turbulence, but I refused to pee the rest of the flight. In fact, I haven't peed on a flight since."

Emma raised her hand. "Hand to God. True story."

As Emma headed out to Sam's bar, she couldn't help but replay what Heather had said to her as she left. "You have to forgive Micah," she said. "He really only interacts with us in the house. He communicates with teachers at school, but only to the extent that he needs to. There's nothing volunteered. I can't get him to join any clubs or sports teams...nothing."

"Oh, Heather," Emma had said. "There's nothing to forgive. I can't imagine what his life is like. And besides, I thought he interacted pretty well."

Heather smiled and looked back over her shoulder at him sitting on the couch reading the comics that Emma had brought. "Much better than usual," she said. "Thank you."

"Anytime," Emma said. "Hey, have you ever tried animal therapy with him?"

Heather knit her eyebrows together. "It's been suggested, but he just never takes an interest."

"Well, I've read that in many rehab situations, people who've had strokes, people in nursing homes, that type of thing, doctors use animals to help connect with the patients. There's a really sweet horse named Roy that I think Micah would get a kick out of."

"Roy?"

"Yeah, he's a horse that Clancy Stephens owns, only I think the horse actually owns Clancy. He's a pretty amazing horse. Very gentle. Practically reads your thoughts. If you'd be interested in something like that, I'm sure Clancy would let you bring the kids out."

"I don't know," she said. "A horse is an awfully big animal."

"This horse is like a puppy."

Heather studied Emma for a second. Then she blinked back tears. "Yes," she said. "I'll bring him. I can't guarantee that he'll engage, though."

"Great, I'll take care of it."

All in all, Emma thought that the evening had gone much better than she anticipated. She pulled into the parking lot at Sam's and noticed the stars twinkling down at her. She remembered the northern lights and couldn't help but wonder if she'd see them again. Or if Clancy would kiss her again. Or if they'd ever...

When she entered the bar, Sam threw his hands up and yelled, "There she is!" Emma smiled and waved back, but he wouldn't settle for that. He came around the bar and gave her a big hug. "You want a beer?"

"Just one," she said. "How about that porter? That was good stuff."

He poured her drink and Emma sat down at the end of the bar in what was becoming known as "her stool." "So, you gonna sing tonight?" Sam asked.

"Uh...maybe? I'm really here just to watch Luella."

He smiled. "Oh, man, that woman's voice...gives me chills," he said and shivered.

A few minutes later Luella walked in and sat down next to Emma at the bar. "How'd it go at the Hollingsworths?" she asked.

"Better than I thought it would," Emma said. "I think his wife was unsure at first."

"Heather's kind of high-strung sometimes," Luella said. "We all deal in our own way."

Before people started singing, they had a heart-to-heart about some of Luella's family and her past. Emma learned that Luella was forty-three, her mother had died last year of colon cancer, and that she had twin girls who both lived in St. Paul with their father, a Swedish architect that she'd met in Denmark back in the nineties, and they were both freshman at the U. Luella and the architect had never married.

Half an hour later the music was going and there was some sixty-year-old man trying to sing Tom Jones' "It's Not Unusual" but he wasn't quite drunk enough yet. Emma thought that if he'd just cut loose, he'd probably be able to do the song some justice. He had a nice deep voice with lots of volume and a good vibrato. Everybody clapped for him just the same and the next person got up to sing.

Emma and Luella clapped and whistled as each person performed. Then they danced in front of their bar stools and finally

Sam said, "Get on up there and sing, Luella. What are you waiting for?"

Clancy walked in with another guy and looked a little taken aback to see Emma there. He made a beeline for her, though. "You've taken over my hang-out," he said and smiled.

"I haven't taken over anything. I'm sharing."

Clancy nodded at Luella then turned to Emma and said, "This is my buddy, Brad."

Brad shook her hand vigorously, looking for all the world like the poster boy for a Swedish children's novel. Pink cheeked, blue-eyed, almost tow-headed...he even had a dimple. He was smaller than Clancy, but not by much. An inch shorter maybe, a little narrower through the shoulders. "I've heard a lot about you," he said.

Clancy had mentioned Brad over the past week that she'd been at his house working with Zeus, but he hadn't gone into a lot of detail about their history. Clancy didn't go into a lot of detail about too many things unless it involved horses or his niece. "Nice to meet you, too," Emma said and gave him a genuine smile.

The two of them ordered beers and stood there next to Emma and Luella while a tiny red head got up and sang, "Kerosene" by Miranda Lambert. There was more volume coming out of that tiny body than Emma thought would have possible. Emma and Luella clapped in time and Luella moved out away from the bar and started dancing, stomping her feet and cheering the woman on. When the song was over the red head said, "What are you waiting for, Luella? Get your fanny up here."

The crowd in the bar went wild and Luella jumped up on the stage and told the MC what to play. She started singing "Before He Cheats" by Carrie Underwood and the hair rose on Emma's arms. Luella held nothing back, in fact she was quite a bit more animated than she'd been at church. She sang about the Louisville slugger to the headlights and the scratched-up leather seats and how that man would think before cheating on the next woman and Emma believed every word Luella was singing. *She's probably done this before. She's smashed some guy's car to pieces because he was a lousy cheating bastard. I totally believe her.*

Then Luella did "Think" by Aretha Franklin and Emma couldn't sit still. The song was over and done with so fast that all Emma wanted was to hear Luella sing it again. She glanced around and even Clancy and Brad were clapping wildly. When she'd caught her breath, Luella said into the microphone, "Come on up here, Em. We're gonna do a song together. Show me what you got."

Emma laughed because she didn't have anything to show Luella. She could sing—her choir took first place in every competition they went to—but that was high school and this was now. But she didn't care. She didn't care how awful she was going to sound compared to Luella. The chance to actually sing with that woman was a thrill. An honor. And Emma gulped down the last of her beer and all but ran for the stage.

Luella told the MC what to play and the bottom fell out of Emma's stomach as she realized that the song she'd picked was "Lady Marmalade." Good God in heaven, there was no way Emma could sing that song. Luella leaned in and said, "I'll do the first and fourth verse, you do the second and third." Emma sighed with relief as she realized she wouldn't have to sing "the note" at the end of the song and she wouldn't have to lead the song off, either. *Bless her.*

Emma took a deep breath, threw a dirty look at Luella, who laughed, and then she gripped the microphone tighter. "Did I mention I'm an *alto?*" Emma said. Luella just laughed again, only that time it was with pure mischief.

Clancy's heart was in his throat. He had no idea what to expect when Emma started singing. He motioned to Brad and they moved up closer to the stage so they could get a better view, and Emma looked like she was going to lose her cookies right then and there. Sam stood on the bar behind them twirling a towel in the air, shouting, "Go Em!"

Luella started the song strong and bluesy like you'd expect from her and Emma started grinding to the music. And when Luella was finished with the first verse, Emma took a deep breath, closed her eyes and started singing. She put everything she had into it and Clancy's heart calmed to a regular beat. She wasn't awful. She wasn't great, but she sure wasn't awful. But who *would* sound great next to Luella? It was clear that the song was out of her range, so on the third verse she took the Lil' Kim route and rapped the lyrics.

She moved out to the end of the stage and rapped to the audience, grinding her hips and making little sexy motions with her hands near her groin and Clancy could feel a twinge in his. She did it just like they did in the video and it was so erotic that Clancy thought dance moves like that, done by her, should be illegal. Then she forgot the lyrics, covered her eyes with her hands out of embarrassment, and then just made stuff up. Something about cows and llamas and horses. Luella heaved, she was laughing so hard. Sam stomped and cheered some more from his lofty position, waving that white towel around like an idiot.

Clancy realized then what he really liked about Emma. The girl had no fear. Except when it came to ticks and vomit. And serial killers, but even then, if her stories were true, she just armed herself. Exactly how many serial killers she'd actually encountered was up for debate, but according to her dead Granny, there'd been at least a dozen.

She'd known she couldn't sing this song and she'd known that she couldn't hold a candle to Luella, but she'd done it anyway. She was making a fool of herself but that just made everybody like her all the more. It made *him* like her all the more.

When they were finished singing, Emma squeezed Luella and gave her a big ol' kiss on the cheek. Luella bowed to her and applauded. Then Emma pulled out her phone and took a selfie with Luella and most likely posted it to Facebook. He'd see it tomorrow because he'd finally accepted her friend request. She jumped down off the stage and ran toward him and he almost opened his arms to catch her, but he stopped himself. "Oh, my God," she said and buried her hands in her face. "I swear I'm not usually that bad."

"You were great," he said to her.

"I'm better in the shower," she said.

I'd like to find out, he thought.

"Fantastic," Brad chimed in.

"Eh, I'm not half bad in my range. But that was *so* not my range," she said.

Part of her hair had flipped over to the wrong side and, against his better judgment, Clancy reached up and flipped it back the right way. Emma searched his eyes, like she often did, for any hidden meaning in his action. It drove him mad. Like if she just looked at him long enough, deeply enough, really concentrated on his eyes, she'd be able to read his mind. On his end, though, when she did that, he just wanted to kiss her.

She skirted around him and she said to Sam, "Can I get some water?"

"Of course," Sam said. "You were wonderful. Don't listen to Clancy."

"Hey," Clancy said. "I told her she was great."

"You guys are too kind," she said.

He watched her mouth as her lips curved onto the glass.

And he wanted to kiss her. Better yet, he wanted to be that glass.

She swept a mass of curls behind her ear, revealing just as many studs in that ear as were in the other.

And that made him want to kiss her, too.

She wiped the sweat from her brow on a paper napkin, laughing at something Sam had said to her. She pounded her fist on the bar, laughed so hard the veins popped out in her neck, and that made him want to kiss her again.

She made small talk with Brad. Asked him a question. Rolled her eyes at the injustice of the song Luella had picked. All around him, the noise stopped, other people blurred into infinity and his mind zeroed in on just Emma. Just Emma and her luscious wine-colored lips, her wild and crazy curls. Those exotic National Geographic eyes.

He wanted to kiss her. Kiss her. Kiss her again.

She glanced over at him when she realized that he'd been staring at her. "What?" she asked, raising her eyebrows. Suddenly the vacuum that Clancy had been in was sucked away and the world came back to him, animated, loud, and in full color.

"Nothing," he said.

Kiss. Kiss and kiss.

If he didn't get drunk quickly, he was going to take her right there on the bar.

17

Emma realized that Clancy was only *slightly* drunk.

Not drunk enough that he was singing to the moon or shouting the Gettysburg Address or even slobbering, which were all things that Emma did when she was drunk. But he was gone just enough that he shouldn't drive home on the snow-packed roads, but sober enough to still be all Clancy-like.

Emma insisted that she drive him home.

"I can drive him," Brad said.

"Shut-up, Brad," Clancy said and smiled down at Emma.

Brad chuckled and said, "Oh, I gotcha. Well, goodnight everybody."

"It was nice meeting you," Emma said.

"Likewise," he said, and he was out the door.

It made sense that Emma should drive him home. After all, they were just across the road from each other, so it wasn't as though she had to drive across town, like Brad would have. After they made a few turns and were on the main road back to Lady Slipper Lane, Clancy turned in the seat next to her. She felt his stare and it was as if one whole side of her face was warmer than it should be.

"What?" she said.

"I was wondering," he began. He reached up and touched her hair.

"You're drunk," she said. "You're not in your right mind."

"Well, you're the reason I'm drunk."

"What? How do you figure?" she asked.

"And I'm not that drunk," he said. "I'm not slurring words or anything. In fact, I may have overstated how drunk I am just to get a ride home."

She glanced over at him.

After their near-death experience on her bathroom vanity, he hadn't said a word about it. It made her think he was sorry for what had passed between them. Well, and she was sorry that he ended up in her shower stall with a knot on his head and a ginormous, wasted, hard-on. But she wasn't sorry about what had led up to that. The man was the sexiest thing on two continents. He was sexier than all the guys in "Magic Mike" put together.

But there was more to Clancy than that. She liked the way he was with the horses. With his Belgians, he moved them gently. He made suggestions to them. Never a harsh word. He hadn't ridiculed her for the collection of pets that she was amassing, like some guys would, and in fact, he'd offered to help catch the parrot that had rapidly taken over her spare bedroom, but they hadn't gotten around to that yet. There was a silent understanding between him and Roy that warmed her heart. He was kind to his animals. And he'd fixed her toilet. And he sang Roy Rogers songs to her while they did the dishes.

But he *was* sexy. And if she wasn't mistaken, he'd sort of lied his way into getting a ride home from her. The implications made her dizzy.

"Wait," she said. "Back to why I'm the reason you're drunk."

He settled back the other way in his seat, moving the seatbelt around to do so. "I needed a distraction."

"Why?" she asked.

"Because all I could think about was taking you right there on the bar."

Emma's stomach clenched and it felt like a horde of butterflies had suddenly been let loose in her chest. "You had to get drunk to tell me this?" she asked.

"No, I had to get drunk to keep Sam from killing me. He doesn't mind public displays of affection in his bar, as long as you draw the line at groping and humping. I'm pretty sure I wouldn't have drawn the line."

"Well, I would have," she said. *I think.*

He held his hands up in surrender. "Well, good. One of us would have been thinking clearly. Anyway, that's why the two drinks too many."

Emma wasn't about to have sex with him while he was drunk. She had a hard and fast rule. Neither person was to be under the influence of anything, except hormones, the first time they had sex. There were no rules for any subsequent encounters, but for the first time, everybody had to be in their right minds so that they were both absolutely sure that what they were doing was what they wanted. No regrets the next morning. And besides, drunk sex was usually sloppy. You do not want your first sexual encounter with somebody to be sloppy.

"Well, buddy," she said. "You're getting food in your stomach."
Because I want sex tonight and you have to be sober!

"Really?" he asked.

"Really. No drunk sex."

"*Really?*" he asked incredulously. "Wait, so you were thinking about having sex with me?"

"Shut-up," she said, smiling.

"I see that smile," he said.

When they returned to her house, Emma let the dogs out, but Tricephus didn't want to go because she hated the cold. Emma gave her butt a little shove with her foot and Tri looked back at her, dejected. Heartbroken. Betrayed. Emma shut the door.

The bad thing about a wood-burning stove was that she would have had to start a fire and wait for the temperature to be just right to start cooking, and at one in the morning, it just wasn't worth it. So, she made Clancy a ham and cheese sandwich on a bun, popped it in the microwave that she'd bought on Thursday, opened a bag of chips and poured him a glass of iced tea. She didn't have any dining furniture yet, so he had to eat on the couch.

When she returned to the living room, she was surprised to find that he'd started a fire. It blazed by the time she served him his food. She sat down on the foot-tall hearth, while he sat on the couch. She didn't trust herself to be any closer to him than that. Thing 1 came slinking toward her and weaved behind her legs. Emma took her boots off and watched Clancy eat. Even his chewing was sexy.

Thing 2 jumped onto the couch and Clancy petted him while he chewed.

Clancy's eyes were tracking just fine and his movements were perfectly normal. He wasn't *that* drunk.

Let him finish his sandwich. And his tea. There is caffeine in the tea.

"So, who was the she-wolf?" Emma asked. *Wow, that's it. Make him think of his ex-girlfriends just before you jump his bones, idiot.*

Clancy swallowed his bite and smiled. He shook his head, "What makes you think I've encountered a she-wolf?"

"The 'I don't like women much' line," she said. *The fact that you look like that and you're single!*

He looked at the cat and tore off a piece of his sandwich for him.

Emma snapped her fingers at Thing 2 and he jumped down and came to her.

"You trained your cat?" he said. "Nobody can train a cat."

"Not true. I had a friend who trained her cat to turn on the faucet and get a drink."

"Well, okay, that's teaching them how to do something. But nobody can get a cat to actually do stuff when you want them to," he said. "It's against the Cat Code of Ethics."

She shrugged and petted both cats.

He took another bite of food and eyed her warily.

"What?" she said.

"I'm not so sure I want to be around somebody who can train a cat. What are you, a hypnotist?" he asked.

Emma laughed.

He finished his sandwich just as Thing 1 jumped onto her lap and nudged Emma's face with her head. Clancy took a swig of his tea and leaned back on the couch and watched her. His gaze was so intense it felt like it penetrated her all the way through and it made her solar plexus trembled. She wanted to just run over there and straddle him, but she didn't. She showed some restraint. She wasn't budging until he answered her question. He was going to give her something, by golly. Some little piece of him. Other than the literal piece of him that she'd been thinking about for a week.

She'd only had one more button to go. Damn you, Marty.

And this time, she knew exactly where those condoms were.

"Her name was Diane. We were engaged. Now we're not," he said.

Emma waited for more, but none came.

"Now, take off your clothes," Clancy said.

Emma smiled. "No."

"You're killing me. How am I supposed to be able to speak in complete sentences when I know that you're naked under your clothes?"

Emma smiled again only bigger. "I'm always naked under my clothes."

"I know and it's maddening!"

Her face flushed. Yeah, she was going to climb all over him.

"All you asked was who she was," he said. "I answered that."

"Why are you no longer engaged?" she asked.

"Because she was the carbon copy of my mother, only I didn't know it at the time."

"How many fingers am I holding up?" she asked, smiling.

"Three very sexy fingers," he said.

Well, he hadn't bared his soul to her, but he had answered her question. Sort of two questions actually. He thought of his mother as a she-wolf, too. She stood and said, "How many cats do I have?"

"Two. But they are not sexy," he said and watched her come toward him with a feral intensity that made Emma shiver.

"And how many hands am I holding up?"

"Two," he said and swallowed as she moved closer. "And I want them all over me."

She knelt between his legs and said, "How many lips do I have?"

"That's a dumb question," he said.

"How so?"

She unbuttoned his shirt. His eyes watched her mouth.

"Because everybody has two lips," he said. "Although, none as good as yours."

Emma giggled. "Doesn't everybody have two hands as well?"

"Maybe not every single person on the planet," he said. "Don't talk. You're confusing me."

She opened his shirt and was slightly irritated by the fact that he wore an undershirt, but this was Minnesota and it was five degrees outside. What did she expect? He leaned forward and tried to kiss her, but she pulled back, teasing him. She pulled his shirt off and he leaned in again, but she avoided him again. Mostly because she wanted to make sure that he had all of his clothes off before he started kissing her because once the kissing commenced, she'd lose her mind and she didn't want to get tripped up on those stupid button-fly jeans again.

She pulled his undershirt over his head, revealing those abs and that chest that she'd barely gotten a look at last week before he'd tumbled into her shower and gotten a mild concussion. She ran her hands over the taut skin and Clancy's eyes rolled back in his head. Then he said, "So, are you going to stay dressed?"

"I wasn't planning on it," she said.

He made a motion then for her take her clothes off. "Come on," he said.

She stood and yanked her jeans down but left her underwear on. Pulling her sweater over her head, she smiled down at him and then he reached for her. His arms disappeared behind her and unsnapped her bra. Her breasts free, he immediately cupped them.

Emma said, "Jeans. Jeans."

"Huh?"

"You can't fondle me until your jeans are off," she said.

"Well, okay," he said, chuckling. "You have weird rules." He shoved one boot off with his foot and the other boot with the other foot, while his fingers, which were used to those stupid button-flies, had them undone in nothing flat. He stood in front of her and dropped his pants. Then he bent down and kissed her and pulled him toward her.

She kissed him back, her hands running along the warm skin of shoulders. Her fingers trailed down his stomach and then rubbed him through his boxers. He was ready and she was ready and they hadn't even done anything yet! That was the shortest foreplay in history. "Um, we need to move this upstairs," she said. "Marty's not here yet, but he probably will be."

"God yes," he said. "Let's move it upstairs."

He reached down, gripped her thighs and hoisted her up. She wrapped her legs around him and they headed for the steps.

"Wait, wait," she said.

"For the love of God, what?" he asked.

"Dogs," she said. "I left the dogs outside."

"Crap," he said and ran for the door with her straddled around him. He opened it but saw no dogs. Cold air poured in on their mostly naked bodies. "I'm not going out after them. You can forget it."

Emma whistled and the dogs came running. Clancy shut the door with his foot and said, "Does Marty have a key?"

"Yes," she said.

"Good," he said and turned the lock.

Emma kissed him along his neck and behind his ear as he made for the stairs. His skin was warm and salty, and he smelled of cedar and leather and the faintest hint of the original Old Spice. He paused at the bottom of the stairs long enough to kiss her on the lips and then he carried her up to the second floor. She sucked on his earlobe and goose bumps broke out along his arm and side. He opened the bedroom door and Emma said, "Wrong room!"

The parrot flew out. Clancy ducked and said, "Bird."

He moved to the next door.

With his earlobe between her teeth she said, "Not that room either."

He stopped in the middle of the hall with her straddled around him and he said, "Emma? Would you like to tell me which room or shall I bang you against the wall right now?"

"It's that one," she said, pointing. Then she kissed him deeply and Clancy dissolved against her, returning her kiss with her back against the wall and her legs wrapped around him. She tightened her thighs, pulling his rib cage next to her crotch and he growled deep in his throat and he ran his fingers along the inside of the elastic to her underwear, brushing the wet sensitive skin.

She whimpered and he moaned.

Finally, he burst open the correct door, threw her on the bed and yanked her panties down. The parrot followed them in, flying around the room, squawking like his tail was on fire. Feathers flew every which way and the bird finally landed on the curtain rod. Emma reached for Clancy. *Must have him right now!* But he stopped, hovering above her. In the moonlight she couldn't tell what he was thinking, if he was thinking anything at all. "What?" she asked. *"What? What?!"*

"You have condoms? Please say yes. And if you tell me they're in another room I'm gonna screw the parrot."

"Oh," she said and wiggled to the bed side stand. Under any other circumstances she would have been howling with laughter but not right now. Right now she was so far gone that all she could think about was getting him inside her. "No, no, no. Don't do anything drastic. I got them!"

"Thank God," he said. He kissed her again and again. Tongues danced as he struggled to open the package. Emma tried to help but her fingers only got in the way.

"Emma?" he said, sounding irritated.

"What?"

"I got this part."

"Oh," she said. "Okay."

Condom on.

Green light. Go.

He gave one good thrust and she came so hard her ears popped.

18

The only thing that kept Clancy from being totally mortified at the expediency of his climax the night before was the fact that Emma had gone first. He'd collapsed on top of her and after a few moments when she finally told him she couldn't breathe, he'd rolled over and gone to sleep. At some point, Emma had woken him up to get under the covers and he felt her warm, soft breasts press against his back and her small hand find its way around his waist. Instead of rousing for round two, which wouldn't have been unwanted or out of the ordinary for him, he'd fallen back asleep.

Just as the sun peeked over the horizon he awoke to the feeling of being watched. He opened his eyes to find Mutt at the foot of the bed, Thing 1 wrapped around Emma's head and the parrot staring down at them from the curtain rod. When he sat up, he found Thing 2 on the rug snuggled around Tricephus, who obviously, couldn't get up on the bed without help. *How thoughtful of Thing 2 to keep Tricephus company.*

He lay back down and reached for Em and ran his hand down her naked back. He wanted her again. He wondered how long she'd be content with things the way they were. Would she start pining for a ring and infiltrating every part of his life as though she belonged there?

Don't borrow trouble, moron.

Why do I care?

Because she trained her cats. Because she worked miracles with Zeus. Because she wasn't afraid to jump up on a stage and make a fool of herself. Because...

Whoa. Stop right there, buddy.

She stirred next to him and he was grateful for the distraction. Because he was thinking crazy thoughts. Crazy, dangerous thoughts.

She opened her eyes from beneath all that hair and smiled at him. She moved toward him, her warm softness spilling into the dip in the mattress and put her arm across his stomach. She nestled her face onto his chest, slid her right leg slightly over his right leg, and tucked her foot just under his calf. *Perfect fit.*

Moron.

She didn't say anything trite or stupid like some women did the morning after. She just rubbed circles on his stomach with her hand and pressed her naked self against him. If she didn't stop...

"Do you smell bacon?" she asked and sat up.

"Uh..." he said. "I smell *something.*"

She threw the covers back and jumped out of bed. Clancy's heart pounded when he saw her standing in the morning sun, completely naked. *Just as awesome in broad daylight.* He noticed a tattoo on her back that he hadn't seen before, but he couldn't make it out in his relaxed and satisfied stupor on the bed. She opened a drawer and threw on a T-shirt, then a pair of underwear—*lucky underwear!*—and some sweatpants and headed downstairs. When Clancy stood, he realized that the events of the night before had made his brain mush. He was fantasizing about being a pair of Emma's underwear, for God's sake. He also realized that all his clothes, except his own underwear were downstairs on the living room floor. Well, he wasn't ashamed of his body in any way, but this was going to be awkward. Especially if there was somebody in Emma's kitchen cooking breakfast.

Who could it be? Aurora would be his best bet. She lived the closest and she often did nice things for people. But how did she get in? Marty must have let her in. Great, he had to go downstairs in his underwear in front of a ninety-year-old woman.

When he reached the bottom step, he was relieved to see that nobody was there, except Emma. But there was bacon and biscuits on the counter. Emma stood with her back to him, reading a piece of paper. "What is it?" he asked.

She turned toward him. "Apparently, Marty made breakfast before he left. He left a note saying, 'I haven't cooked in ten years. Hope it's eatable.'"

"Eatable?"

"That's what it says," she said. "Then he thanked me for the clothes. He said the shirt was a bit big but it would do. But the boots didn't fit at all."

"Clothes?" Clancy asked. "What clothes?"

Emma covered her mouth and her eyes grew wide. "Oh no. You left your clothes down here last night, he probably thought they were for him! Anytime I get him something I just leave it out for him."

Clancy ran into the living room and looked frantically for his shirt and jeans. They were gone. He ran his hands through his hair. "Oh, great," he said. "Your bra was on the floor, did he think that was for him, too?"

Emma just laughed.

"Em! How am I gonna get home with no clothes? Even if I wasn't worried about the humiliation factor, it's subfreezing out there!"

But Emma just laughed harder.

When Emma was finished with her hysterics, she did the only thing she could think of. She offered him clothes. "Well, I guess you'll have to wear a pair of my yoga pants home."

"*Yoga* pants?" Clancy screeched. "*Freakin' yoga pants?*"

"Well, you won't fit into my jeans," she said. "Look, at least you still have your boots."

"*Do I look like a guy who would ever, ever, ever, wear yoga pants?!*"

Emma laughed so hard she could barely stand up.

Clancy glared at her and then a smile tweaked at the corner of his mouth. Next thing she knew he was laughing as hard as she was. "Go get me your goddamn yoga pants," he said, resigned. "Just try to make sure they're not pink or flowered."

A few minutes later he sat on the hearth with an old Rams sweatshirt that had belonged to Emma's ex-boyfriend—why did women always keep at least one item of oversized ex-boyfriend clothes when they broke up?—her teal yoga pants, and his cowboy boots. He glowered as she brought him his breakfast. "May as well eat something," she said.

"Don't laugh," he said.

"I'm not laughing. Your butt looks really cute in those pants and I can see the outline of your circumcision. Nothing to laugh at, let me tell you."

He mumbled something as he shoved the biscuit with jelly into his mouth. Tricephus moved in on his bacon, though, and Clancy was too slow. "Mangy mutt!" he said to her.

"Wrong dog," Emma said and gave him her bacon.

When they opened the door to take Clancy home, Roy stood on the porch, looking bored and put out. Clancy hung his head and took Roy by the reins. "I'm gonna walk him home," Clancy said.

"You want me to drive you home so you can get on a pair of jeans first? You can always come back to get him."

"No," he said. "My dad's gonna see me no matter what. My dignity is in shreds. What does it matter?"

"Okay."

"I mean, who else is gonna see me between here and my house, anyway?" he asked.

Emma shrugged.

She wanted to kiss him good-bye but that would sort of be like they were in a relationship or something and she didn't want to scare him away. She waved instead. "I'll be over later to work with Zeus."

He waved back and she watched him and Roy head toward Lady Slipper Lane. His spine stiffened as a car pulled in her driveway. It slowed as Clancy walked past, but Clancy never even acknowledged the driver, and then it stopped in front of her house. A man got out, young, under twenty-five and said, "Hi. I'm Brandon. Clancy's cousin. I'm here about the repairs."

Emma smiled.

"Roy get out of his pen?" he asked.

She nodded.

"Was Clancy wearing ballet pants?"

Emma giggled and looked up in time to see Aurora speeding by on her snowmobile. Then the trash truck went the other way. Who is going to see him between here and his house? Apparently, lots of people.

19

Aurora had made tuna fish and cucumber sandwiches and more of those sinful chocolate chip cookies. She'd stopped by earlier that morning on her snow mobile to invite Emma to lunch, so Emma decided she'd work with Zeus *after* indulging in Aurora's cookies.

"So, I hear you're interested in the history of the Quail Bottom Saddle Club," Aurora said. "I talked to Luella this morning. That woman makes the best hash browns in the world."

"Well," Emma said. "It seems as though my mother may have been, for lack of a better word, a saddle club groupie."

Aurora's small dark eyes narrowed on her. "Your mother from around here?"

"No," Emma said. "Her mother was from Maine and her father, my grandpa, was from Wisconsin. They met in Chicago. So, my mother and her sister were raised mostly in Illinois and Missouri. I think there was a time when they lived in Iowa. I'm not really sure. Why?"

"Just curious why she'd be up here that summer in the first place," Aurora said.

"Oh, that's easy. She followed a guy up here. They lasted a few weeks, so my mom made the best of it. She'd just go through guys like plastic cups. You know, trying to reassure herself that there was nothing wrong with her."

"Looking for Mr. Right among all the Mr. Wrongs?" Aurora asked.

"No, I don't think so. She never talked about a Prince Charming or somebody who would make things all better. It was more like when one guy stopped reassuring her or stopped making her feel beautiful, she'd find one who did. Or like one guy telling her she was wonderful wasn't enough. What if he was wrong? But if she had fifty guys telling her she was awesome, then she could come closer to believing it."

"Was she a trust fund baby?"

"What do you mean?" Emma asked.

"How could she afford to just take off for the summer?"

As Emma began to speak, she realized that she could have been talking about herself. "Oh, until I was born, I don't think she ever had a real job-job. Just temporary jobs. She'd save up all her money and then just go...until she ran out of money. And she'd start over."

Emma had been the thing to make her mother settle down, although that term could be applied quite loosely. They hadn't moved around a lot once Emma was born, but her mother had changed jobs and men as often as she changed hair color. She'd been trying to be wild and free when she no longer was. Because of Emma. If her mother had only looked, she would have realized that the one person who thought she was wonderful was sitting at her knee the whole time.

Me.

Aurora got up slowly and pulled a scrapbook off the counter. With ancient, wrinkly hands, she pushed it in front of Emma. "That's the scrapbook for 1986."

Emma opened it and began flipping pages. The book was shoved full of newspaper articles, photographs, ribbons, statistics. There were as many pictures of horses as there were people. It was a saddle club, after all.

On nearly every page, images of horses galloping around barrels and guys on bulls and riders in cowboy hats and jeans, frolicking under a huge blue sky. Emma pointed to a photo of a man with a Wyatt Earp type of mustache and wearing a big white hat. He led his horse away from the barrels by the lead rope and the smile on his face was almost as huge as his hat. The caption told Emma that it was taken August of 1986. Emma smiled and Aurora said, "That's Marty Pepper."

"What?" Emma said. She looked closer. She studied the image and was struck by how his life had gone off in a direction that, at that moment, he couldn't have foreseen. Probably couldn't have fathomed. The homeless man who slept on her living room floor looked completely self-possessed and healthy in this picture. "Wow."

Emma scanned the crowd for her mother's familiar face and big poufy mousse-filled hair. She didn't see her in the picture of Marty. But then a few pages later she saw the image of Helen presenting a trophy to somebody. "Wait, that's her!" she said.

Aurora turned the book around and looked.

"Why would she be handing out trophies?" Emma asked.

"Oh, sometimes the show officials would get pretty girls from the audience to do the honors."

Emma stared at the image. "Wow." She couldn't help but wonder who the man was. Had they hooked up later or not? Was that her father?

She turned the page and came to a big group photograph taken on the bleachers at an event. Everybody smiled, some held trophies, and others had belts. A banner that hung above the stadium said: Winchester Saddle Club Barrel Races. August 25th, 1986. There were as many men as there were women. "I hadn't expected so many. There must be sixty pairs of cowboy boots in this picture."

"Oh yeah," Aurora said. "And those are just the members who were at that event. There were probably a hundred members."

"A hundred? Well, what's the population of Quail Bottom?"

Aurora smiled, "About eighteen hundred. Give or take fifty."

"So, do you still remember who everybody is?" Emma asked.

"Well, that's me," she said, pointing to a tiny, smiling woman who sat on the shoulders of two brawny cowboys. A huge turquoise band decorated her ten-gallon cowboy hat. The hat was almost bigger than she was. "I was flashy. They thought of me as their mother."

Emma did the math. If Aurora was ninety, then in 1986 she still would have been almost sixty. She didn't look it. And there she was perched up on top of those two cowboys' shoulders like she was a sixteen-year-old gymnast.

Aurora ticked off names. "That's Sam Sherman, and that's Jimmy Hollingsworth. Oh, that's the current mayor of Quail Bottom, Roger Olson, and his wife, Tammy, although she wasn't his wife, then. They found love in the stables, like so many other couples. And that's Ned Barstow and next to him is the sheriff, LeRoy Chatham. That's Reuben Stephens, and that's my brother Hugo—he won the overall championship that year. But then Marty came along the next year and broke his barrel racing record. Hugo was so mad. Because the horse that Marty had broken the record with was the horse that Hugo had sold him!"

Aurora laughed. "Oh, what was that horse's name? Sonny! That was it."

"Wait..." Emma said. "Did you say Reuben Stephens?"

"Yes," Aurora said. "He was president for a few years. Why?"

"Well, any of these guys could be my father, right?"

"Well, I suppose... Depending on whether or not your mom got the name of the town right and the years right and..."

Emma thought of the photo that Jim Hollingsworth had. And she thought of the picture she'd just seen of her mother. "Oh, I think she got the year and the town right," Emma said. She wasn't sure about anything else, but of those two things she was certain. So far none of them had the name Doug or Tug or Larry, although LeRoy sort of sounded like Larry. If you were drunk or stoned enough. Aurora clicked off more names and Emma tried to listen for anything that sounded close. Harry maybe. Lug? Lug was a name, wasn't it? But she couldn't hear a whole lot because the blood rushed in her ears at about a hundred miles an hour.

Reuben Stephens had belonged to the saddle club. He'd been on the circuit that summer.

Emma felt sick to her stomach. What if...?

Had she just had sex with her brother? Oh, God.

"Technically, it would be a half-brother," Granny said.

Well, gee, Granny. Don't you think you could have mentioned that before now?

Her heart beat faster and faster until she thought it would just turn into one long beat. The room spun sideways and Emma reached a hand out to the table to steady herself.

"Emma, are you okay?" Aurora asked.

But Emma just kept playing the moments of mindless passion between her and Clancy in her head. Over and over. Clancy moaning on top of her. Her snuggling into his back to sleep. *Her brother?!*

"Half-brother, dearest."

"Shut up, Granny!" Emma said.

"What did you say?" Aurora asked.

Okay, well as far as crazy went, this was the craziest of all crazy-ass shit and she was going to hell. Her Granny would never forgive her, and there weren't enough Hail Marys in all of the world to get her out of this mess. This was it. She'd finally done it. Being thrown off of a balcony into a sea of drunken testosterone during Mardi Gras, getting hit by lightning, the whole city block in Louisville up in flames—an accident, but still!—even that thing that happened with the nun, *none* of it came close to being *THIS FLIPPING CRAZY!*

"Emma, you do not look good at all," Aurora said.

"No," she said. "I'm fine."

I'm hyperventilating and my ever-loving soul is on fire—set aflame by Satan himself—but I'm fine! Could a person go to hell more than once?

"Aurora," Emma said. "Can I take this book with me?"

"Why sure," she said.

"I hate to eat and run but...I have to go order more DNA tests."

20

As Emma headed across the road to Clancy's she got a text message from Sam: *The fishing shacks have to be off the ice in a few weeks. You want to go ice-fishing before the season is over?*

She texted back: *ABSOLUTELY YES.*

Sam: *Tomorrow?* 10:00 *AM? Breakfast first?*

Emma: *Sounds great.*

She looked up the driveway and Roy clopped toward her with determination in his eyes. It seemed unusually cold today, but maybe that was just because she'd learned she was going to hell and she was in shock. She glanced up at the cobalt sky and on the very edge of the horizon she saw a front inching its way toward them. She pulled out her phone and glanced at the weather. Sure enough, snow tonight. Winter storm advisory.

When she reached Roy, she noticed that he had no lead rope and no halter. He was a naked horse. "Hey, Roy," she said. As she approached him, he turned around back toward the Stephens ranch, but he just stood there. Without a lead rope, how was she supposed to take him home? What was she thinking? It wasn't like he didn't know the way. She glanced up to see Marty lumbering toward them with his cart of belongings.

"How's it going, Marty?" she asked.

"Good," he said. "You get my breakfast?"

"I did," she said. "It was wonderful. Thank you."

Emma smiled at him because she liked what she saw. He seemed taller. He was also wearing Clancy's ill-fitting shirt and jeans under his Army ration coat. She blushed and hoped he didn't notice. "Do you need anything, Marty?"

He looked up at the sky and said, "Storms coming. Do you mind if I ride it out with you?"

"Not at all," she said. "Just put your cart in the garage."

"And...can I use your address...to get mail?"

What sort of mail was he going to get? But she nodded her head and he looked relieved. Marty raised a shaking hand and rubbed Roy under the forelock. She studied her houseguest. He needed a shave. And a haircut. And his eyes were blood shot. But he looked more alert. "I got food for the parrot."

"Oh, good," she said, and her heart swelled. Where had he gotten the money for parrot food? Had he used his tin cup donations?

"You headed to Clancy's?" he asked.

"Yes, but Roy here doesn't seem to want to go."

"You just rub him on the rump and tell him he's a good boy."

Emma laughed. "Is that the secret code for all horses?"

"Just this one," he said. Marty's hand trailed down Roy's back and Roy twisted his head around and kissed Marty on the top of the head. The two stood there in silent communication, one old rider to one old horse. Although, in truth, she wasn't sure how old Roy was. He just seemed old because he never made any sudden moves and he seemed wiser than most horses. Marty rubbed Roy's rump and told him he was a good boy and Roy blew air and flapped his nostrils. "Let's go," Emma said, and Roy followed her.

As they walked across Lady Slipper Lane to the Stephens ranch, Emma unloaded her troubles on him. "Boy, I tell ya, Roy. I've been in some serious doo-doo before but this time..."

The horse threw his head up and whinnied.

"I know. I get what you're saying. And I should just walk away from this. Clancy won't care, I don't think. I mean, I don't get the feeling that I mean *that* much to him."

Roy was silent.

"No? Nothing from you?" she asked.

"*He made sure you didn't miss the northern lights,*" Granny said.

True.

"I just thought, you know, we were two consenting adults who were attracted to each other...who hadn't had sex in a while..." She gave a sideways glance at Roy. He nodded his head. "I'm not sure what's more disturbing. The fact you can understand me or the fact that you know the details of Clancy's love life."

He snorted. She stopped and looked at him. "All right, seriously? Are you putting me on?"

I am talking to a horse.

"I'm going insane. One, two three..."

Roy abruptly turned around in a circle and gave her a sheepish look. If horses could look like sheep.

"You are so strange," she said and continued walking. "The bad part is, if he's my brother, and Reuben is my father...well, I was sort of hoping to have a relationship with my newfound family. Will I be able to think of Clancy as a brother then? Will Clancy be okay with it? Is that whole sex thing going to ruin what chances I had at a normal relationship with them?"

"*Obviously,*" Granny said.

Roy was silent.

"I mean, nobody knows we had sex. Just the two of us. Unless Marty remembers the bathroom incident, but he was pretty drunk. Oh, well, and Brad might have figured it out. But, if nobody knows, we could just go on like nothing happened. I'd have a father, a brother, a sister and a niece. And a wicked stepmother that I wouldn't even have to worry about killing because she's already dead. It works out perfectly," Emma said.

Except that she and Clancy had had great, fantastic, wonderful sex.

Roy had nothing to say on that, either. She pulled out her phone and said, "Come on, let's get a picture." She held the phone up, placed her head next to Roy's and snapped a picture. She checked the photo and giggled. Roy had raised his head just a notch and bared his teeth. She posted the picture to Facebook with the caption: *Hangin' with my bestie, Roy.*

"I mean, it wasn't the greatest sex in the world. It was over with too fast to rank up there with phenomenal sex," she continued. "Of course, I don't ever remember being that turned on. But still... Oh, just...*damn.*"

Roy suddenly stopped and bowed to her, one leg out in front of him and his butt up in the air. She blinked at him. "Seriously, what is your problem?"

He stayed like that until she rubbed his hindquarters. Then he continued walking.

"But the thing is, I was kind of hoping to have *more* sex with him to find out if it was going to be the best sex in the world. I mean, he could potentially be the Orgasm Wizard of the World and he's living right across the street from me and how convenient is that? How am I supposed to find that out if he's off limits because he's my brother?"

Roy walked along in silence.

"That sounded weird. You can tell me. I won't be offended."

He snorted. Twice.

"That's what I thought," she said. Emma expelled a huge sigh. "But, I keep thinking Granny would have said something. If she could let me know there was a valley to land a flying inferno in, don't you think she would have said, 'Uh, gee, Em. Clancy's off limits.' But I guess it doesn't work that way. But it does make me feel a little better. Because even though she's quiet on a lot of things, usually the big ones, and this one is big, she's pretty vocal."

They finally made it to the farm and Roy nudged her with his nose and headed to his stable. She glanced about, trying to find everybody, but only saw Zeus in the corral. She'd made a promise that no matter how comfortable she felt with the horse, she wouldn't go in his pen by herself again. Not until Reuben said it was okay. So, she walked on past and down to the other stables which were heated inside. She stopped and petted the Belgians: Tyrone, Lilly, Edna, Liberace and Duke.

She headed to the other stables with the Appaloosas and found Clancy inside mucking out the compartments. "Hey," he said and smiled at her. It wasn't just a smile, it was a I-just-had-sex-with-you smile. Things could be worse. He could have frowned. Or ignored her. Or spat on her. The sizzling, sparkling, afterglow smile was awesome. And at any other time in her life she would have taken that as encouraging. Now, all she could hear was Sister Mary Josephina cackling in a voice that was a cross between the Wicked Witch of the West and Gollum, *"There's a special place in hell reserved for you, my pretty precious."*

Or Father Hadrian, with his matter-of-fact tone, *"That's four billion Hail Mary's, Emma. We'll work on the Our Father's later."*

"Hey back," she said.

He leaned the shovel up against the stall and went to the sink and washed his hands. "Did you tell Heather Hollingsworth that she could bring her son out here to meet Roy?" he asked.

"Oh, well, I told her I'd ask first. But, I...didn't get the chance last night."

He abruptly whirled on her and leaned her up against the wall in one swift motion. Before she could think or protest, he kissed her. When he managed to tear his lips away from hers, he said, "That's because I was too busy kissing you."

She kissed him back. "Yes, I know. I was there."

"And doing other things to you," he said. He kissed her neck and then her ear. And then the other side of her neck. And back to her lips.

Sweet Jesus. Her stomach flip-flopped.

"I know," she said breathlessly. "So, do you mind if Micah comes out and meets Roy?"

"Not at all. I told her she could come out tomorrow afternoon," he said. He had her pinned against the wall with his thigh between her crotch and his hands on her hips. He kissed her again, soft and slow this time and without her realizing it, he unzipped her coat. Emma leaned into him and forgot herself for a minute. She forgot she was being stared at by a bunch of equine Peeping Tom's, and she forgot that she was supposed to protest because he was her brother. Well, *could* be her brother. Could be her *half*-brother. There was a difference. Maybe there wasn't a difference on the scale of sins, but biologically there was. Should she tell him?

Hypothetically speaking, if she got pregnant, they could have a three-headed baby with blue skin. She wasn't sure, since this had never been covered in any of her schooling, but if there was the potential to have blue-skinned three-headed babies, it seemed that the guy ought to be made aware.

Reuben had seen the ad the same as everybody else. He hadn't come forward, so maybe that meant he hadn't slept with her mother! That's right. Just because he was on the circuit that summer did not mean he'd had sex with her mother. He would have been a married man. Clancy would have been four or five then. There was no way Clancy could be her brother.

Her heart began to beat faster and she thought, *but what if Reuben had cheated on June with Helen?* Then not only would Clancy be her half-brother but her mother was the woman he cheated with! This couldn't get much worse.

But he didn't answer the ad. Which means, he didn't have sex with her.

Or else he didn't want to admit it. Or he was lying. Or he couldn't remember. There were people who did forget the people they slept with, believe it or not, and people were not beyond lying about indiscretions, especially if they were married!

No, no, no. There was no reason to tell Clancy. No reason to bring it up, because she chose to believe that if Reuben had slept with her mother, he'd have said something. She was giving him the benefit of the doubt. That was mostly because Clancy had her coat off and his hands were up her shirt and his thumbs were doing magical things to her nipples, and he tasted good and...

"A special place in hell!" a chorus of nuns screeched.

Oh, stuff it!

"What did you say?" Clancy asked, pulling away from her and looking down at her with sparkling blue eyes.

"I'm sorry, what?" she asked.

"You just told me to stuff it."

"No, no, I said...I..." she stammered. She couldn't even think of anything that sounded remotely like stuff it, so she just kissed him and ran her hand up the front of his shirt feeling his abs beneath. He pulled her to him and kneaded her butt with his big, capable hands, and she was pretty sure that she liquefied from the inside out. She was a big puddle of goo. They'd mop her up in the morning.

His hands seemed to be everywhere. Leaving a trail of warmth wherever they touched. It was as if he had five of them. And she didn't care. She wished he had eight of them. Good god, what could this man achieve if he had eight hands?

But what if he was her brother? Shouldn't she mention it?

No!

"Oh, God," she said.

"My thoughts exactly. I have condoms in my pocket."

"I'm not having sex...with the horses..." she said.

"Of course not," he said into her mouth. He felt for the button on her jeans and she tried to fight him. Sort of. Okay, not really. "You're having it with me. They're just watching."

"Doesn't that creep you out?" she asked.

"Not in the least," he said. "I watch them have sex all the time."

That statement should have made her pause, but it didn't because he'd knelt down and licked her belly button and her mind was buzzing and...and...yeah.

There went her zipper.

Stop him now!

Because she might talk God into forgiving her for last night because she hadn't known there was the possibility of siblingness between them, but today, she knew there was that possibility and yet..."Don't stop," she said, suddenly. "No matter what I say...*oh, wow*...um...no matter what I say, just don't stop."

Clancy said, "I wasn't planning on it." He pulled her pants all the way open and licked her hip bone. Emma rolled her head against the wall of the barn and only slightly noticed when one of the horses whinnied. She ran her hands through his hair, reveling in the sensation of his tongue. He went back to her belly button then and she thought she'd go insane from the sensation.

He stood and kissed her, sucking on her upper lip and Emma forgot everything and tore at his pants. She forgot her name, how old she was, what state she was in, what *his* name was...she just flat out forgot everything there was to know except that her skin was ferociously alive and she wanted to rub her skin with his skin. She ached everywhere for him. Especially...

He ground his pelvis into her.

...*there*. Yeah, especially there.

"Emma Rose! Even if he is not your brother, you're keeping vital information from him. This could break all trust he has in you!" Granny's voice said.

"Okay, wait," she said.

"You said not to stop. No matter what. I'm holding you to your word."

"No, really," she said. "I...I just want to run something by you."

His blue eyes clouded over with lust and searched her face. *"Now?"*

She nodded.

"Later," he said.

"Now," she said.

He ran his hands through his hair, took a deep breath to get his bearings and said, "What? What? *What?*"

She was never particularly good at mincing words. "So, Aurora showed me her scrapbook from the summer my mother was hanging around the saddle club."

"Yeah? And?" he said.

"Well, I saw your dad in the pictures. One of them was at a show in Winchester Hollow."

"Yes, he belonged to it for years. So?"

"Well...what if...?"

His eyes grew wide. "Are you suggesting that my father cheated on my mother with your mother and that you're my sister?" He blinked. "Please, say no."

"W-what I'm saying is, what *if* they were together? I mean, his marital status wouldn't have stopped my mother one way or another."

He blinked again, soaking up her words. "Did he answer your ad?"

"No."

"Then he didn't sleep with your mother."

"You believe that?"

"Yes," he said. "Absolutely. Besides, if there was even a doubt in his mind, he would have said something to me. He's been here with us, Em, he's not stupid. He knows there's something going on between us. He's seen the way I look at you. He would have nipped that in the bud right away. He wouldn't want me having sex with my half-sister, even if it meant he'd have to admit that he cheated on my mother."

She'd never thought of that! If there was the smallest chance in Reuben's mind that they were going to hook up, he would have immediately said something because he wouldn't want blue-skinned, three-headed grandbabies, either.

"Oh, thank God," she said, with her hand on her chest. She let out a long relaxing breath and inhaled again. "So did I kill the mood?"

Clancy laughed, a deep and devilish laugh. "Where's that stool?"

21

"Well, a lot of good you did me," Emma said as Roy walked her home.

Roy blinked at her but kept walking.

The sunshine was gone, hidden behind a thick cover of low-hung clouds. And dusk was only an hour or two away. The world had gone still and quiet, and silence announced that a storm was coming. Funny how the animals could tell that.

The snow crunched beneath her feet and it seemed especially loud.

"You got nothing to say?" she said.

Roy tossed his head about.

"Reuben seems like an upright, honorable guy. If he'd had sex with my mother, he would have said something. I'm sure of it."

Roy stopped and leaned into her, placing his ginormous head on her chest. He just stood there for the longest time, listening to her breathe, and she realized that she was absolutely in love with this horse. They walked the rest of the way to her house and as she climbed the porch stairs she said, "Go on home, Roy. You don't want to get caught out in the storm."

Inside, Marty had a fire going and was covered with animals. All of them except the parrot were seated next to him on the floor. He wouldn't sit on the furniture because he told her that he was too dirty, even though he'd been taking showers at her house pretty regularly.

She popped two potatoes in the microwave and steamed some broccoli and put some cold turkey on each plate and brought dinner into the living room. Carb, protein, green. Just like her grandmother always taught her. She really needed to get some dining room furniture.

When she sat down, legs crossed, the animals came for her food, but she snapped her fingers and three of them jumped up onto the couch, while Tricephus sat in front of it on the floor. It was a bit disconcerting to have four pair of eyes watch every bite you took.

Emma watched Marty as he flipped through the scrapbook from Aurora. "Oh," Emma said. "That reminds me." She pulled out her phone and dialed Aurora's number. "I promised Zoe and Luella to check on Aurora now and then."

"Yes?" Aurora said.

"It's Emma."

"Oh, Emmie, what can I do for you, dear?"

"Nothing," she said. Then thought better of that. "Well, something. You can tell me if there is anything you need before this storm hits."

"Why?"

"Because we're supposed to get ten inches."

"So what? You think I'm old and can't take care of myself?"

Oh, great. "No. I think I'm paranoid and worry about people. You're just like number eight on my list of people that I was checking up on," she lied. That's it, put it back on herself.

"Oh," Aurora said.

"You okay on firewood?"

"Yes."

"Is it in the house?"

"Yes. And I went to the store yesterday. I'm fine."

"Alrighty then," Emma said.

When she hung up the phone, she noticed that Marty had grown very still. He ran his fingers across the picture of him with the Wyatt Earp mustache. "Took first place in cattle roping that day."

He pulled his whiskey bottle out of his pocket and took a swig and then put it away. He ate his dinner as he flipped pages. When he came to the picture of her mother handing out the trophy he said, "There's your mother. Right there."

"Yeah," Emma said.

The wind kicked up outside and Marty said, "It's starting to snow."

She hadn't bought a television yet and honestly, she'd been too busy to watch it anyway. So, Emma went into the kitchen and hauled down the chess set that still had the pieces in place from the game they were playing on Saturday. Marty was about three moves away from taking her queen. "Guess we'll just ride out the storm," she said.

He smiled up at her and she started singing REO Speedwagon's "Ridin' the Storm Out."

"Are you playing guitar or am I?" she asked.

"I'll do the guitar," he said and proceeded to play air guitar while Emma sang.

Clancy could not stop thinking about Emma. That whole idea of having sex and getting her out of his system had completely and utterly backfired. Instead, she was all he could think about and he wanted more. The way she smelled like sunbeams and lilacs, the way she moved like warm honey, the way she chewed on her lip when she was deep in thought. The way she made everybody, including the four-legged everybody, feel special. And warm.

And holy crap. What was wrong with him?

He'd had an earthshaking, all-encompassing shudderfest in the barn yesterday. That's what was wrong with him. *In the barn!* The thought made him smile. Why, of course in the barn. Because any woman that wouldn't have sex in the barn was no woman for him.

Not that he was in the market.

Almost a foot of snow had fallen last night, and he looked out on a world that was white and gray. While he drank his coffee, he stared across the road at Emma's house. Ned Barstow's old house. It'd be hard to get used to thinking of the house as belonging to anybody but him. That old coot had lived there for ages, then decided, out of nowhere, to retire in Florida. True Minnesotans would never give up pine trees for palm trees. It just wasn't done. But Emma was making it her own with little touches here and there. And Brandon was going to fix her porch for her next week.

He couldn't really see that much of Emma's house because of the overgrowth and the trees, and in the summer all he could see was the roof and one window on the second floor. It was a good thing that wasn't her bedroom window or he'd stand here all day staring at it. Even though it was too far away to actually see anything. He'd know she was in there. Sort of like how he stood and stared at the house in general because he knew she was in there.

He had to laugh at her though, all worried that they were siblings. He was absolutely convinced that there was no way on this Earth that they were siblings, but he'd ask his dad about it anyway. Just to put her mind at ease.

Caitlin had arrived late yesterday afternoon in time to watch Emma in the pen with Zeus. She'd just stood there in the cold, clutching her stuffed horse, watching every move Emma made, almost forgetting to blink.

For some reason, some parent-teacher conference or something, Caitlin was off from school. He might just call his sister and tell her not to come and get Caitlin this evening because of all the snow. He just wanted another day with her. And Heather Hollingsworth was due out with Micah later today, too, and it might make him feel better to see Caitlin with the horses. A little girl, somebody his age, could go a long way in relaxing him.

"Uncle Clancy," Caitlin said from behind him.

He turned to find his bleary-eyed niece, still clutching Chester, standing in the doorway in her pajamas. "I'm hungry."

"You want pancakes?" he said.

She nodded.

By the time he finished making her breakfast, the girl was wide-awake and talking a mile a minute, whereas Clancy still had at least three cups of coffee to go before he'd be human. Still, he tried to keep up.

"Did you know that Emma's birthday is almost the same as my Mom's? Just a couple of days apart. They're even the same age! I want to be just like Emma when I grow up," she said.

"Yeah?"

"I want to make the horses talk to me," she said.

Clancy gave her a sideways glance.

"I've seen her. She talks and they listen and then, sometimes, they answer her. Then I can help horses like Zeus," she said.

Clancy grew still. "Caitlin, you have to promise me that you'll never get in the corral with Zeus," he said.

"I know," she said, stuffing a bite of blueberry pancake in her mouth. "And Emma said that one time she had to run into a raging river and rescue a bag full of cats."

"She did?"

"Yeah. She said that some asshole had tied them up in a bag and threw them in the river!"

Clancy choked on his coffee. "Caitlin, we don't say that word."

"Well, that's what she said. And I agree with her. That's what that person was!"

"Okay, but you're eight. You can't use that kind of language."

"Whatever," she said and took another bite. "And then one time she picked up this stray dog on the street corner. He wasn't wearing no tags. She was going to take him to the humane so...society. But before she could get there, she found another stray and picked it up, too. Only one was a boy and one was a girl..."

Caitlin blushed and started giggling. "And she said the boy dog started humping the girl dog, right there in her backseat!"

"Caitlin!" Clancy said, trying to stifle a laugh.

"Eh," she said and waved a hand. "I've seen the horses do it."

Clancy just rubbed his forehead and laughed. "Eat your pancakes and shush," he said.

"Not enough coffee yet? Emma says that coffee is God's way of controlling the crime rate. He knows if you take away coffee everybody kills each other."

Clancy smiled.

"And Emma also says that Minnesota is colder than a witch's tit in a brass bra."

Clancy spit coffee everywhere.

22

Sam came and got Emma in his big ol' truck because he didn't want her to drive out to his lake in her "toy car." They stopped in Luella's Café and had breakfast. Aurora was there having her daily dose of hash-browns. *Those snowmobiles are awesome,* Emma thought. A foot of snow didn't stop a ninety-year-old woman.

After their bellies were full and they had coffee to-go, they headed out to Odin Lake. As they came over the hill, the frozen lake spread before them. Emma hadn't yet seen the lake in the daylight and she was transfixed. Right now it was covered in newly fallen snow and there was no way to even see the frozen top. Little huts dotted the landscape like a mobile village. A big, white expanse stretched out in front of her. She could only tell where the edge of the lake was because majestic pine trees bordered it and boating docks and houses were wedged in there as well.

"Okay," she said. "What's the deal with ice-fishing?"

Sam smiled and said, "It's a nice alternative to hamburgers."

She laughed.

"Unfasten your seat belt," he said.

She glanced over at him. "Why?"

"Because we're driving out onto the lake now."

"*What?!* You're going to drive the truck onto the lake?"

"Yes. Don't worry."

"Won't the ice break?" she asked.

"No," he said.

"So, why am I taking off my seat belt?"

"In case the ice breaks," he said. "You won't get trapped in the truck."

"But you just said..."

"Precaution, my dear."

Emma giggled and said, "Okie dokie." Off came the seat belt. Her heart gave a flutter as the wheels of the truck made contact with the ice.

"You got all of these houses and huts out here," he said. "It can take a truck."

"Uh-huh," she said. *We're driving a pick-up truck onto a lake! This. Is. Awesome!*

"All of the huts have to be off by mid-February. That gives everybody plenty of time before a thaw. If they're not gone, the authorities go out and haul them off."

She noticed that some shacks looked like outhouses and some looked like little miniature trailers. Some people were just perched over a hole with poles, with no protection from the elements whatsoever. "So...are there guidelines on how thick the ice has to be?"

"Oh yeah," he said. "To bring a truck like mine out, it needs to be fifteen inches or so of clear ice, because clear ice is stronger than milky ice. But even with just two to four inches, you can come out with a lawn chair."

"It still seems...iffy to me," she said.

Sam laughed. "The cars need to be fifty or so feet apart and if you drill a small hole next to them and you start to see water lapping over the top, it's sinking and you need to get off."

"Oh, nice to know," she said. It was so weird, because even though she knew she was on ice, it didn't feel like it.

"Some guys, they got big elaborate buildings out here. Bunk beds, big screen television, mini refrigerator stocked with beer, a heater. Basically, they say they're going fishing but this is their man-cave on ice. They're getting away from their wives."

Emma laughed and waved out the window as one fisherman looked up and nodded. A minute later Sam pulled up next to a shack and killed the engine. "That's mine," he said.

The shanty was about eight foot by eight foot with a door, one window and a heater built into the wall. At one time it'd been painted bright red, but now it had faded to an orangey-brick color. "Home away from home," he said.

Emma stood on the ice and looked out at the tree line. They had to be a half a mile away from the shore, at least. She glanced down at her feet and jumped up and down.

"Oh, God, don't do that!" Sam yelled.

Emma screamed. *"Why?"*

And then Sam pointed his finger at her and laughed.

Her heart pounded in her chest. "You're a jerk!" she said.

He was still laughing as he unlocked the shack and escorted her in. "You probably scared all the fish away," he said.

Inside there were four holes in the floor and Emma knelt down and stuck her arm in one of them until she reached the frigid water. "Holy cow!" she said.

Sam smiled at her. "Never saw anybody stick their arm down a jigging hole before."

Emma laughed. "Well, I've never seen ice that thick from this angle! How deep is it?"

"Last time I checked about eighteen or nineteen inches," he said.

He didn't have bunk beds or a refrigerator, but he did have blue gingham curtains hanging on the window. "Curtains are a nice touch," she said.

"The ex-wife made them," he said. "Just never got rid of them."

He had a recliner in the middle of the hut and a radio with Bose speakers, and two fold-up chairs sitting next to two of the holes. He scratched his beard and said, "Well, let's bait them up and catch some fish."

Half an hour later they sat in their chairs staring down into the dark holes, Puccini on the stereo. A wonderful soprano sang lush Italian words and Emma imagined Sam, out here by himself, reclining in that chair with his eyes closed, surrounded by fish and that music. She would have never pegged him for a lover of opera.

"What happened?" she said.

"What do you mean?" he asked.

"With your wife."

He shrugged.

A moment later he said, "Things happen. I wasn't the greatest husband."

"Did you try?" she asked.

"I did," he said. "But I think it was Garrett that really did us in."

"Your son?"

He nodded. "She just kept giving him chance after chance and giving him more money and he just kept using her. I tried to tell her what he was but she couldn't see it. She wouldn't accept it. She kept saying, 'He's my boy. I can't give up on him.'"

"And you gave up?" Emma asked.

He nodded again. "I know maybe it wasn't the right thing, Em, but he was killing us. I don't mean our marriage, I mean he was physically killing us. We weren't living any kind of real life. We both had trouble sleeping. Eating. Communicating. Not just with each other, but the outside world, too. I didn't want to turn him loose. I *wanted* him to be normal. But when your own son will break into your house when you're not home and steal his mother's jewelry for drugs, well..."

Emma got a nibble on her pole, but she ignored it.

She thought very carefully about how to word her next sentence. "I can't imagine what that must have done to him."

"What do you mean?"

"Well, somewhere inside him he was aware of what he was doing. You think he wanted to steal her jewelry? Like a payback for something? Or was he just that desperate?"

Sam blinked at her. "I think he was that desperate," he said.

"Well, if it wasn't a payback, some sort of revenge, then it probably bothered him as much as it did you. He just didn't know what else to do. He knew that you guys had the means to keep his demon at bay. Even if it was for only a few days."

"You think that he doesn't enjoy doing drugs?"

She cleared her throat. "I'm not sure I understand the question."

"If it didn't feel good, he wouldn't do it. Right? Like how people get a little tipsy because it's fun. How can you steal your mother's antique pearl necklace to have fun?"

"I think maybe the first couple of times was probably fun. But what he's doing now...oh, now he's just trying to outrun the demon. What that feels like when you wake up straight...like razor blades crawling around in your skull. You'd want to stop that, too. He has, in essence, given up his life already. And so many addicts won't get help because they've destroyed everything they've ever loved, and they've got nothing to go back to. Or so they think."

He took a deep breath. "Are you speaking from experience?"

"Not first-hand. Second-hand. I knew somebody who was a heroin addict."

"Did he survive?"

"Last time I checked. But he put a gun in his mouth more than once. Luckily, he either talked himself out of it, or somebody was there to stop him."

"You?"

She nodded. "I walked in on him. I...was so scared when I saw him that I didn't even think. I just lunged for him. The gun went off in between his ear and my ear—neither of us could hear for days—and the bullet hit a lamp, shattered it, the glass flew back and cut me right here," she said. She pulled her sweater down to reveal a small scar on her collar bone.

"Look, what I'm saying is, the walking away...I get it. I did it. You're right. He was killing me. It's like trying to swim to shore with fifty-pound weights on your ankles. Just as you're almost there they add more weight and you get dragged farther out. Anger? I get that, too. But, eventually I realized he was sick. I quit taking it personally. Does that mean that I'm going to invite him back into my life? No. I would die if I did. But I stopped hating him. Because I wouldn't hate somebody if he was sick. I wouldn't hate him if he'd had a stroke and was a vegetable."

"It's different," he said. "His illness is self-imposed."

"Poor diet, smoking, no exercise...that's responsible for a lot of illness and death in this country, Sam. It's not all genetic. Regardless, I don't hate them for it, and I don't take it personally."

Sam took a deep breath and messed with the fishing pole. He cleared his throat and when he looked up at her he had tears in his eyes. "But why weren't we enough for him to not start using in the first place?"

"All children go through the phase of burning that umbilical cord. They want to be their own people. Make their own mistakes. Sometimes during that phase, they get turned around and forget where they're going. And they do really, really, stupid things. You can't blame yourself for that. You didn't hand him the drugs and say, 'Take them or else.'"

Sam nodded and rubbed his eyes. "But maybe I was too hard on him. Maybe I made him feel like a loser. Then that made him do the drugs."

"Why didn't he choose to become a rocket scientist and prove you wrong, instead? There were about a thousand directions he could have chosen instead of the one he did. *That* is not on you. What's on you is how you react to it."

"You really think?" he asked.

She nodded. "Wasn't an easy lesson for me to learn, but it saved me." Something bent her pole and she was grateful for the distraction. "I think I got something," she said.

Sam stood and said, "Good! We'll have dinner!" He swiped at his eyes before he came over to help her, but she'd already picked up the pole and started reeling the fish in. She could see the pale underbelly of the fish, but somehow she'd managed to get it stuck on the underneath side of the ice. She yanked on the pole and Sam came rushing over and the fish practically flew out of the water and smacked him right in the face. Emma screamed and Sam laughed. When it was all said and done, she'd caught a fourteen-inch yellow perch.

"Good eatin' indeed," Sam said.

23

Clancy approached his dad in the barn just before the Hollingsworth boy was supposed to arrive. Reuben was brushing down Roy, humming some old cowboy song, when he saw Clancy and nodded.

"Hey, Dad, I was wondering if I could talk to you for a minute."

"Yeah?"

Clancy had rehearsed in his head what he would say to his father but all of it sounded dumb. Or confrontational. *"Hey, Dad, are you Emma's father?"* Seemed really...out there and bold, and yet hinting at the real question seemed juvenile. Like bad reality T.V. writing. He wasn't accusing his father of anything, because he didn't for a second think his father was Emma's father, but he just wanted to make sure. It would make Emma feel better. He was simply asking a question. There was a difference. He just hoped his father would see the difference, too. Because, if there was one thing Clancy knew for sure, it was that his dad was a good guy. His dad was his rock. And he didn't want that to change.

"What do you think of Emma?" Clancy asked.

Reuben smiled at him. "Think how? As a person?"

"Just in general. How would you describe her?"

"She's a nice girl. Warm. Open. A good person."

Roy raised his head and whinnied.

"I know, we're talking about your girl," Reuben said to Roy. He looked up at Clancy and smiled. "If she were anything else, the animals wouldn't like her."

Clancy thought about that for a moment. Diane had been ambivalent toward the animals. He'd mistook her interest in the business as interest in the animals. Then he realized that she hated the smell. Hated the mess. And although she was not cruel to the animals and wouldn't have tolerated cruelty toward them, she hadn't even known their names. Roy was the only one whose name she'd bothered to learn. And well, how could you not know Roy's name? No, her interest had been in the bookkeeping only.

But Angie had liked the animals and they had liked her, so he wasn't entirely certain that his father's philosophy wasn't flawed. Angie had liked all of it. The problem had been that she'd wanted to own the whole thing, and it didn't really seem to matter if Clancy came with the deed or not.

"So, you don't think she's capable of deception?" Clancy asked.

Reuben looked taken aback. "Everybody's capable of deception, son. This is a fine time to be thinking of that now. Shouldn't you have thought of that before you slept with her?"

It was Clancy's turn to look surprised.

"There was a pair of teal colored yoga pants in my laundry," Reuben said. "You'd never be caught dead in teal yoga pants. Besides, anybody who's seen you two this past week could see that it wouldn't take long for you guys to collide. In the Biblical sense. I've never seen two people enjoy washing dishes as much as you guys."

Clancy thought he should be insulted simply because he liked to believe he wasn't that transparent, but he couldn't bring himself to feel the indignity.

"Look, I'm happy for you. You've encountered some not-so-nice examples of the female sex, son. And it's been a year since I've seen you even take an interest in a woman. Emma...well, Emma's special."

"Okay, so...about this search for her father," Clancy said.

"What about it?" Reuben asked.

The reaction I was hoping for!

"Did you know her mother?" he asked.

Reuben shrugged as he held the halter out for Roy. Roy nudged his nose into it. "I'm sure I woulda had to have seen her at some point. But nothing sticks out. Why?"

"Well, you know, any of the guys in the saddle club could potentially be her father...I just wanted to make sure that she and I...that we weren't..."

Reuben laughed and Roy did his fake mocking laugh a split second later.

"Again, something you should have thought of sooner. But, I did not sleep with her mother, if that's what you're asking."

Clancy held his hands up in surrender. "I just...you know...wanted to make sure."

Reuben studied Clancy for a minute and then shook his head and laughed. "You were worried?"

"Well, not really, which is why it never occurred to me until she brought it up. I told Em that I thought you would have said something. But I also know that my mother was not an easy woman to live with and...I could see how..."

"The second I thought something might be up between you two, I would have said something," he said. "I was gone most of that summer, Clancy. That's one of those times that I'm not proud of. I left you and your mother for almost four months. April to like, late-July. I called you every day, and every day you'd tell me how much you missed me and wanted to know when I was coming home," he said. "A lot of the guys, they'd drive to the shows and rodeos and then drive back home on Sunday nights to their jobs and families. Then the weekend would come and they'd hitch up the trailers and back out they'd go. But not me. I took my horses and my trailer and I stayed gone. Not proud of it. But at the same time, I know that it was for the best or I'd probably be rotting in jail right now."

Clancy smiled and understood. It was an exaggeration, but still. The fight had been one of *those* times. Usually, his mother was the one to leave, but at least twice she'd made his father so incensed that he'd left just for the safety of everybody involved. Clancy didn't really remember those times, because they occurred before he'd even started kindergarten, but his mother would always use them against his father in arguments.

"And I'll tell you that I got propositioned plenty of times, I did," Reuben said. He took a deep breath. "And I'm gonna tell you, son...I broke my marriage vows only once, but it wasn't with Emma's mother."

Clancy's heart almost stopped beating.

"It was a lady barrel racer from North Dakota. I met her when I was a kid on the charity wagon trains that we used to do. Couldn't have been more than fourteen when I first met her. Anyway...her name was Mary Beth Turner, not Helen Wisniewski. I know for sure I never slept with Emma's mother, and I know for sure I'm not her father. I did, however, have an affair, the summer of eighty-six, with Mary Beth. And I'm sorry if that hurts you, son."

Roy snorted and stole Reuben's hat with his teeth.

Clancy was speechless, but at least his heartbeat was back to normal.

"I... uh, well, that's okay. I'm not hurt by it." And then he thought about it a second. "Why did you come back home? You could have stayed with her. Gone to North Dakota. Was it because of me?"

Reuben nodded. "Among other things. I had all of this," he said and made a broad sweeping motion to the farm. "I love my life here. And Mary Beth loved hers. Neither of us was willing to give up what we had for the other. So, when the season was over, I put my priorities in order and came home to my family."

Clancy leaned against the stall for support. "Wow," he said. Roy bit Clancy's hat off his head, too, but Clancy caught it before it hit the ground.

"But as for Emma," Reuben said. "That's one fine woman."

"Yeah," Clancy said. Still reeling from the new information, he rubbed his chin and shook his head. And he wasn't related to her! That was even better.

Later that day, Clancy saw the Hollingsworths arrive with their two children, just as Emma pulled into the driveway. As she got out, the dogs came with her. Mutt jumped into the snow, almost right in front of her, but Tricephus didn't land so gracefully and had a face full of snow. Then a third dog, a big blackish sort of monster who reached Emma's hips, got out of the car.

Clancy laughed. "Who's that?" he asked.

Emma rolled her eyes and said, "I don't know. I found him on the lake when I went ice-fishing with Sam. Just as we were getting ready to leave, he came barreling out of the woods and onto the ice. I thought he was a wolf at first, so I jumped in the back of the truck. He's got a collar but when I called the number it had been disconnected."

"What's his name?" Clancy asked.

"Well, according to the tag it's Valentine," she said. The dog gave a quizzical look at her when she mentioned his name. "He doesn't look like a Valentine to me."

Just then she saw the Hollingsworths farther up the driveway and went to greet them. She signed to the little boy, "This is Clancy. He's got a fantastic horse for you to meet!"

The boy gave a casual smile and Clancy waved. He watched Emma as she interacted with all of them and was amazed at how at ease she was. As far as he knew, she'd only met them the one time, but she talked to them like she'd known them for months. Like she did with everybody. That was the thing about Emma, once you met her it was like you'd known her forever.

Caitlin came outside then, bundled up in her deep purple coat that Peri insisted on buying her. "Why should my kid have to wear pink just because she's a girl?" Peri had said. Not that Clancy had been arguing with her. He didn't care what color coat she wore. But Peri had been incensed that the store had offered twelve different shades of pink coats, one purple, one black and one green. So she bought the purple out of protest.

Caitlin had left Chester inside, for once, and ran up to Emma to give her a hug. "Emmie!"

"Caitlin," Emma said. And then as she spoke, she signed. "These are my very good friends, Micah and Jamie. Micah cannot hear. So, if you want to communicate with him, he has to see you."

"You know sign language?" Caitlin said.

Emma nodded and translated for Micah.

Caitlin turned to Micah and spoke very loud and over enunciated her words. "Hoooowwww arrrrrree yyoooooouuuu?"

"That won't help, Caitlin," Emma said. "Talking like that won't help him understand."

Caitlin blinked. "You mean...like, he can't hear even explosions?"

"Nothing," Emma said. "Just talk to him like normal. For one thing, if you talk to him differently than you do other people, it will only make him feel weird."

"Oh," Caitlin said. "I'm sorry."

"It's okay," Emma said. "Now you know."

Clancy took them out into the arena and said, "Do you want to see some of the wonderful things that Roy can do?" Everything he said, Emma signed. Heather and Jim stayed outside the arena with Reuben, who'd just come out of the barn and wandered over. Heather or Jim could have stood in to translate for Micah, but Roy would concentrate better with Emma in the ring. If she'd been standing outside, he would have kept wandering over to her. Not to mention, kids often did better when the parents were close enough to save them, but far away enough that they felt independent.

"First of all," Clancy said. "I need you to promise me that you will not ever approach him, or any horse, from behind. That's their blind spot and they can't see and if you spook them, they could kick you. Also, never go in a corral or a stable stall with a horse without an adult. And never feed them anything without asking, because horses cannot throw up. So, if you give them too much food their stomachs can explode. Or if you give them something poisonous, they can get really sick because they can't get it back up."

Emma glanced at him and said, "I didn't know horses couldn't puke. They are the best animals ever!"

Clancy wasn't sure why he found that funny, but he did. He laughed at her and touched her lightly on the shoulder.

"So, here we go. I'm going to count to three. One, two, three," he said. Roy spun around. He counted again and Roy spun the other way.

"How many fingers am I holding up, Roy?" He held up four fingers and Roy pawed at the ground four times.

Micah signed something and Emma said, "Micah wants to know where he learned to do that?"

Clancy studied Roy and his heart swelled. How many times had he and Reuben doubled over in laughter at this horse? Too many to count. And the sheer shock of discovering that on certain verbal commands Roy would stop what he was doing and perform tricks was disconcerting to say the least. Especially if you were on him at the time! "We don't know," he said. "We found him...found him in terrible living conditions. I could tell immediately that he wasn't like other horses. We brought him home and found out that he could do all sorts of tricks. So, we think he might have been a circus horse at one time."

But it was so much more than that. Roy could understand. He understood people and situations. He could sense that you wanted to go left, and he'd go left before you even suggested it.

"Come here," Emma said. "Sometimes when I'm upset, Roy will put his head right here on my chest. Like he's listening to me breathe or listening to my heart."

She placed her hand on her chest and Roy snuggled his head against her. Clancy watched as Micah and Jamie observed with wonder. He realized then that these two kids could be her siblings. The thought of it was surreal.

Micah signed, "Let me try!" Micah took Emma's place and Roy placed his head on Micah's chest. Micah stood there for the longest time. When he looked up at Emma, tears glistened in his eyes and he signed, "He's talking to me."

Emma asked, "You feel him?"

"No," Micah said. "In here." He pointed to his head. Micah trailed his hand down the length of Roy and stopped when he got to his mid-stomach area. Micah placed his head against Roy's chest, like the horse had done to him. He closed his eyes and felt the horse breathe.

When Emma looked up at Clancy, tears streamed down her face. He struggled to keep his emotions at bay watching Micah. With his eyes still closed the little boy reached his hands around the girth of Roy as much as he could and hugged him. "Emma," Micah signed. "I love him."

Then he made a sign, the two middle fingers down and the other two, plus the thumb, up.

"What does that mean?" Clancy asked her.

"It means, I love you," Emma said. "Micah just said that he loved me."

Clancy cleared his throat and had to look away.

Damn horse.

Damn woman.

24

The next day Emma had her first day of work at the wildlife refuge. It was situated on a hill looking down over the St. Croix River, and as she got out of the car, she walked to the edge of the parking lot and looked out over the mostly frozen water. She was reminded again of how quiet winter was as the snow acted like insulation to muffle most of the excess noise. The hawk flying overhead, the songbirds twittering above her, the scurry of squirrels on the forest floor—the sounds they made were all muted, almost smothered, instead of crisp and sharp like they were in the summer.

"Some of the cleanest river water you'll find," Zoe said, startling Emma.

"I can't wait to see what this place looks like in the summer," she said. "It's gorgeous now all snow-covered and frosty. I can't imagine what it'll be like when it's green."

"You know, I've lived in a couple different states in my life," Zoe said. "But none of them have this river."

"Did you pick the location for the refuge?"

Zoe nodded. "I wanted the animals to feel like even if they were in a building, they were at least in the middle of the wilderness. Plus, if I've got to come here and work every day, the view may as well be something I want to look at, too."

Emma glanced up at the structure. It was a mix of stone and big wooden logs. A dozen or so outbuildings spread out from there, along with chained pens and cages and even a stable. A bubble of excitement squiggled in her belly. "So, what's my job?" she asked.

"You can muck stables. You can answer the phone and feed all the guests. Keep them calm. I've seen the way you are with Zeus. If you can do a fraction of that for some of these animals, it'll help me a lot. I don't know what gift God gave you, but it's really something."

Emma looked at her sharply. "You think I've been given a gift?"

Zoe shrugged. "Maybe. I think part of it is the animals can sense that you mean them no harm and you're not afraid. You're in total awe of them and you should be. Animals are smarter than we are. They may not be able to work out complicated math equations, but they can tell when it's gonna rain and they can tell if they're in danger from a predator by the scent on the wind. Humans, not so much. Most humans can't tell when there's a criminal sitting right next to them. In fact, every time somebody uses the term 'dumb animal,' I want to get out my whip and lash them."

Emma studied Zoe. She was small, as short as Emma, petite but yet a total powerhouse. Zoe came across as one of those women who could wear down a mountain with a feather.

"I'll show you around," she said. "And Emma, I never ever want you to be afraid of any animal that comes in here, but you do have to have a healthy respect for their power."

Zoe pointed to the scar on her own chin. "Fox got me right there. And I've got a dent in my shin that'll never go away from a cow that kicked me."

Emma nodded.

"I've got volunteer zoologists and other vets who come out and help me with the surgeries and that sort of thing, but their hours are sporadic. And I've got one teenager who does my record keeping. But the rest is on me and has been for a few years now. Sometimes it's not so bad because we don't have a whole lot of animals. Other times, I don't even go home."

Zoe showed Emma all the buildings and the animals that were currently housed there. There was a bald eagle, an owl, a turtle, two hawks, a few rabbits and a deer who'd been hit by a car. They made their way back into the building that held the office. Inside was Zoe's desk, a couch, a refrigerator and a television. The walls had spider and snake identification charts on them. Emma thought the spider charts were a bit...unsettling. Those were some angry looking arachnids.

"So, if this is a wildlife center, how'd you get kicked by a cow? Are there wild cows in Minnesota?" Emma asked.

Zoe laughed. "I get called sometimes on domestic cases, too. I am a licensed vet and a lot of times, I'm closer than the animal abuse groups. I'm the one that got the call for Roy."

Emma glanced up at her. "What do you mean?"

"I don't have a trailer," she said. "So, I called Reuben and Clancy out to help me. You cannot imagine the conditions of those animals. Well, some were already dead. They'd been left alone for weeks. Some of them could get to a water source, which is the only reason they were still alive when we got there. Some of them couldn't. I'll tell you what, I thought Clancy was going to kill something."

Emma had no doubt.

"I've never seen a guy so torn up...he had to go outside to collect himself. Roy'd been tied up, but luckily with enough slack that he could get to the water, but he'd gotten tangled up just before we got there and it had been a while since he'd drunk anything. He was so dehydrated. Thought we'd lose him for sure. He can get out of any pen, but he couldn't pick a padlock. Poor thing."

Tears welled in Emma's eyes and she felt like she was going to burst with hatred for whoever would do that to any animal, let alone Roy. He must have been so scared.

"I'm glad those people were long gone, because Clancy left that barn ready to break down and sob, but when he came back in, he was full of rage. I really think Clancy would have hurt them," she said and sighed. "So, if you don't think you can handle a domestic abuse case, I won't take you with me. But if you think you can, I can always use an extra pair of hands when I get those kinds of calls."

Emma nodded. "Hopefully, we won't get those kinds of calls."

Zoe nodded but Emma had the peculiar feeling that Zoe was just trying to make her feel better.

She got the grand tour of the "operating" room. There was a metal table in the center of the room with a rack above it fortified with plastic goggles, spray bottles with solution in them and different types of plier-looking tools. Barred cages nestled against the perimeter of the room. One of the hawk cages had a sign that said, "Male handlers preferred."

Emma questioned Zoe about it. "Female red-tailed hawk. She does not like women. I don't have a regular male employee but when one is here, I always send him to take care of her."

Emma tilted her head. "Really? I've never heard of such a thing."

"Very common," Zoe said.

Emma filled out W-2 information and background information and then she mucked out the deer pen, fed everybody and checked the stockroom. Zoe had been very meticulous about labeling the shelves, and anytime that Emma saw that something was getting low, she wrote down the information and then gave the list to Zoe.

At five she snapped a picture of the rehab center and then got one of her and Zoe and the bald eagle and posted it to Facebook with the status: *My new boss, Zoe! So excited!* She went home to find Sam and Brandon fixing the front porch. Darkness had just fallen, but they'd turned on the porch light to finish up what they were doing.

"What are you doing here, Sam?" she asked. "Thought I was paying Brandon."

"Fish weren't biting," he said. "Ran into Brandon and he told me he was headed out here. This is a favor for him. Marty is..."

"What?"

"Cooking," Sam said, eyebrows raised.

A mixture of happiness and dread filled her. What on earth was he cooking? She reminded herself that the breakfast he'd made her was quite edible.

When she entered the house, all three dogs attacked her at once. She crouched to the floor and petted them and loved them and cooed at them, telling them they were all the best doggies in the whole wide world. *And we believe you! Yes we do, yes we do, yes we do!* Thing 2 sauntered over and did a figure eight in and out of her legs, and Thing 1 just stretched on the couch and looked up at her as if to say, *"Oh, the human's home."*

"Marty?" Emma called out.

He stuck his head from around the corner of the kitchen and said, "I'm in here."

He was clean as a whistle and freshly shaven and wearing Clancy's clothes. She glanced down at his feet and noticed that he had new boots. As Emma made her way into the kitchen, she noticed his tiny whiskey bottle sat on the counter, but it was only half empty. It could be a new bottle, but she'd sworn that he bought that the day of the storm. If so, that meant he'd cut his drinking down. "Smells great, what are you making?"

"Stew," he said. "And cornbread."

"You know how to work the oven? How do you know what the temperature it is in there?"

He smiled. "I grew up with one of these. I'll have to teach you."

"Or I'm going to buy a new stove," she said. "One with buttons and temperature gauges."

"Don't you dare!" he said.

Laughing, she turned and opened the refrigerator, and inside was a banana cream pie. She stood up and glanced over her shoulder at him. "Did you make this pie?"

"No," he said. "Luella did. I think she's coming for dinner. Aurora dropped off something, too."

"Oh," Emma said. "But, Marty, I don't have any place for anybody to sit. You and I always eat in the living room."

He shrugged.

Emma heard a knock at the door and went to answer it. Jim and Heather Hollingsworth stood on the front porch. "Oh, hi guys, come on in," Emma said.

"We can't stay," Heather said. "We just-"

"Well, we heard that you didn't have a whole lot of furniture," Jim said.

Emma blinked. "Not yet," she said, wondering what this was all about.

"I hope you don't mind, Em, but we just bought new furniture and we were going to have a garage sale and sell the old stuff, but thought maybe you'd like it instead," Jim said.

Emma looked past them to the truck in the driveway.

"It's an old dining set," Heather said apologetically. "And a dresser and a bed, but we kept the mattress and box springs, is that okay?"

"Oh," Emma said. "Of course, that's fine."

What in the world is going on?

Brandon and Sam stopped what they were doing and helped Jim get the furniture unloaded and into Emma's house. They didn't have far to go with the dining furniture, since the dining room was on the left just inside the front door. Then they carried the dresser upstairs to the spare room and set up the bed and the frame, even though there was no mattress.

On their way out, Heather said, "I want to thank you for what you did for Micah. Roy is all he's talked about all day. And horses.

And you. He said he wants to join 4-H," she said, tearing up. "He's never wanted to do anything but sit in the house. He's always been so cautious..."

Emma rubbed Heather's arm.

"I just want you to know that I will be forever grateful. And...if it turns out...if the DNA comes back...well, there's not many people who would make a better sister for him."

"Oh," Emma said as the breath rushed out of her. "I..."

Jim tapped her on the chin in a fatherly way, like she was six, and they turned to leave. Emma stood there blinking back tears. Finally, after she'd watched them pull out of the drive, kicking snow up as they went, she turned and looked at the dining room furniture. It was old, like Heather said, but it was beautiful. One very large mahogany table and eight chairs. *What am I going to do with eight chairs?*

"Feed people," Granny said. *"You're awfully dense sometimes."*

Marty hobbled past Emma and opened the front door. "Food!" he yelled.

Brandon and Sam came in, stomping snow from their boots and taking off coats. They made their way to the sinks in the house and washed up, and then Luella came through the front door with two jugs in her hand. "I brought my world-famous sweet tea," she said.

Emma smiled. "Fantastic!" They hugged and gave loud cheek smooches and Emma almost backed into Sam because she hadn't realized that he was behind her putting bowls on the table.

Another knock at the door and Luella yelled, "Come in!"

Clancy walked through, tossed his coat on top of Thing 1 and announced that Reuben wasn't coming because he'd eaten too much lasagna for lunch at the Italian restaurant in Winchester Hollow. "That's okay," he said. "I'll eat his share."

Aurora pulled up on her snow mobile less than thirty seconds later.

Marty carried the stew pot to the dining room table, and Luella followed right behind him with the biscuits. Emma just stood there trying not to blink because she was afraid if she closed her eyes it would all go away. Then Marty grabbed onto the back of his chair because his hands were shaking and he said, "I hope it's as good as I remember it being."

"Well, it smells fantastic," Emma said.

"Let's eat!" Luella announced.

"I want dessert first," Brandon called out.

"You touch that pie and I'll take a hammer to your head," Luella said.

"There's pie?" Clancy asked.

"Banana cream," Emma stated.

"Oh," Clancy said. "I don't like bananas."

"That's okay," Aurora said. "I dropped off a cheesecake earlier, too."

"I love you," Clancy said.

"I know," Aurora countered.

"Hey, somebody grab the butter," Brandon said. "Can't have biscuits without butter."

"I'll get it," Clancy said and headed to the kitchen.

When he came back with the butter, he sat down next to Emma and said, "So how was your first day on the job?"

Emma tried to speak but she was so overwhelmed with emotion that the words sort of stuck in her throat. There were people—guests—in her dining room eating with her. And she liked these people, so that made it even better. And Marty had made dinner.

Tricephus barked and Clancy reached down and gave the dog the edge of his biscuit. "Well?" he said. He was still bent over, feeding Tricephus, but when he glanced up at her, Emma's heart did a double beat. He looked so unguarded then, so at ease, so comfortable. At that moment she wanted to curl up next to him and watch T.V. He of course, had no idea that her thoughts were off in fantasy land, so he pushed on. "Your first day on the job. Did you like it?"

"I...I liked it just fine," Emma said.

"I knew it would be a good fit for you," Clancy said, smiling at her.

"Well, Marty," Emma said with a deep breath. "I want to thank you for making dinner."

"It was Clancy's idea," Marty said.

Sam smiled at her from across the table and winked.

"Why?" she asked.

"People gotta eat," Clancy said with a shrug. "Plus, it was your first day at work. Figured you'd be too tired to cook."

Emma stared up into his eyes, searching for an explanation, but all she saw was warmth and contentment.

"But Marty did all the work," Clancy said.

"And it's your food," Luella said, laughing.

"Who cares?" Brandon said. "Can we just eat it already?"

25

The next two weeks were mostly a blur. Emma went to work several days and watched as the eagle gained more and more strength. She went ice-fishing two more times with Sam and then helped him get his shack off the ice because the deadline to remove huts from the lake was approaching. She went to church both Sundays and Luella talked her into singing harmony with her. She wasn't sure what the rules were about singing in Sunday services if she wasn't a member of the church choir, but she did it anyway. Luella had asked. That was enough.

She worked with Zeus to the point that she no longer needed to warn him of her every move. He came to the fence to greet her if she was alone. If anybody was with her, he hung back.

She helped Aurora muck out the llama stables and Aurora made her cookies.

Her Facebook statuses had mostly been: *Shoveling more crap.* Or, *Did I mention I'm shoveling crap today?* But it didn't matter how much she shoveled, she loved her new life.

There had been dinner at her house both Tuesdays with the same group of people, plus Reuben. Sam had brought fresh fish the first week, and Marty had cooked it. Brandon had finished the porch and had moved on to the railings on the stairwell in her house. She supervised Micah and Jamie's visits with Roy twice each week and attended Jamie's dance recital. Jamie had worn fuchsia-colored feathers in her hair and a matching tutu, and her cheeks had been flushed with that innocent child pink. And when Jamie had twirled around she'd accidentally smacked another girl in the face and caused a domino effect all across the stage, but she never stopped smiling. A kid after Emma's own heart.

And every night Marty came home at ten o'clock sharp.

She wasn't sure when he'd officially moved in. She'd never asked and neither had he, but there was a silent understanding between them. Emma's house was there as long as he needed it to be, and she felt in her bones that he was trying hard to stand on his own and not need it. She had no idea where he went during the day or what he spent his time doing when he was away from her. But each day his color looked better than the day before. Each day the puffiness left his face, replaced by healthy muscle and normal flesh.

And as the days ticked off, she wondered: *Which one of these wonderful men is my father?*

She almost didn't want to know. Would it be selfish of her to ask the universe for three fathers?

And then there was Clancy. He'd stayed both Tuesdays to help with dishes and then spent the night. They'd made love furiously at first. They'd barely get their clothes off after the door shut on their last guest before pouncing each other with tangled limbs and rushed kisses. They'd panted and clawed their way to the finish, collapsing in a near dead faint from lack of oxygen and utter exhaustion. And then later in the night one would reach for the other and repeat the coupling. Slower then, more tenderly. The kind of sex where you explored every part of each other and took your time getting to the top of the mountain. There had been another encounter with him in the barn, which was always exciting. The chance of getting caught was exhilarating and they'd been a little more inventive, since lying down wasn't an option and there was no furniture. Except for that stool. And there'd been an incident in a fishing shack that Reuben owned that was only about four foot by four foot. The two had accidentally slammed into the door, mistaking it for a wall, and tumbled out and onto the ice, pants down, butt cheeks freezing on the spot. Thank goodness that had been at night and there had been no witnesses.

If Clancy went more than three days without her, she could almost feel his need for her from across the room. It emanated off him like silent gamma sex rays. She'd caught him watching her when she was with Zeus. He watched her when she was with Micah. He'd even brought her lunch at work, twice, claiming he'd been "in the area," and he'd bought her a cage for "that damn bird." And she was no less skin hungry when it came to him. She was ridiculous with the need to touch him. Even if it was just the back of his hand at the dinner table. It was electric and sizzled her right to the core.

But it was his thoughtful habit of calling her at eleven o'clock every night that had made Emma pause. "Just calling to say good night," Clancy would say. And she would reply, "Good night, Clancy." And he would follow it up with, "Good night, Em." As if he just wanted her voice to be the last thing he heard before he went to sleep.

She hated to think beyond that. He was gun-shy, and even though Emma didn't agree with his defense mechanism of just assuming every woman he met was a she-wolf who wanted something from him, she could understand how he could come to believe that. His sister had mentioned a few more details of life with their mother, and the woman had been as hideous as the rumors. Never satisfied. Always complaining about the horse smell and how Reuben never did enough for her. Still, Emma wasn't sure that a guy like Clancy could ever really be open and fearless even if he hadn't experienced bad relationships. And that's what a relationship was. You had to lay it all out there with no fear. No resentment or niggling thoughts of imminent doom. For now, she was happy to just be with him and take their relationship for what it was. It was clear he liked her, clear he liked having sex with her, clear that he thought about her even when sex wasn't on the menu—always a good sign. But he'd yet to take her out on a date for the world to see, and he'd yet to classify her as anything other than his neighbor. And Emma was careful not to behave as though she expected those calls at eleven, or he'd bolt for sure.

Because she loved being with him, dressed or naked. She didn't want to lose that.

At the end of those two weeks, Emma stood in the walkway leading to Zeus's corral. Clancy saw her coming, finished talking to his dad and came over to her. Clancy and Reuben were both extremely cautious about her being alone with Zeus, and any time she came for her sessions with him, one of them would drop what they were doing and go to her. They'd stand right outside the fence, ready to save her if Zeus went spastic.

"I think we should try getting you in the ring with him," Emma said. "I think he's ready."

Clancy immediately said, "No."

"Why not?" she said. "It's been weeks. He trusts me now."

Clancy worked his jaw as he looked away, and she suddenly realized what was wrong. He was worried that Zeus would reject him. Again. And the pain of that was too much for him. Whereas if he never tried again, he wouldn't have to face that rejection again. "Hey, if we don't ever try..."

"No," he said.

She took his hand, one of those hands that were rough and big and had worked magic all over her body, and said, "Please?"

"Emma, if he goes wild...I can't protect you. He'll move too fast. If I'm injured, who's going to drag you out of there?"

"He's not going to hurt me," she said.

"Fine," he said, after a moment. "But you go first. Get him relaxed."

Emma went leg first into the corral and then approached Zeus like she always did. She used normal movements, like she had that very first day. Nothing cautious or overly slow. She'd gained his trust enough to do that. But she hadn't tried to put a saddle on him, mostly because she didn't know how to put a saddle on a horse. But she had put a blanket on him and he'd stood and taken it, like she'd hoped. She was able to groom him. She'd even cleaned out his shoes after she'd practiced on Roy a dozen times.

If she told Zeus that Clancy wasn't going to hurt him, he'd believe her. He trusted her. If she showed she trusted Clancy, Zeus would too.

She hoped.

Zeus nudged her hand and rested his chin on her head. She smiled and ran her fingers down the length of his neck. "We're going to have a visitor today, big guy. Okay?"

She walked back to the corral and took Clancy's hand and he stepped in, careful to stay flush against the fence. "Em," he said. "Wait."

"What?" she asked.

"My heart is pounding," he said. "Hang on."

He took a couple of deep breaths and then approached Zeus. Zeus eyed him cautiously but didn't move. Clancy took another step and Zeus backed up. Emma was hoping to stay on the sidelines, but realized that Zeus might do better if she was right there next to them. So she walked over to him and petted him. She took his face in her hands and said, "You're just going to pay attention to me, okay? I'm right here like I always am and nothing bad happens to you when I'm here. Right?"

She motioned to Clancy to move closer, and he did.

"There's somebody here who loves you a whole lot," Emma said to Zeus. "And he's missed you. He wants to say hi."

She let his head go so that he could see Clancy was a little bit closer. His muscles quivered but he stood his ground. His tail flicked and he kept his head up, ears perked. That was good. Finally, Clancy slowly caressed Zeus's neck.

"Okay," Emma said to Clancy. "I don't care what he does, don't make any sudden moves. If he snorts, jumps, whatever, you just stay steady. He might try to test you."

Clancy gave her an incredulous look. "How do you know this stuff?"

"Because that's exactly what people do. Basically, I treat him like I would a person in the same situation. The difference is it's easy for me to gauge him because he's got no ulterior motives like people do. All his emotions, no matter how upsetting they are to us, are pure."

Zeus put his head on Clancy's shoulder and then snorted. He raised his head and whinnied and Emma said, "Steady."

"Hey, Z," Clancy said. He stroked the horse's nose and then down the side of his face, under his forelock. "You're tense, buddy."

Zeus stammered again, made fussy noises. It was as if he was telling Clancy off. Letting Clancy know how wronged he'd felt. But Clancy just kept petting him, soothing him, telling him how sorry he was. "It's going to be okay," he said.

Emma felt tears sting the back of her eyes. "Looks like my work here is done," Emma said, smiling up at the two of them.

A few minutes later, Emma was at the edge of the corral headed home. Just as she was about to put her foot through, Clancy came over and grabbed her hand. He pushed his hat back off his forehead and kissed her deeply, passionately. It felt like she was kissing the real him for the first time. As if he'd been holding something back all this time. It stunned her to the bottom of her toes.

When he finished, he cupped her face in his hands, rested his forehead against hers and said, "Thanks. For that."

"My pleasure," she said.

It was later, around eight, when she was curled up reading a book with as many animals as she could get on the couch with her, and the parrot now safely in his bird cage by the window, that Clancy knocked on her door. As he came in, he shut the door behind him, locked it, and took her by the hand. Turning off all the lights, he pulled her up the stairs behind him without saying a word. He entered her room, kissed her and unbuttoned her blouse.

"Clancy..." she said because she could tell something was different. But he only kissed her deeper and she kissed him back, leaning into his body, drawing her hands along his back and up his shoulders. His kisses were slow and deep this time, not hurried or rushed. He felt like an ember to the touch, burning hotter and hotter.

He moved her to the bed and when he'd settled between her legs, she wrapped her arms around him, pulling him as close as she could get him. She was weak with anticipation, dizzy from the rush of her blood and pounding heart. When he was deep inside her he stopped and said, "Emma?"

"What?" she asked, breathless. She was on the cusp of spilling over the edge of desire and was amazed that she could even form the word. She was delirious with need and she could no longer tell where her body ended and his began. She clutched at him, afraid he would move and push her over the edge—when clearly, he had something to say—but yet, at the same time, she wanted him to *move*. Because she wanted to go over that edge and take him with her.

"What is this?" he asked, staring at her with moonlit eyes. She didn't completely understand what he meant and she didn't want to misunderstand. Not now, not at this moment. So she said nothing. She urged him to move in her, but he wouldn't. He held back. "Between us. You and me. What is it?"

Love, she thought. But what she said was, "Whatever you want it to be."

He moved and she gasped. She ran her hands over his naked hips.

He leaned down and whispered in her ear. "You're the most amazing woman I've ever met."

She kissed the nape of his neck in response.

"I want this to be an us," he said. "Not just physical."

This hasn't been just physical for a very long time. In fact, she wasn't sure that it had ever been. It had never been meaningless, anyway. Of that she was sure. But she didn't say that.

He kissed her deeply then and she reveled in it. She knew what it cost him to say those words. Especially at his most vulnerable point. They moved together into the night and when, a little later, he called out her name, her heart melted at the sound of it, knowing that at that moment, he thought of nothing but her.

Emma Rose Gordon, it would seem, was in love.

26

A few days later, Micah had asked that Emma attend one of his 4-H meetings and, of course, she didn't hesitate. She was his show-n-tell, after all. She arrived at the C&B Ranch five miles northwest of Quail Bottom at 3:30 in the afternoon. Heather and Jamie greeted her in the parking lot, and they made their way toward the indoor corral, making small talk about the weather.

"So, what am I supposed to do?" Emma asked. "Are there any special tricks?"

"I think you're supposed to lead him around the pen."

"He's riding a horse that's not Roy?"

Heather nodded. "This is like his sixth time out here. I can barely keep him away. He really wants you to see what he's accomplished."

"Oh, I can't wait."

"And he might want you to ride, too."

Emma froze. "Wait, what? You do realize that I've never been on a horse in my life. Well, unless you count mules."

"You've never ridden Roy?"

"No," Emma said. "God, he's so human-like that I'd feel guilty for getting on him."

Heather waved a hand at her. "Piece of cake."

That's what the chef said to her just before the fire in Louisville.

Micah came running toward her, waving wildly, and she waved back. He threw himself in her arms and hugged her. The event was really low-key, with parents and grandparents and other children all standing around or hanging off of the fencing. Micah climbed on a sorrel horse that was pretty low to the ground, which made Emma feel better because he wouldn't have as far to fall. She took the lead rope and walked Micah and Jonesie around the indoor corral and everybody clapped. Heather snapped a few pictures and as Emma went around again, she tossed her phone to Heather. "Get a picture for me!"

The instructor, a middle-aged woman with her salt-and-pepper hair pulled up on top of her head, spoke into a microphone. "A horse has four basic gaits. Walk, trot, canter and gallop. Our newest members mastered walking in no time, so we've moved on to the trot."

Emma signed to Micah. "Trot."

And he did. He rose up just as the instructor described. "The trot is a two-beat gait. The rider should come up out of the seat on the horse's outside leg. That's the leg closest to the fence."

A huge smile flowered on Micah's face and Emma felt a swell of pride.

Then the instructor told everybody to switch places. The special guest was to get on the horse and the rider was to take the lead. Emma's hands started to shake and then realized she was being silly. Getting her leg over the horse was a little trickier than she thought it would be, but she managed. She signed to Micah, "Now what do I do?"

He answered, "Don't pull up on the reins. The bit will hurt, their head will follow. He'll buck you right off."

Oh great. The instructor gave the sign to go and horses and riders began walking around the corral. After they did three laps like that, it was time to trot, but only if you wanted to. Emma didn't want to trot. Walking had been just fine. In fact, it had been soothing and calming. In what could only be called unfortunate, Micah misunderstood Emma and thought she wanted to trot. Either that or he ignored her and decided she could handle it. He ran a little too fast and then Jonesie wanted to go faster. Micah tried to keep up with Jonesie and Jonesie tried to keep up with Micah, and before she knew what happened, Emma was passing all the other horses, with her hair flowing backward and a scream of holy terror tearing from her lungs.

"Hoooow do you maaaake it sttttooooooooopppppp?" Emma said to Heather as she flew by her. But Heather was too busy snapping pictures.

Emma looked down and Micah was gone. She looked around frantically for him and he stood in the middle of the ring, signing as fast as he could. "Say whoa!"

"Whoa," Emma said and remembered to pull straight back and not up on the rein. "Whoa. Whoa. *Whoa!*"

Finally, the horse stopped with a jolt and Emma was off that saddle in the time it took to blink. Micah ran to her signing madly. "That was the most awesome thing I've ever seen."

Emma ruffled his hair, looked around and said, "Thanks." She decided to let him believe that it had all been carefully planned and that Emma had been in complete control the whole time.

As she sat in her car, hands shaking from adrenaline, she posted the pictures to Facebook. "Me and Micah showing the horse what's what." Even though in the picture of herself, Emma's mouth was wide open and her eyes were bugged out of her head.

Brad was in the barn shoeing a couple of the Belgians and Clancy was supposed to be dispensing the barley, but he found it hard to concentrate.

Peri and Caitlin were in town and Clancy had invited them to dinner at Emma's tonight. Emma had a few extra chairs she could pull around the table and Clancy knew she wouldn't mind. Emma loved Caitlin, he could tell, and although she hadn't spent as much time with Peri, he could see that they hit off, too. That made things easier. It was always easier when the family liked...what exactly? His girlfriend? Did he really have a *girlfriend*?

He smiled to himself. How had that happened?

It was a little disconcerting to think that he was "dating" the girl across the road. His neighbor. But then he thought of Emma with Zeus. She'd given four or five days every week, several hours of every day, to come and sit with Zeus. Talk to him. Coax him. Work bloody miracles on him. And why? As much as Clancy would like to think it was for him, he knew that the overwhelming reason she'd done it was for Zeus. Because she couldn't stand to see him suffer and if she had the means to make him better, then she felt like she owed it to him. She might never have thought of it in those specific terms before, but Clancy knew that was exactly why she did it. Did anything, really. He thought of her soft and naked, climbing on top of him this morning, spilling herself over him as though she were a warm waterfall, and he realized that there was nothing disconcerting about dating his neighbor after all. He'd run his hands through her hair and down her body matching every move she made.

There were times Emma was completely wild. His untamed wolf-girl who straddled him in the fishing shack. And other times, she was his delicate flower, unfolding beneath him. Revealing a little more of herself with each encounter. Each conversation. And there were other times that even his own lust couldn't match hers. But always, always, she was good and kind and the one and only place he found complete solace. And nobody was more surprised by that revelation than he was.

"You're smiling like the goddam Cheshire cat," Brad said. "Stop it."

Clancy looked up at his friend and he smiled wider. "Can't help it," he said.

"Well, I'm leaving unless you stop that shit," he said. "I'm trying to work here. You can't expect me to work in these kinda conditions."

Clancy laughed, but Brad wasn't finished. "You need some alone time, buddy?"

"No, no," he said. "I'm fine. Just do what I'm paying you to do and shut up."

"Sure you don't want to talk about your *feelings*?"

Clancy glared at him and Brad went back to work, chuckling.

Later, Clancy arrived at Emma's for dinner with Caitlin hanging off his hip and Peri bringing up the rear. Reuben stayed home because he wanted to watch the hockey game and he was nursing a sore hip, anyway. Marty had made two batches of lasagna and Peri made a huge salad. As usual, Aurora brought dessert, a chocolate pie and cookies, and Luella showed up with jugs of sweet tea and German chocolate cake with a cherry filling. Sam brought the bread. So far, it seemed to Clancy that Brandon was getting a lot of free meals without contributing. And that was so like his cousin.

As Clancy came through the door, Brandon drove the last nail in the railing. Emma's steps were now fixed. Clancy took the salad from Peri and set it on the table, and Caitlin jumped from his arms to the floor in one swift motion chasing after poor Tricephus. "This dog's only got three legs!" she shouted.

"Don't you make fun of her!" Marty said. "She can't help it."

The parrot squawked and said, "Gimme the money. Gimme the money."

Caitlin looked up, forgetting all about Tricephus and said, "That bird just talked."

Clancy laughed at her and turned to Marty, "Where's Em?"

"Getting dressed," he said.

Just then Emma came down the stairs in a flowing emerald green dress that stopped just above her knees. It had straps but no sleeves and Clancy wondered if she was cold. The fabric swished about her bare legs and he thought; *Who cares if she's cold? She looks great.* He smiled and then he decided to announce to the world that they were a couple by yanking her to him. She slammed into his chest, her warm yellow curls bouncing every which way. "Oh!" she said.

"Emerald green has just become my favorite color," he said.

Then he kissed her. He didn't know what kind of fabric that dress was made out of but it swished and slid around her thighs and suddenly, that's all he could think about. Sliding around Emma's bare thighs.

When she pulled away she was smiling at him. Smiling. At him. Because of him. Because of each other. And he'd never been quite so content in his whole life, which was terrifying. In fact, terrifying wasn't a strong enough word. He was excited at the same time, which was just weird. It was all new. There was so much they didn't know about each other and so many different directions their relationship could go. The future was no longer set. It was no longer: *I will breed horses until I die and give my ranch to Caitlin.* There was so much more. So much more that could happen. But yet, there was contentment, too. Which seemed completely at odds with the excitement, but he didn't really care. Bring it on. He'd take any of it. As long as it meant he could have Emma. Every day.

Everybody clapped at the kiss and Emma blushed.

"Oh, wow, it's about time," Sam said. "Everybody's known there was something going on with you guys for a few weeks now. Was wondering if you were ever going to let us in on it."

Everybody sat down. Plates were passed around, glasses were filled with tea, and conversation began to pass back and forth. Clancy studied Marty and he couldn't believe the changes in him. Emma had been here seven weeks? And Marty had made significant changes every one of those weeks. Everybody noticed but everybody was also afraid to say much about it. Afraid they'd jinx whatever was happening with him.

"You look lovely in that dress," Aurora said.

"Oh, thank you," Emma said. "I saw it in town. I couldn't wait for spring. So, I bought it as an early birthday present."

"When's your birthday?" Luella asked.

"Next week," she said.

"Same as Mommy!" Caitlin said.

"Really?" Aurora said.

"Yeah," Emma said. "Even the same year. We're like five days apart."

"Well," Sam said. "You should be getting your DNA results back right about the same time. We should throw a big party. See who the lucky guy is and celebrate both your birthdays."

Emma laughed nervously.

Clancy touched her leg under the table because he felt her unease.

"What's wrong?" Aurora said.

Emma shrugged. "I don't know. Now I kind of don't want to find out," she said. "I want it to be all three of you."

"Aw," Luella said. "How sweet."

"Well," Sam said with a twinkle in his eye. "I think it's gonna be me."

"Shut it, Sherman," Marty said. "It's me."

"How nice that you've got three guys who all want to be your father," Peri said.

"Yeah," Emma said. "We were worried for a while that Reuben was going to end up being a candidate!"

Luella laughed and so did Sam and Brandon. Marty concentrated on getting his food to his mouth, which seemed almost more than he could handle. "That would have been awkward, considering," Brandon said.

"You have no idea," Emma said. "I was already starting on the Hail Marys, let me tell you."

"Why would you even think that our dad could be your father?" Peri asked.

"Well, he was gone on the circuit the whole summer," she said. "And Mom was seriously into cowboys at the time."

Clancy felt a niggling at the back of his mind, but he swept it aside and kept eating. "Marty," Clancy said. "This is really good."

"Th...thanks," he said. Marty was more alert and looked better, but there was no doubt that he was plagued by the shakes. *He's trying to quit drinking,* Clancy thought.

"Wait," Brandon said. "If Uncle Reuben was gone the whole summer, then how did he knock up Aunt June?"

Forks stopped in mid-air.

"What do you mean?" Emma asked.

"If you and Peri are the same age and Uncle Reuben..."
"Stop," Clancy said.

"...was gone all summer..."

Clancy stood and said, "Brandon, stop."

That was what had been niggling at the back of his brain. Reuben could not be his sister's father. He knew it as sure as the sun would come up the next day. It all made sense now. How his mother would always come home and say, "You've no right to Peri. Let me take her with me." She'd never asked for Clancy. Because Clancy was Reuben's. She'd always asked for Peri because his father had no legal right to keep Peri in a divorce or separation. Clancy had always thought it was just because she didn't love him as much. Now it all made sense.

"Peri," Clancy said, but it was too late. His sister sat stunned, the color drained from her face. Her complexion was like the underbelly of a fish.

"Well," she said. "There must be some mistake."

"Oh, crap," Brandon said. "Oh God, I'm really sorry."

Emma raised a shaking hand to cover her mouth. "Oh, I'm sure that your dad came home to visit," she said.

But he hadn't. Reuben had told Clancy he'd been gone for several months straight. He came back home in August and finished out the summer saddle club activities here in Quail Bottom. But June, when Peri would have been conceived, he was on the western side of the state with the woman he'd met as a teenager. Anger swelled at the injustice of his mother's betrayal. Even from the grave she managed to reach out and hurt them.

And his father had raised Peri as his own without a word.

"What's happening?" Caitlin asked and shoved a big bite of lasagna in her mouth.

"No," Peri said, shaking. "It can't be. I...I...I have to go home and talk to Dad."

"Come on, Caitlin," Clancy said. "We've got to go." But Peri was already out the door.

"But I'm *eating*," she said.

He started to protest, but Emma reached out and touched him. "Clancy, it might be better if Caitlin wasn't home for this conversation. Let her eat. I'll bring her home later."

Clancy knew she was right. But he was so angry that he just wanted to yank Caitlin out of her chair and run home after his sister, who had already made it out the front door and probably halfway down the driveway. He was angry with his mother, who'd gotten pregnant by another man. He was angry with his father for being gone those months. He was angry with both of them for the lies! He was angry with Emma for bringing it up. Angry with Emma for being here. If she hadn't come looking for her father, neither he nor Peri would have ever known the truth. And as much as it hurt that they'd been lied to, it was nothing compared to the hurt of this. Of finding out you're not who you thought you were.

He took a deep breath, trying not to make eye contact with anybody at the table. "It's probably better if you don't. Have Brandon bring her home."

27

"Well, I don't know about you all," Luella said. "But I'm going straight for the chocolate cake."

Emma sat stunned.

"Can I have cake?" Caitlin asked.

"A-after you eat your dinner," Emma said. She studied Caitlin. Her grandpa wasn't her grandpa. *Oh, my God. What have I done?*

"Now, Emma"...she heard Granny's voice. But Emma shoved it back. There was no way to make this right.

Emma glanced up to catch Sam staring at her across the table. "Emmie," he said. But Emma wanted nothing to do with rationalizing right now and ran from the room. She took to the stairs, green satin swirling around her knees, every step feeling as though it were Mount Everest. When she reached her room, she flounced onto the bed and cried.

Sam knocked on the door frame but didn't wait for her to invite him in. "Em?" he said. "Aw, girl. Don't cry."

"Go away," Emma said.

Sam stood there, unsure of what to do, but then finally made his way to her bed and sat down on the edge next to her. He rubbed at his five o'clock shadow and sighed. "Well," he said. "That was an unexpected turn."

Emma sobbed harder.

"Oh, Sam," she said. "Do you realize what I've done?"

"You haven't done anything," he said. "All of that is June Stephens' doing. May she rot in Hades, the selfish bitch. Pardon my language."

"No," Emma said. "Caitlin is going to hate me forever. She asked me to heal Zeus so she could have her Grandpa back. Instead, I just took him away from her!"

"Emma Rose," he said. "Listen to me."

But Emma just shook her head and cried harder. Her mind reeled. How could she fix this? *I have to fix this!*

"It's done, child," Granny said. *"There's no fixing it."*

For the first time in Emma's life she wanted to shove a sock in Granny's mouth.

"Reuben is her grandfather in every sense of the word. He loves her. He claims her. That's all that matters. Do you hear me? He claims her and he claims Peri, and none of the rest of it matters," he said.

"How can you say that?" Emma said. "I'll bet Peri and Caitlin disagree with you! Can you imagine what they're feeling right now? Can you?"

"No," he said, shaking his head.

"Well, I can. I can't understand the betrayal part, but Peri is now in the exact same place I was. She doesn't know who her father is!"

"It's not the same. Reuben is her father," Sam stated. "He is. Even if he's not biologically. You never had one at all."

Emma wiped the tears from her face and looked up at Sam. His blue eyes were filled with compassion and love and understanding. And suddenly she understood.

"What?" he said, reading the change in her expression.

"You knew, didn't you? You all knew."

"Knew what?" he asked.

"That Reuben wasn't her father. It'd be hard for you not to know, considering. You all went out to your ridiculous rodeos and horse shows and June wasn't pregnant, and you came home and she was. You had to know! Even Aurora."

"There've been whispers about town. But any time anybody said anything about it, Reuben declared, 'She's my daughter and that's that.' Nobody's mentioned it in years. Emma, stop crying, sweetheart."

Sam put his arm around her, and Emma melted into him and sobbed some more. "I...I...did this."

"No. June Stephens did this," he said.

"Nothing you can say is going to make this okay. If I'd just let the past lie... If I'd never come here."

She hiccupped and snuffed and wiped snot on the back of her hand. "Do you know what kind of pain Caitlin is going to feel because of me?"

"Not because of you."

"Oh, Sam," she said and sobbed some more.

"What's your Granny got to say about this?" he asked. "She's never wrong."

But Emma said nothing. She just buried herself deeper into Sam's chest.

"You're breaking my heart, Emmie. Breaking it clean in two," he said.

But she clung to Sam as though he was life itself, and he didn't move. He sat there, shushing her and stroking her hair, and when she'd cried herself dry, Sam tucked her into bed. "I'm sleeping on the couch," he said. "Even if it means I have to sleep with Marty."

As he left her room, all the animals trotted in. The two cats found their spots, one on each side of her head, while Mutt lay on her feet. Tricephus barked from the floor, and Emma lifted her onto the bed, and snuggled the dog in her arms. Valentine clomped down the hallway and made a running jump onto the bed and bounced all of them three inches off the mattress, and then snuggled into her back. She had no idea how she'd ever managed to sleep without animals before. And she was grateful they were there now.

28

Clancy made it in the door three minutes behind Peri and he almost wished that he hadn't made it home at all. Peri stood in the kitchen, trembling from head to toe. His father, coffee mug in hand, looked down into the cup as though it held the secrets to the universe. "I'll ask again," she said. "Are you my father?"

When Reuben looked up he had tears in his eyes. "I was expecting this conversation," he said. He motioned to Clancy to come the rest of the way in the room. "My whole life I've struggled with what to do. Then the other day in the barn with Clancy, I...I put the information out there. Sort of. And figured somebody would do the math eventually."

"You bastard!" she said.

Clancy flinched. His father was anything but a bastard. He was the greatest man Clancy had ever known. But Clancy certainly understood how his sister would feel this right now. "Peri," he cautioned gently.

She held a hand up to him. "Don't talk to me right now."

Clancy shut up.

Reuben went on. "I will admit and own up to anything, but I just couldn't figure out a way to bring it up. So, I dropped that hint the other day... Peri, I love you. You and Clancy are my whole world. I feel no difference between the two of you. I never have. I love you both the exact same. You are my daughter."

Clancy reached for Peri as she crumbled onto the kitchen chair. His father turned his back to them, using the sink to steady himself. Peri sobbed into Clancy's shoulder, but his father was no less stricken. Reuben slumped over the sink and Clancy was torn between cradling his sister and cradling his father.

Finally, Reuben turned to face them. "I'd called your mother from Fargo and told her I wasn't coming back to her, but that I'd be back to get Clancy. She could take me to court, she could do whatever she wanted, but Clancy and I were done with her. We were gonna start a new life. Then she told me she was pregnant. I came home assuming you were mine. Then I did the math, too. And during one of our fights, she told me the truth. But I couldn't leave her like that. I said I would stay through the birth. And then you were born..." Reuben said. His voice broke and he took a deep breath. "Then you were born, and I was so in love with you that I knew I could never leave again. I was done leaving."

"Oh, Jesus," Clancy said, a lump forming in his throat. How could everything have gone so completely sideways? Ten minutes ago he was admiring the love of his life in a green silky dress and now his family was falling apart.

His sister stood finally with Clancy's help. "Who is my real father?" she asked.

"I am your real father," Reuben said, a little indignant. "I don't know the name of the man June had the affair with. She never told me. And honestly, I didn't ask. I didn't want to know."

Nobody said anything for several moments. The silence was accusatory and crushing.

When he finally spoke, Reuben was in a place mentally that Clancy couldn't fathom. What must it feel like to hurt the one you love this much? He hoped he would never find out. "I'm really sorry, Peri. What are you going to tell Caitlin?"

Clancy's gut clenched. *Caitlin!* "Let's not tell Caitlin anything right now," Clancy said. "She doesn't need to know this. Not now."

"Well, when is she going to find out?" Peri said, anger replacing hurt. "When she's twenty-eight like me? After she's been lied to for decades?"

"Peri," Clancy said. "You're angry right now. I get that. I am too."

"No!" she said. "You don't *get* to be angry, Clancy. You just don't."

"At least calm down before you tell her. If you're crying and upset, it's going to traumatize her," he said.

Peri shook her head and looked up at the ceiling as if the light fixture had all the answers. "Fine. I'll wait for now," she said. "But I don't want her around Emma anymore. Your girlfriend's done enough damage."

"That's unfair," Clancy said. "You're the one who suggested I go out with Emma in the first place."

"Right," she said. "But I didn't know she was going to ruin our lives."

"Wait," Reuben said. "Emma didn't intentionally do anything. It was an unfortunate consequence of her searching for *her* father."

"Unfortunate or not, I don't want Caitlin around her. In fact, I'm not sure I want her around any of you," Peri said to Reuben and stormed out of the kitchen. Clancy ran after her as she headed to the guest room to get their things. He grabbed her by the arm and she swirled on him, yanking it away. "Don't touch me."

She's angry. She's not being rational.

"Peri," Clancy said.

"I don't even know who he is anymore!" She pointed down the hall where they'd left their father. "He's a total stranger to me. He lied to me. Has lied to me my whole life. How is this possible?"

Clancy decided not to say anything else to her. There was nothing he could say right now that she would hear anyway, and he didn't want her anger to get to the point where she said things that she didn't mean or said things that couldn't be taken back. She had to calm down, work through it, and then he could maybe talk to her.

He thought of Emma and how she must feel. She was most likely hating herself right now. But then he thought of Peri's face and realized that anything Emma was feeling had to be trivial by comparison. He should call and check on her. But somehow, to do that right now would seem like he was picking sides. Like he was choosing Emma over Peri, and he'd made a promise to his whole family after Diane that he'd never put anybody before them ever again. Peri needed him the most right now. So, he wouldn't call. At least not tonight.

29

Emma awoke to brilliant sunshine and the smell of muffins baking. Clancy hadn't called to say goodnight. Not that it would have mattered, since Emma had fallen asleep way before eleven. When she stretched, the cats did the same and leapt for the floor. Mutt yawned and Emma set Tricephus on the rug and then lay back down. She stared up at the ceiling and a wave of sadness came over her as she replayed what had happened yesterday.

She rolled over to find Valentine lying on his stomach with his head on Clancy's pillow.

Clancy's pillow. When had she begun to think in terms of his and hers? She reached over and stroked the dog's head. He opened his eyes and licked his teeth. Mutt crawled in between Emma and Valentine, shoving his nose under her arm. Then he scooted farther up until he lay directly in between Emma and Valentine. He blinked at her. *I'm cute, right?*

She had to get up and face the day, even though that was the last thing in the world she wanted to do. She made her way downstairs with the entire zoo on her heels. She went straight to the front door and let everybody out. Everybody went except Thing 1 who would rather die than be caught in the wild.

Sam was gone, but Marty was in the kitchen. "Coffee?" he said from the other room.

Emma went into the kitchen and grabbed the mug that he held out for her. She took a sip of it and then stared at Marty. He was freshly shaven and it appeared as though he'd gotten a haircut. He flipped the eggs over and then pulled the muffins out of the oven. The magic he could work on that wood-burning stove was mind-boggling. "Where'd you learn how to cook?" she asked.

"I used to do all the cooking at home. My mother was a working mother, back when most moms stayed at home. I would come in from school, do my homework and then cook dinner so that it was ready for my parents when they got home. My brother, he hated to cook."

Emma nodded.

"Gimme the money!" the bird said from the other room.

"You gotta name for him yet?" Marty said, gesturing to the parrot.

"I've just been calling him the bird," she said. She took another drink and realized in horror that she was still wearing the green dress from last night.

"You working today?" he asked.

"Yes," she said. "Marty?"

"What?"

"You're looking good," she said.

He nodded. "Some days are better than others." There was a knowing silence between them. But neither said anything else.

"I've got to get dressed. Can't wear this to the animal shelter."

"Emma," he said.

"What?"

"Don't you blame yourself for what happened last night." She blinked against the sting of tears that suddenly welled. "I...I just...can't even."

He turned to her then and Emma saw the concern in his eyes. The tracery of little red lines along his cheeks that were so prominent weeks ago were no longer as inflamed. His head shook slightly, like a palsy, but she realized that it was probably caused from withdrawal. She hadn't seen a whiskey bottle anywhere in days. "No matter what," he said. "I...I'm here."

She hugged him and stole a muffin from the pan and then headed upstairs to put on her jeans and work polo. Half hour later, after she'd eaten her eggs and was headed for the door, Marty stuck his head out of the kitchen. "I'm thinking about an herbed pork tenderloin with a peach glaze sauce for dinner," he said.

"Wonderful," Emma said. "I'll be here."

She opened the door to find Roy. He bowed to her, nose almost touching the porch floor, hind-end high up in the air. She nearly burst into tears. She glanced over at the Stephens farm. "Marty?" she called.

"Yeah?"

"Can you take Roy home?"

"Sure," he said.

When she got to work, Zoe treated her no differently than normal, but Emma was fairly certain that Luella had called her and filled her in on what had happened the night before. It was the way Zoe's eyes had cut around when she inquired about dinner and then added, "Everything okay?" in such a casual voice that it was obvious.

Emma had fed and watered everybody and had helped Zoe unload a truck full of feed when a car pulled up out front of the building. Emma thought it was probably the load of hay that they were expecting and went outside to meet the driver. Instead, it was Jim Hollingsworth. "I've come to take you to lunch," he said.

Emma pulled her phone out of her pocket and sure enough it was lunch time. Where had the morning gone? She smiled at him. "Okay," she said. "Let me just check with Zoe to make sure she doesn't need me for something."

"Great," he said.

Five minutes later she left with Jim, and he took her to Winchester Hollow. Winchester Hollow was a bit bigger than

Quail Bottom in square miles and population, but it was still a quintessential Midwest small town. They passed older homes from the turn of the twentieth century with American flags in the front yard and Easter flags hanging from the porch. Easter was weeks away, but being buried in all this snow made one anxious for any sign of spring. They passed a shop that boasted eighteen flavors of ice-cream and three flavors of gelato, and a bead store. "Hey, I wonder if that's where Aurora gets her beads?" she asked.

"Probably," Jim said.

They arrived at an Italian restaurant called Luigi's and took seats in a booth near a window. The whole room was decorated with white tablecloths, candles made out of green wine bottles, and pictures of overweight cartoonish chefs. Right above the door was a sign that said, "Mama Mia!"

"I know there's every cliché imaginable in here," he said. "But they really do have good food."

"I'm not complaining," Emma said.

Jim ordered the chicken spiedini and Emma the pasta con broccoli. They'd been chit-chatting about Emma's visit to Micah's 4-H meeting the day before when the salads arrived.

"Heather's pregnant," Jim said out of the blue.

For the first time all day, Emma felt real joy. "That's great!" she said. "I think. I mean, you're happy, aren't you?"

Jim shrugged. "Of course I'm happy, just a little surprised. We were only going to have the two and I'm forty-six. I'm not a spring chicken. And really, neither is Heather. She's thirty-six now and they say that women have more problems over the age of thirty-five...so there's some concern."

Emma grabbed his hand from across the table. "She'll be fine. And so will the baby. I had a friend in Kentucky who had her very first baby at forty and they were both perfectly healthy. And that was even after jumping from a tree."

Jim visibly relaxed. "You think?"

She nodded. "Oh, I'm sure everything will be okay. Plus, Heather's done this before. How exciting! When is she due?"

"August," he said. "We've known for a few weeks. Like I said, we were shocked. We're still not even sure how it happened."

"My mother always told me it was the result of sex," Emma said and they both laughed.

The main courses arrived and Emma's mouth watered as she looked down at the sauce-covered broccoli, mushrooms and shell pasta. It smelled like sin, which was why she couldn't wait to taste it.

"It's funny. We were all set with our foursome. We'd begun to plan out our lives with the members in place and then this happened. Once we got over the sheer shock of it, we felt like, yeah...this feels right. Then the worry set in."

Emma took a bite and savored it. This little hole-in-the-wall place in a small and unknown town had fantastic food!

"I'm getting fixed after this," he said. "I just wanted you to be one of the first to know about the baby."

"Aw," she said. "Thank you."

They kept eating and Emma's stomach began to swell. If she ate any more she'd explode. But it was so good, so she kept stuffing her face. And it wasn't as though she wasn't going to work it off later. She had to muck out cages and pens.

After a moment, Jim grew serious. "I heard about what happened last night."

Emma swallowed and that bite hit her stomach like a rock. "Does the whole town know?" she asked.

"Probably," Jim said. Emma took a deep breath. "I know I'm probably the tenth person to tell you this, but don't blame yourself. You can't be held responsible for the fact that June Stephens got pregnant by another man, nor can you hold yourself responsible for Reuben keeping it a secret."

Emma shrugged and set down her fork. "Did you know Reuben wasn't her father?"

He shook his head.

"I know I shouldn't blame myself, Jim. But yet, it feels like I've done something wrong. Clancy didn't call me last night after they got home. He wouldn't even let me bring Caitlin home. He made Brandon do it."

"Well, there could be lots of reasons for that."

"He calls every night," she said. "Eleven o'clock sharp."

Jim smiled at her. "So there is something going on between you two. Heather said she thought there was, but I wasn't so sure. Should have known. Women's intuition."

Emma looked at him sharply. "Why wouldn't you be so sure about us?"

"Clancy's over thirty, set in his ways. Hasn't had a girlfriend in well over a year. You seemed like entirely too much fun for him."

"How many girlfriends has he had?" she asked.

"Two or three, not counting high school. Diane dazzled him. Toppled him right off his horse, if you know what I mean. We could all see what was happening."

"And what exactly was happening?" Emma asked.

"She tried to come between him and his family. Not just the usual misunderstandings that go with introducing a new person. You know how it is. Bringing the significant other home to the family is a scary thing. You're scared the family won't like her and you're scared she won't like them. There's this established unit already. No matter what, for better or worse, a new person is going to upset the structure. Some people resent that. Some welcome it. But Diane...well, Peri didn't trust her at first, but gave her the benefit of the doubt. Later...it became an all-out war between them. Each one tugging at Clancy in two directions. Reuben wasn't too thrilled with her, either, but didn't say much. I'm not sure how she did it, but Diane managed to convince Clancy that his family was mistreating her for no reason. That they were jealous of her and their relationship."

"What did his mother think of her? June was still alive then, right?" Emma asked, forgetting about her food.

"June couldn't stand her. Which, I think in the early days, is what pushed Clancy to love Diane even more. He saw somebody who could stand up to his mother and beat his mother at her own petty games, without realizing that meant Diane could turn that same venom on him. Which she did. But the fact is, for a long time, in the beginning, anyway, Clancy chose Diane over his family at every turn. And what do you do? Sometimes families really are territorial and really are unfair to the newcomer. You want to give the woman you love the benefit of the doubt. But sometimes...the newcomer is out to destroy you from the inside. And sometimes, both sides just act like babies."

Emma thought for a minute.

"I'm glad to see Clancy has found a decent woman. I like Clancy. He's a good guy."

"Well, we'll see," Emma said and shrugged. "After last night...He didn't call."

"That doesn't mean anything, Em. His sister had just had the shock of her life and I'm sure he was up all night comforting her. That family, aside from June, they are really good people, Emma. Really good. Reuben showed me the ropes when I first joined the riding club. One of the most generous guys I've ever met. Generous with his time, his emotions and his money. He loaned me a couple thousand one time. Took me five years before I could even pay him one dollar, but in all that time, he never asked for it. They are all just upset right now. They'll come around."

Emma took a deep breath. "I know that June and Reuben are to blame here, Jim. But I still feel like I've caused all the pain. Like I've done something wrong." She glanced out the window and noticed that there was an honest-to-goodness bookstore across the street. "Maybe I shouldn't have moved up here. Maybe I was wrong in thinking it was time to settle down. I just..."

"Just what?" he asked. The concern was obvious in his face, and Emma's heart swelled to know how much she mattered to him.

"I just wanted to know the other half of me. I wanted to see if this is where I'd belonged all those years. If this was the life I should have been leading. But now? Now it all seems so selfish."

Jim wiped his mouth with his napkin. "So, when do you get those DNA results back?"

She shrugged. "Should be around my birthday."

"Well, Micah wants to adopt you as it is, so, we're hoping we get a positive result. It'll be weird having my children range in age from zero to twenty-nine, right?"

She nodded and swiped at a tear.

"But who cares?" he said and smiled. "Everything will be fine. I promise."

Emma laughed. "You promise? Like, what are you, Santa Claus?"

"Nope," he said. "But it'll all work out. Any time I say that, it always happens."

She nodded and tried to think positive.

30

Wednesday night came and went. Clancy didn't call.

Thursday. Clancy didn't call.

Friday.

Clancy.

Didn't.

Call.

"Just freakin' call him yourself," Luella said.

It was Saturday and they sat at the end of the bar at Sam's, with the jukebox playing Hank Williams "Why Don't You Love Me." Hank got to the part about being a worn' out shoe and Emma felt as though she could relate. She'd never related to a Hank Williams song before. Her life was headed in a downward spiral for sure.

"I can't call him."

"Why not?" Luella asked.

Emma thought about the things Clancy had said to her the night before everything went sideways. *What is this?* The ends of her fingers tingled when she thought about it. *I want us to be an us.* How many couples didn't talk to each other for four days? Especially when they lived right across the street from each other. He hadn't even texted. God, even your enemies texted you.

Clearly, he had some issues to work through, and she was not going to push him. That would just make him run. If she was the one to call or text, he might think she was wanting him to pick sides. "If he wanted to talk to me, he would have called me."

"Well, what...Oh, Jesus. That is the stupidest thing I have ever heard of! What if he's thinking the same thing?" she said. "Then you both deserve to not have each other."

Luella shook her head and motioned for Sam, who brought tequila shots and fried pickles. "Here, drink this, stupid," she said. "Maybe it'll make you smarter."

Emma didn't really even notice what was in the shot glass. She just picked it up and swigged it back, and then coughed up a lung as her eyes bulged. Juan had always tried to give her tequila. He would tell her it was the nectar of the gods. But she'd always said no. Now she knew why. It was like somebody took a vacuum cleaner to her mouth. That stuff was nasty. She scooped a fried pickle into the horseradish/ranch dip and ate it.

"I think I've gained five pounds," she said.

"Where?" Luella asked. "Between your ears?"

"I'm serious. Everybody has fed me this week."

"People feed broken hearts. Just like colds," Luella said.

"I thought you fed a fever, not a cold," Emma said.

"Potato, pot-ah-toh."

"Aurora brought me a whole batch of cookies," she said. "Not just one or two. I got the whole batch to myself. Well, until Valentine helped himself to the tray. Still, I probably ate ten of them."

"You eat all ten of them in one sitting?"

Emma nodded.

"Aw, hell," Luella said.

Emma pounded her forehead on the bar.

"Come on, honey," Luella said. "Ain't no point in damaging the bar because you got a broken heart."

Emma ran her fingers through her hair and expelled a deep sigh. She really just wanted to cry. Actually, she wanted to climb the stairs behind the bar to Sam's loft and curl up on his sofa with a whole bottle of alcohol—something that wasn't tequila—but that would solve absolutely nothing. "I just want to go home," she said.

"Well, then I'll take you home," Luella said.

"No, not to Lady Slipper Lane."

"Well, then where? You want to go back to St. Louis?"

"That's not my home, either. It really never has been. It was just where my mother was."

Luella rubbed Emma's arm.

"That's my problem, Lu. I've been trying to go home my whole life, only I don't know where it is. I thought it was here. Maybe I'm one of those people who just don't have a home."

"All right girl, shut up," Luella said. Then she turned to the bar and yelled at Sam. "Turn that sappy sad garbage off the juke box! We got a lady in distress down here."

Sam nodded and changed the music on the jukebox himself. He played "Blurred Lines" and came back to the bar proud of himself. Luella just rolled her eyes. "So, he puts on a song about a naughty girl and a misogynist. Well, it's an improvement. At least we can dance to it."

Luella pulled Emma on to the dance floor and began dancing. Luella had a nice little stripper-hip-movement going and it made Emma laugh. They did the bump for a while and when the song was over, they headed back to the bar, where there was another round of shots waiting. Emma looked at the glass and thought, *that glass looks awfully big.*

She drank it anyway.

Now she was buzzing pretty good and dancing to the music in front of her stool. George Thorogood screamed from the jukebox and his guitar sounded like an outboard motor. Her hips bounced to the song and she ate more pickles.

"What do you think his problem is, anyway?" she asked.

"I assume you mean Clancy?" Luella said.

"Yeah, the guy with the...and the...and the really great..." she bit her lip.

"The chiseled jawbone, the sparkly blue eyes and the great butt?" Luella asked.

"I was going to say great cowboy hat."

"No you weren't," Luella said.

"I was. Honest."

"Uh-huh."

"Have you seen his abs?"

"No," Luella said. "Not all of us are that lucky."

Emma shrugged. "Doesn't matter. Because he's a...doesn't matter."

"A doesn't matter? That's a new one on me."

Just then a woman with long, dark, silky hair came up to Luella. "Well, hello there."

"Oh, God," Luella said. "I mean, hello, Diane. How have you been?"

Diane? Emma thought.

"Emma," Granny said. *"Do not do anything stupid."*

"Um, Emma Gordon, this is Diane Irwin."

"Soon to be Hudspeth," Diane said and wiggled her ring finger, revealing what must have been a two-carat diamond, in front of Luella.

"Dang, I'm surprised you can lift your hand," Luella said.

"I know," Diane said. "He's so wonderful."

The Diane?

"Emma Rose! Do not do anything stupid!"

"Nice to meet you," Diane said to Emma.

Emma smiled and nodded.

"Emma bought Ned's old place," Luella said.

Diane faltered, but for only a second. Ned's place meant, right across the road from Clancy. The recognition was there. Emma wasn't sure if it was painful, like a reminder of what got away, or if it was anger as in, this was the one she couldn't win. Diane was tall, thin, with a wonderful profile and pink full lips. Her hair was so annoyingly straight and silky that Emma wanted to stick the woman's finger in an electrical socket. The lights in the bar gleamed off it. It moved like a river of oil. She should be on *Sports Illustrated*. The swimsuit issue, not the rugby issue.

Emma imagined Clancy running his fingers through that midnight waterfall and not getting his fingers tangled once. Then she thought of them naked. Together. Although, thinking of them naked separately wasn't nearly as rage inducing.

"Oh? That old dump? I didn't think anybody was desperate enough to buy that place. I mean, no offense Lu, I know it was your brother's. But really, he let it go to pot," Diane said. She turned to Emma and gave a smile that didn't quite reach her eyes. "Have you met your neighbor across the road?"

Luella closed her eyes.

"Oh yeah," Emma said. *Of course I've met the neighbor across the road, you bitchy bitchface bitch! And just what is wrong with my house?*

"So then you are intimately familiar with the smell of horse crap," Diane said. "That family...I was sad to hear about their mother, although I can't say that I didn't see tragedy coming."

Deep breath Emma. Deeeeeep breath.

Her lungs weren't deep enough.

"If I owned that farm, my office would be in town, away from the stench. Really, Clancy has his head so far up his horse's vaginas he doesn't even know what day of the week it is. Just try getting him to notice a two-legged female. He's only got eyes for the four-legged. He could tell me the ovulation date of every female on the property, but he couldn't even tell when I was in the mood."

"Maybe the horses' vaginas are prettier than yours," Emma said, and Luella slapped her on the back of the head. Emma rubbed her skull and shot Luella a dirty look.

"What did you say?" Diane asked with a rigid smile frozen on her face.

"Oh, crap. Did I say that out loud?" Emma asked. No wonder Luella had hit her.

Diane gave Luella a quizzical look, but kept talking. She must not have heard Emma.

Thank you, George Thorogood.

"Everything comes second to those animals," Diane continued. "I told him he should hire out the work and run it all from town. He could wear a suit and tie. Oh, and he looks great in one, by the way."

Emma had never seen him in a suit and tie. *I hate her!*

"They really are sitting on a gold mine over there," Diane said.

"I kind of got the impression that everything came second to Caitlin," Emma said. "Not the horses."

"Oh, yeah, her. Clancy spoiled her and I can't for the life of me figure out why. I mean, she was okay, so far as kids go. I didn't see what was so special."

Emma's blood boiled. Deep breath. Deep breath. Deep breath. No matter how much she tried to breathe deep and relax she found herself panting like a dog. She balled her fists.

"Did you know that Zeus was injured pretty badly when June was killed?" Luella said, obviously trying to change the subject.

"Zeus...which horse was that?" Diane said.

And that was the last straw. All Emma could think was, *the bitch must die!* And the next thing Emma knew, she was pulling back her fist and punching Diane right in the face. And as Diane hit the floor, Luella busted out laughing and Sam jumped over the bar.

Note to self: Next time, open-face slap. Punching hurts. Like, a lot.

The door to the bar opened and Clancy and Brad walked in.

Things went downhill from there.

31

"I think I broke my knuckles," Emma said, slurring her words and staring out at the snow-covered pine trees as Sam drove her home. Those same pine trees had seemed so exotic, so gorgeous, so otherworldly when she'd first moved up here. Now they just looked like dumb old pine trees. The stupid things didn't even have the sense to go dormant in the winter like most trees. Their optimism ticked her off and she wished they'd all die.

She thought a moment about what the future held for her if a tree could make her this angry.

"What were you thinking?" Sam said.

"That pine trees are really stupid," she said.

"At the bar, Emma. At the bar! Wait, you weren't thinking, were you?"

"Yes I was! I was thinking Diane's attitude needed rearranging with my *fist!*"

"Emma..."

"That *woman* didn't even know who Zeus was," she said. "How can you be in a relationship with Clancy and not even know *which horse is Zeus?!* I just wanted to punch her face. Punch her, punch her, punch her."

"I get that," Sam said. "Do you have a habit of punching people in the face?"

Emma thought about it. She flipped through her mental index file. She'd slapped a girl in high school for calling the size twelve cheerleader a cow. Really? A twelve? Marilyn Monroe was a twelve. She'd tripped a waiter at a restaurant in Arizona once because he'd insulted a nun. Sorry, you just didn't insult nuns. Then there was the groom that she slapped silly on his wedding day because he'd been hysterical. He'd thanked her. She'd saved the wedding and the marriage. And then there was the time that she'd shoved her cousin Suzanne into speeding traffic. She hadn't realized, of course, that there was speeding traffic, she was just trying to get Suzanne out of the way of the copperhead snake that they'd stumbled on while walking on the side of the road. Everybody was fine. The cars swerved and missed her.

"Emma?" Sam asked.

"I'm thinking..." There was the guy in Toledo. That was a kick to the shin. The guy in New Orleans. That had been a kick in the butt. Oh wait, that had been a woman. No, a guy. She couldn't remember clearly and it didn't really matter anyway. The woman in Tampa...a slap. Oh, and there was that whole mess in Louisville, Kentucky, that wretched, wretched state, with Louise Bromley, but Emma had only pulled Louise's hair and dumped a can of paint on her head. "No, I've never punched anybody before."

"Emma..."

"I know, I know. But I was just punching her for good measure. Like, for the whole Stephens family."

"Okay," he said. "But calling her a...wait, what was it you called her?"

"A scum-sucking, slop-slurping gutter-slut."

They pulled onto Lady Slipper Lane. "Yeah, that. I think that might have been overkill."

Emma smiled. "It really ticked her off," she said, rubbing her chin where she would have a bruise the next day.

"A bit," he said.

"But, hey, if I recall, you let go of me and told me to hit her again when she called me Clancy's latest brood mare," she said.

"I did not. Well, I did let go of you, but Brad was the one who said to hit her again."

"Well, I didn't mean for Luella to take that jab to the stomach," she said. "She just sort of got in the way."

"And the broken chair over my head?"

"Totally Diane's fault. She went psycho crazy on me."

"I might need stitches," he said.

"No you don't. I've seen worse," she said and waved her hand in his direction.

"And the four bottles of beer that went flying through the air and broke my juke box?"

Emma winced. "I did that, didn't I? Jesus, I'll pay for it. I got the money. I'll write you a check."

"You're damn right you're gonna pay for it," he said.

"I'll never think of 'Brown-Eyed Girl' in the same way again," she said. "It's always been such a happy song to me. Now...it was like, just as he got to the shalalalalalalalalalalalalala part, that first bottle hit. Then Van Morrison sounded like a demon. How many la la's are in that song, anyway?"

"What about Clancy?" Sam asked.

"I never touched the jerk."

"No, but he now has horseradish and ranch dipping sauce in his hair."

"Not my fault."

"Emma?"

"That one is not on me," she said in utter indignation.

Silence.

"Well, not completely."

Sam turned into her driveway and Roy waited for her on the porch.

"Dumb horse," she muttered. "I love that stupid horse."

They got out and Sam helped her up the steps, but somehow she still managed to miss one of them. She threw her arms around

Roy and said, "I love you, Roy. But you really have to stay at home from now on."

"Come on," Sam said.

"I broke the heel on my boot," she said.

"The least of your worries," Sam said.

"No, no, these were really cute boots."

"Now they're asymmetrical. Install them in a gallery somewhere and call them art."

"Oh, I never thought of that," Emma said. "You're so smart."

"Sometimes. Never when it counts."

When they stepped inside, the animals attacked, and Marty sat up from his sleeping position on the couch. He looked at Emma and then his gaze went to Sam's hand that gripped her arm.

"The only reason any of it happened is because Luella gave me tequila," she said.

Clancy sat on the edge of his bed with a bath towel around his waist, clutching the phone in his hand. His ritual for the past week had been that at eleven o'clock sharp he sat down, picked up his phone and then stared at it for ten minutes. He could not bring himself to call her. He wanted to. God knew he wanted to talk to her, but then he'd see his sister's face, crying, stricken. *I don't want Caitlin around her. Your girlfriend's done enough damage. If I'd known she was going to ruin our lives...*

It was stupid, he knew. Emma wasn't responsible for what happened to his sister. But she was sort of responsible for why she found out. It was as simple as it was stupid; Peri was blaming the messenger. But if he couldn't have a relationship with Emma without upsetting his family then what kind of relationship was that? And the last time a woman tried to come between him and his family, his family had been right.

But Emma hadn't intentionally meant harm, like Diane had, and he knew it. And he kept thinking that Peri would eventually cool off and everything would be fine. But Peri hadn't called, emailed, texted or been down since the whole thing had happened. She wouldn't return calls, either. So, clearly, Peri's time for forgiveness hadn't arrived.

And the longer he waited to call Emma, the harder it was going to be.

The real problem, and this was the kicker, was that Clancy had begun to associate Emma with Peri's pain. He hadn't meant for it to happen. When it first started he wasn't even aware of what was going on. Just, he thought about Emma smiling up at him in the barn, and then he saw Peri's tear-stained face. He thought of Emma gliding down those stairs in that emerald green dress, and he saw Peri screaming, "You bastard!" at their father. Thoughts of Emma had become a source of great pain. So he tried not to think about her. Well, not thinking about her wasn't exactly the foundation for a great relationship!

But tonight...tonight he'd walked into Sam's bar and saw Emma with a handful of Diane's hair and Diane kicking the crap out of her, and he wanted to just grab Emma and run with her to safety. Luella had then pounced on Diane and Sam had lunged for Emma, grappling both of her arms behind her back. Diane and Emma had both turned to Clancy and said, "Oh, great, it's you."

Then all hell broke loose, with beer bottles flying and food going everywhere. Somehow, just before Sam managed to get Emma out of the bar, she'd stopped in front of Clancy and said, "She insulted my house. She insulted Caitlin and she insulted you. And your horse. *Horses.* Plural. And she has serious issues with horse vaginas."

As Sam dragged her out the door Emma screamed, "You haven't seen the last of me, Diane! I'm gonna unload the fury of my rebel ass all over your scrawny Yankee butt! I'm coming for you! *'And hell's coming with me!'*"

"Shut up, Emma," Sam had said, dragging her.

Diane had tried to gather herself as best she could. As she made her way to the door, lipstick smeared all over her cheek and her silky dark hair in knotted tangles, she said, "You haven't broken her in, I see. Better get on that."

And Clancy wanted to hit her, too. He didn't, of course, but he sure wanted to.

Now he sat rubbing his eyes, knowing that Sam was over at Emma's house tucking her into bed, hopefully. Either that or he was holding back her hair while she puked.

Clancy needed to speak to her. For the sake of any future. If he ever wanted to hold her again, ever wanted her to smile up at him with those curls flying around her face and hear that wicked, throaty little laugh that she had, well, then...he needed to call her.

Just as he moved his thumb to push the number his phone buzzed. It was a text from Emma. *Come get your house. Horse. Damn auto correct. Come get your horse and get out of my labia. Life. Life. Get out of my life. WTF is wrong with this phone?*

She was still drunk. He dried off, got dressed and went to get his horse.

32

Clancy walked up Emma's driveway, wondering just what had gone wrong in the past week? On Tuesday he'd been gazing at the most amazing woman in the world, ready to throw caution to the wind and plunge into what he hoped would be the most wonderful relationship of his life. The next thing he knew, his family was shattered and Emma...and Emma was...

Well, he didn't know. Because he hadn't called to find out.

"Come on, Roy," he said from the driveway. He glanced up at the second floor and noticed that her bedroom light was on. She'd be up there curled on the bed with all of her animals around her with her hair fanning out on the rose-colored pillow and her hip swelling under the covers and she'd be warm and soft and... Well, she might also be puking. But still. She was right there. All he had to do was go in and talk to her.

He should at least check in with Marty and Sam and make sure she was all right. As he reached the porch, Roy nudged Clancy in the shoulder. "All right," he said. When Clancy hadn't knocked fast enough, Roy bit his ear. "Ow, dammit!"

Then the door opened and there was Sam with blood on his forehead and Marty in the kitchen saying, "I don't think we have any Band-Aids."

"What in the devil's arse is going on?" Sam asked Clancy. Then Marty walked into the living room with his hands on his hips in indignation.

"What do you mean?" Clancy asked, rubbing his ear and checking for blood.

"Why haven't you called Emma?" Sam asked. He shut the door behind Clancy and glared at him.

"It's complicated," Clancy said.

"You want to be with her?" Sam asked.

"Yes," Clancy answered.

"Then what's so complicated?"

"I've got my family to consider," Clancy said.

"Are your dad and your sister gonna keep your bed warm at night?" Sam asked.

"No."

"Make you laugh your ass off at three in the morning?" Sam asked.

"No."

"They going to drain your gravy hose until your eyes are sunken in your head? Until your donuts are all outta jelly?"

"Um..."

"Are they going to heal your horse? Give you a skip in your step?"

"No, no, no. Look, I get it," Clancy said.

"Then what's the problem?" Sam asked, incredulous.

"He's a friggin' idiot, that's what," Marty finally chimed in.

"Hey!" Clancy said.

"You're an idiot," Sam said. "The longer you go without talking to her, the more stupid you make her feel. Your silence is convincing her that she's done something wrong!"

Clancy took a deep breath. "Look, I'm just trying to give everybody time to calm down. So that nobody says anything they can't take back. I can't choose between them. I almost lost Peri the last time."

"Well, you're gonna have to, you wimp," Marty said.

"Hey!" Clancy said.

"Can it, Marty," Sam said. "Nobody should be asking you to choose. The minute somebody does, you walk away. Making you choose is not love."

"You can't put demands on love," Marty said.

"So is somebody making demands?" Sam asked.

"Not exactly," Clancy said. "And who said anything about love?"

Marty and Sam both flounced onto the couch and said, "Idiot."

"Look, I just came here to get my horse," Clancy said.

"No you didn't," Sam said.

Marty stood then. "Fine. Go. You don't deserve her."

"Wait," Sam said. He stood and walked toward Clancy. "What do you mean 'not exactly'?"

"Emma has said nothing," Clancy said.

"Obviously, since you haven't called her," Marty said.

"But my sister..."

"Peri's making you choose?" Sam said, surprised.

"No. But she said that she doesn't want Caitlin around Emma. Or any of us, for that matter."

"It's a whole friggin' family of idiots!" Marty said, flailing his arms about.

"Now, listen here," Clancy said, taking offense.

Silence. They *were* listening and now suddenly Clancy didn't know what to say.

"If Emma can't be around Caitlin," he began. "I cannot abandon that child. So, so, so what? I have separate celebrations on the holidays? I can't take Emma to any of Caitlin's games or recitals or barrel races? It puts me in a tough spot. Just tell me, where does that leave me?"

"With an idiot for a sister," Marty said. "I'm gonna talk to Reuben. He can be reasoned with. You and Peri, you got too much of June in you to listen to reason."

Sam held up two hands. One at Marty, to shut up, the other toward Clancy telling him not to kick Marty's butt up between his ears. "I'm not breaking up another fight tonight. So don't even start," he said. He turned to Clancy. "Look, I get it. That does confuse things. But Peri is being unreasonable. That girl upstairs, crying into her pillow right now...she's only shown you kindness. Tell me she's ever shown you anything else."

Clancy blinked at him.

"You can't, can you?" Sam said. "You know why? Because that's all she's ever shown any of us. Well, except maybe Diane, but Diane was being awfully condescending."

"And the tequila contributed," Marty said.

"True," Sam agreed.

Clancy stood watching both of them. Her guardian angels.

"And she fixed your friggin' horse, or have you forgotten?" Marty said. "I hear memory loss is strong among idiots."

"Look," Clancy said. If Marty insulted his family one more time he was liable to pop him a good one, truth or not. "I gotta go. I'm not going to stand here and be insulted by a homeless, jobless, drunk and...and...a..."

"I'd be careful of your next words," Sam said in a steely voice. "And in case you haven't noticed there, pal, Marty is no longer homeless, or a drunk, and Luella gave him a job cooking in her diner weeks ago."

The bottom fell out of his stomach. He couldn't believe he'd just said those words to Marty. And his scalp prickled with the realization that Marty, indeed, was no longer any of those things. And it was because of Emma.

They were right. He didn't deserve her. He swallowed the anger and the bile rising in him. "Would you at least tell her that I checked in on her?"

"When you *do* actually check in on her, we'll tell her," Marty said. "This was just you hoping for absolution from us. Well, you ain't friggin' getting it."

"And that's the last word on that," Sam said and then gently pushed Clancy right out the door and shut it.

Clancy looked at Roy in the darkness and Roy bit him on the other ear. "Stop doing that!" he said. "Let's go."

But the horse refused to leave. "Come on, Roy. This is no joke. Emma doesn't have any food for you here."

But Roy just blinked at him. Clancy rubbed the horse's butt. "You're a good boy. Now let's go."

Roy wouldn't budge. The horse took his nose and shoved Clancy in the middle of the back, right off the porch into the snow. The front door opened, and Sam said, "Leave that poor horse alone, Clancy. We'll bring him home in the morning."

33

There was an e-mail in Emma's in-box that had been sitting there for a week. It was the result of the DNA tests. Inside it had the answer as to whether Jim, Sam or Marty was her father. But she couldn't bear to look.

It was March now and her birthday was tomorrow. The snow was starting to melt, although she'd been told by everybody that this area of Minnesota often got the biggest snowstorms in March so not to expect lilacs and daffodils any time soon. They'd all lived here much longer than she had. In fact, she hadn't experienced a spring in Minnesota ever. But she couldn't help feeling that spring was in the air. She could smell it, rustling through the bare trees and pooling in the mud left behind from the dissolving snow.

Clancy had texted her on Monday. *Working through stuff right now. Talk later?*

And she'd responded: *Don't bother.*

It might not have been the most mature thing to do, but if he was having that much trouble deciding whether or not to talk to her, then he clearly didn't want to. Did he really think Peri was the only one hurt by this? Did he not realize that she needed to hear, "You are not responsible for this," from *him*? Or that she needed to hear that what happened changed nothing between them? Of course, that was what she needed and he hadn't said it. So it no longer mattered. Actions spoke louder than words anyway, and his actions had just said that on his list of priorities, she ranked pretty low.

There was a knock at the door, probably Aurora. She'd called and said she was coming over. Emma answered hoping that Aurora hadn't brought any more cookies. She didn't need them and, of course, if Aurora brought them Emma would feel obligated to eat them. It was better if they didn't exist at all.

"Hello there, Emma," Aurora said, and the dogs went crazy. Valentine bayed and Tricephus yapped and Mutt just barked like a normal old dog. It was an odd sounding trio. Small, medium and large.

The sun shone through the trees like always, but it looked different today. Like it shined from a different angle. Emma smiled at Aurora and took a deep breath. It had to be forty degrees at least. "Come in," Emma said to the dainty woman.

"I've brought you *wiingashk*," she said as she came through the door. "I haven't lived with my people for a very long time. But I do still observe some of the traditions. This is sweet grass."

"Do you smoke it?" Emma asked. She shut the door and remembered Zoe's warning about not inhaling anything that Aurora offered.

"You smudge it. You just burn it and it purifies your house. When sweet grass is harvested, it is cut rather than pulled, and then it's sometimes braided because it signifies the hair of *Ogashiinan*, the great mother, mother earth. Sweet grass purifies by replacing negative with positive. You should do this. I braided it myself."

Emma took the bundles from her. They sort of looked like horse's tails when they were braided, only they were a greenish brown. She sniffed. True to the name, the sweet grass smelled sort of like vanilla. "You want me to do this now?"

"Nah," Aurora said. "Whenever you like."

"Should I say or do anything special when I burn it?"

Aurora shrugged. "You don't have to. But you could imagine that you are an eagle and that you are taking a prayer to *gitchi manitou*, the great spirit, the creator. Or, think of basketball, if you want. It's your ceremony."

Emma laughed. "Won't you stay? I can make tea."

"Only for a minute. I've got to see a man about a dog. I'm getting one of those big Pyrenees," she said. "Big white dog."

"Oh," Emma said. "How wonderful."

Just then Valentine, who had snuggled back onto the couch, farted, forcing Mutt to find a new place to sit by the fire. "Idiot," the parrot chipped. "Idiot."

Emma laughed. "I don't know where that bird learned that phrase. All he used to say was 'gimme the money,' but for the past week or so he's been calling everybody an idiot."

She put the tea kettle on to boil and got down two mugs. She'd compromised with Marty and bought a hot plate so that she could heat things quickly without firing up the wood- burning stove. She became aware suddenly that Aurora was studying her. "What?" she asked.

"Your spark is dampened," she said.

Emma shrugged because that's exactly what she felt like and she couldn't really argue with her.

"Did I ever tell you how I got my name?" Aurora asked.

"I assume you were named after the northern lights," Emma said.

"Ahh, yes, but do you know why?"

"No," Emma said. She got down the tin with the chai tea bags in it.

"My parents first kissed under the northern lights," she said.

Emma stopped as she reached for the refrigerator door. Had Clancy told Aurora about their first kiss? "My mother told me that she wanted me to carry the magic of that first kiss throughout my life," Aurora said.

"Oh," Emma replied. She got out the milk and took the kettle off just before it started whistling.

"She said that anybody who lost their virginity or had their first kiss beneath the aurora borealis would be forever blessed."

Emma poured the water. "Did Clancy tell you that we kissed under the northern lights?" she asked, defusing the moment.

Aurora's eyes grew wide and she placed a hand on her chest. "Why no," she said. "What gave you that idea?"

"You're lying," Emma said, giggling.

"No, I'm not," Aurora said. But when it was clear that Emma wasn't buying it, she came clean. "I was out on the lake in one of the fishing huts that night and saw you two."

Emma laughed and handed Aurora her mug. Of course she was out on the lake. Where else would a ninety-year-old woman be at midnight in subfreezing temperatures but out on a frozen lake fishing? Made perfect sense. The truth was, that was probably the reason Aurora had lived to be ninety, because she didn't sit in front of a television waiting to die. "You want to sit?"

"Soon enough I'll be resting forever," she said. "I'll stand as long as I can."

Emma nodded. Aurora's comment bothered her, but maybe that was just the sort of thing people said when they were ninety. Like her own Granny. She'd known when her time was coming. Of course, that was most likely because a doctor had told her that her heart was worn out and to say good-bye to those she loved. But still. In any case, Aurora certainly didn't *look* any different. "So, all that stuff about being forever blessed is baloney?" Emma asked, not wanting to follow the age and dying thread.

"No," Aurora said. "That's true. I've only known three couples who had their first kiss under the northern lights. And two of them have had long, lasting, loving relationships."

"What about the third?" Emma asked.

"I'm waiting to see how that one turns out," she said and winked.

"I don't think there's going to be one," Emma said. "I hate to break it to you."

"Things have a way of working out."

"No, things work out because people are willing to put the effort in. They don't just magically work out."

"True," Aurora said. "But things have a way of working out."

"You're impossible," she said.

"So, tomorrow's your birthday?"

Emma nodded.

"Doing anything special?"

"No," she said. "Last time I went out in public I gave a complete stranger a black eye, yanked her hair out in clumps, broke Sam's juke-box and trashed the bar. It's just me and the animals tomorrow. All day and night. Well, until Marty gets home."

"Are you going to read that e-mail?" Aurora said. "The one about your DNA results?"

"How did you know?" Emma asked.

"All week long, you keep checking your phone, hesitating. Like there's something there to read, but you don't ever read it."

"I don't want to be alone when I read it," she said.

"Then don't be," Aurora said.

Emma swallowed and fought back the tears. She wanted to know who her father was, and yet she suddenly, irrationally, passionately didn't want to know. But she wanted to share the news, whatever it may be, with Clancy. But now she wouldn't. Because things had changed.

"I'll read it tomorrow," Emma said. "It seems appropriate to do it on my birthday."

Aurora took a drink of her tea. "It's what you came here for, right?"

"Right," Emma said, gripping the cup.

After Aurora left, Emma was seated on the couch with Thing 1 licking the fuzzies off her sweater when her phone buzzed. It was a text from Clancy: *I cannot get Roy to eat. Would you please come over and talk to him?*

Emma texted back: *Right. Resorting to using your animals as an excuse to talk to me?*

Clancy: *Em, I'm being serious. He won't eat. Barely drinking.*

Emma: *Clancy, I can't come over there every time one of your horses won't do something you want it to do.*

Clancy: *This isn't just any horse, Em. It's Roy. And he will not eat.*

Emma: *I'll be right there.*

She pulled on a jacket and her boots and hopped in her car. It wasn't that far of a drive and she usually just walked, but it was really muddy and she wanted to get there quickly and she wanted a hasty retreat, too. She pulled in front of the house and Reuben met her in the driveway. "You here about Roy?"

"Yeah," she said.

"He won't eat. Going on three days now."

Emma's brows knit together and worry pounded in her chest. She hadn't really believed Clancy. She thought this was a ruse just to get her here. The skin prickled along her spine and panic settled in her stomach in a twisted knot. She headed for Roy's stable, but Reuben grabbed her arm. "Prepare yourself."

"What do you mean? How bad is it?"

"Not for Roy. For Clancy. It's as bad as when Zeus had his accident."

Emma bolted for the stable, sliding in the mud, her heart pounding with each step she took. She rounded the corner and stopped in front of Roy's pen. Roy was lying down in the straw and Clancy was lying right next to him, stroking his mane. Clancy never even acknowledged when she arrived, but she knew he knew she was there. "Clancy?" she asked.

His eyes never left Roy's face. "Just please, make him eat."

She lifted the latch on the door and stepped inside and Roy's head shifted sideways to take note of her. "Is he drinking?"

"Some."

"Have you called the vet?"

He nodded. "They did an ultrasound to see if there was a blockage anywhere. There's nothing physically wrong with him."

Roy's coat was as dull as his eyes. She felt a piercing pain in her chest and she wasn't sure if it was for Roy or if it was for Clancy, and then realized it was for both. "He's gone to your place about four times a day, but I bring him back before you realize he's even been there. This...this is a broken heart, Em. He wants you."

"Oh, God," she said. A knot formed in her throat and it wouldn't go down no matter how much she swallowed. "Clancy, how long have you been lying here?"

"Since last night," he said.

"Go," she said. "Go in the house, get something to drink. Go to the bathroom."

"I'm not leaving him."

"Look," she said, raising her voice. "He's going to be fine. Go clean up."

He sat up then and looked at her and her heart cleaved right in two. His eyes were hollow, sunken and spiritless. His fear was so palpable she could practically feel it radiating off his skin. He tried to speak but words wouldn't come out. He shook his head in anguish and buried his face in his hands.

"You know I'm right. Maybe he's not eating because you're not eating," she said.

Clancy nodded. "Okay, maybe." When he stood, he seemed weak and stiff. It was four in the afternoon. How long had he been in the barn? Sixteen hours or so? As he walked away, she sat down next to Roy with her back against the wall. "So," she said. "What are you, three years old? You're pouting?"

Roy didn't look at her.

She felt something under her butt in the straw and fumbled to grab it. It was Clancy's phone and when she picked it up, the screen lit up. He'd been looking at her Facebook page. She had about sixty photo albums on there, thousands of pictures, and he'd been flipping through them because he'd stopped on the picture of her at the Grand Canyon with a donkey named Toby and her guide Carlos. Carlos with the long stride and narrow hips. Carlos who said she reminded him of the sun. She smiled at the memory. It was a nice line, but it hadn't gotten him anywhere.

She reached out and touched Roy. "Hey, I'm talking to you. Now this is complete and utter poppycock. Do you know what you're putting Clancy through?"

His ears perked forward.

"Right, I'm talking to you. You know I am. Now what's all this nonsense? If you're dead, who am I supposed to talk to the next time I think I've had sex with my brother? Huh? You gotta eat, dude. You just have to. If you don't eat then there's no poop, and if there's no poop then there's nothing for Clancy to shovel. And if there's nothing to clean out, then there's no fertilizer and without fertilizer there's no garden. Seriously, you could end up starving the entire family."

She crawled over and grabbed the bucket that had barley and oats in it and then came back to her spot. "Nom nom nom, good...grains. Nom nom nom."

Roy nickered at her and snorted.

"Well, okay, I get that," she said. "It was a rather sudden separation."

He blew air out of his nose.

"I know. I know. Well, you know, shit happens. I...my presence here has caused a consequence that I did not foresee. And it's hurt some feelings and..."

He shook his head like he was trying to get water out of his ears.

"So," she said, putting the bucket under the nose. "You want this. I know you do. You just want it from me. Which, I'm telling you, is the ultimate definition of spoiled."

Roy shoved his nose in the bucket and blew air out of his nostrils, tossing feed into the air. He didn't eat any of it, but he was at least aware that it was there. Emma stuck her head in the bucket. "Nom nom nom."

He made some weird sound in his throat that she'd never heard before. "Look, don't get prickly with me. I realize that Clancy could have just called me and made everything okay. He's a guy. What did you expect? Oh, sorry, so are you. Well...he's... I *thought* he was everything I ever wanted. Man, Roy, the first time I saw him with that beard and those coveralls, I thought he was something right out of 'Deliverance.' And I'm not sure how many movies you've seen, but that one ranks up there as one of the scariest things ever made. Scarier than Freddy or Jason or...or those 'Saw' movies. But then...honestly, when I saw that stupid beaded flower on his hat and he told me that Aurora had made it for him... What big tough guy do you know that would wear a beaded flower on his hat? And risk the chance of getting made fun of?" She laughed. "That's the guy for me right there."

Roy stretched his neck and placed his head on her shoulder.

"And then he shaved and showed up at Sam's and, have you ever seen him dance with a woman, Roy? He practically makes love to her right there on the dance floor. I get hot just thinking about it."

Roy blinked.

"Sorry, please eat something." But Roy just sniffed her hair. "But it's not to be. That doesn't mean that you stop eating."

Roy pulled her toward him with his head. "I know," she said. "I love you, too. I mean, honestly. I think I love you more than just about anything on this planet. But you're not mine to keep and neither is Clancy."

She sniffled and gave a little sob. "Who would have thought that the craziest thing I would ever do in my life would be falling in love with a horse?" The tears were warm on her face and she rubbed his neck. "Now, you're a good boy. Please, for the love of God, eat."

And Roy dipped his head into the bucket and took his first tentative bites.

"Oh, thank God," she said. "That's it boy, keep eating."

Then Clancy and Reuben both stuck their heads around the door with hopeful expressions on their faces. Reuben blinked away tears and Clancy took big, heaving breaths of relief. They'd been standing there the whole time. Clancy had never left. Emma swiped at her tears and made a motion for them to go away, which they did this time. She sat there in the straw until Roy finished eating. Then she took Clancy's phone, pressed her cheek against Roy's head and said, "Say cheese."

And took the picture.

"Open it," Jackie's voice said. Emma clutched the phone, knuckles white. She reached for her laptop, logged onto the internet and pulled up her e-mail. She decided not to wait for her birthday to learn the identity of her father. She decided that the memory of what she learned would color all her future birthdays and so there she was, on her couch, an hour after coercing Roy into eating.

"I can't."

"Emma, I swear to God, if you don't open that e-mail I'm going to march up there myself and mop the floor with you."

But suddenly she couldn't. She loved all three men. She wanted it to be all of them. Her father's identity didn't matter to her anymore.

"Emma!"

"No," she said. She took the e-mail and then dragged it to the trash bin. "I deleted it."

"What?! Oh my God!" Jackie said. "I'm getting in my car right now!"

And then just as quickly, Emma retrieved it from the trash can, opened it and scanned the e-mail. Her heart pounded. The blood raced through her ears. She was completely flushed from head to toe. Her blood pressure felt like it was a thousand over five hundred. She scanned it, she read the first paragraph and, blah, blah, blah, and then she saw the words... NO MATCH.

Her heart sank. She crashed and said, "It's none of them."

"What?" Jackie said.

"None of them matched."

"Oh, honey," she said. "Whoever he is must not have answered the ad."

Emma started to cry. All of this and it wasn't *any* of them!

"Emmie, baby, look. There could be lots of reasons why he didn't answer. He could be dead, for one thing," she said.

"You think?" Emma said. Somehow the fact that her father could be dead and not ignoring her made her feel better.

"Of course," Jackie said. "Lots of guys die. Look, don't give up. Maybe he moved out of town and he hasn't even seen the ad. Put another one in the paper. Branch out. Put one in the Minneapolis paper. Call your mom and see if you can get more information. Maybe she's thought of more details since she went to the tropics. Paradise will do that to you. You have more time to think. Maybe that one lady, um, Aurora! Maybe she can help you do more digging. Go through all of her pictures with a fine-toothed comb."

But Emma only sobbed louder. The dogs howled, the cats licked the tears from her face and the parrot just kept saying, "Idiot. Idiot. Idiot."

"I...I've got nothing, Jackie. No father. No Clancy. No *mother*."

"That's not true. You've got a lovely house that you like and you've made lots of really good friends and you've got all the animals. And you still have me and Suzanne. Look, please don't do anything stupid. The last time you got your heart broken you snuck into Mexico for three weeks and came back with two tattoos, your tongue pierced and a case of the crabs."

"Not true," Emma said, hiccupping. "That was the time before."

"Whatever. Just, please God, give it time."

"Don't worry. Canada is the closest foreign country right now and I don't think they get crabs up there."

Jackie was silent.

"How am I going to tell these guys?" Emma asked.

"Well, you were going to have to tell two of them that they weren't your father one way or another," Jackie said.

Emma hadn't thought of that. The potential to hurt these men hadn't occurred to her when she came up here looking for her father. Because she'd assumed she wouldn't matter that much to them. They'd be relieved if she wasn't their daughter. Plus, she'd honestly thought only her *real* father would have answered. Like some stupid fairy tale. She'd been so incredibly selfish. As long as she got her answer, she'd had no regard at all for the kink she would throw into these men's lives!

"I am a horrible person," Emma said.

"Idiot," cried the parrot.

"Emmie," Jackie said. "You are not a horrible person!"

"For once in your life, listen to your cousin," Granny said.

"Idiot," cried the parrot.

Emma wailed even louder.

"I've got to go. I need a hot-fudge sundae," she said.

34

The next day, Clancy stood in front of Roy's stall with his hat in his hand and his head hung. "Don't you ever do that to me again, you shit head. You hear me?"

Roy blinked and spun around in circles.

"No, I don't think you're cute. And you're going to run into the wall if you're not careful. Now stop," he said.

He swallowed back disgust. Disgust at himself. He'd let Emma leave yesterday without saying a single word to her. It wasn't that he'd planned it that way. He just couldn't figure out what to say. Nothing he came up with sounded even remotely appropriate. It all sounded trivial. That was because there were no words for what he'd felt at that moment. What he had wanted to do and what he would have done under any other circumstances was to smother her in kisses. He'd stood as rigid as he could because if he'd let go of his senses even for a second, he'd have grabbed her and kissed her and if he'd done that and she'd rejected him, not only would it have hurt, but he would have been mortified.

So after she saved Roy's life he just let her leave without saying a word to her.

Out of the corner of his eye, Clancy saw Peri step into the stable. He so didn't need any lip from her today. He wanted her to go away. Right now, all he could think about, all he *wanted* to think about, was Roy, Zeus and Emma. Not necessarily in that order. He'd heard what Emma had said to Roy. *I think I love you more than just about anything on this planet. But you're not mine to keep and neither is Clancy.*

He'd thought about it all night. Had she meant that she loved him, too? She'd lumped him into the sentence with the horse, which oddly enough, felt appropriate. Because the woman for him would love his horses as much as she loved him. They'd never talked about love before. They'd barely gotten to the "us" part. But ever since he'd held her that first night at Sam's and danced to "The Third Degree" he knew that no other woman was ever going to make him feel like that. And she made him laugh. And she was absolutely fearless.

And he was so obviously afraid.

"I came as soon as I heard about Roy," Peri finally said.

"That's nice," Clancy said.

"Look," she said.

"No, you look. I have called, texted, e-mailed. So has Dad. You're behaving like..."

"Like what? Like somebody who just had her life turned upside down?"

"I get that, Peri. I really do. But, you're killing the messenger. Emma is the cause for you learning the truth, but that doesn't mean she's to blame. If you got bit by a snake and the doctor told you he had to amputate your leg, you don't get mad at the doctor. You get mad at the snake. Look, Peri, everybody screws up at some point."

She rolled her eyes. "Well, on the scale of screw ups-"

"I know," he said, cutting her off. "It's a big one. But everybody makes mistakes. We all do. For ninety-nine percent of his life, our dad has been a tremendous human being. He's one of the good guys. Do you know how many people have crappy fathers? Lots. Do you know how many men don't even stick around and raise what's theirs? Or contribute to the raising? Lots. Just ask Emma. But you, you'll never know what it's like to feel abandonment, Peri. You were wanted your whole life and you were given everything a person could ever dream of. By a man who had one not-so-shining moment."

Peri covered her face as she began to cry.

"And the not-so-shining moment wasn't his affair, it was the lie he told you."

"I...just want to be *his*."

"You *are* his."

"I..."

"Now, I told you when you divorced that I would never abandon you and Caitlin. And I know after the fiasco with Diane that I had a lot to answer for but Peri, Emma is..."

"I know," she said.

"She's..."

"I know," Peri said. "She's perfect for you. And I really like her. I just hated her for a little while."

Relief swelled through him. "What changed your mind?" he asked, almost unable to form the words.

"Time," she said. "And Caitlin. I told her the truth."

He felt like he'd been punched in the stomach.

"And she thought it was no big deal," Peri said. She laughed and shrugged her shoulders. "She wanted to know if anything was going to change? And I told her no and then she said that Emma must feel really bad, and I thought, yeah. And I didn't help matters. Then she wanted to know if she could meet her other grandpa. She didn't look at it like she'd lost one Grandpa, she looked at it as she gained one. Which is how I should look at it. She amazes me, Clancy. I couldn't go on being bitter if she wasn't."

Clancy opened his arms and Peri ran to him and hugged him.

"I don't think I'll ever know who my birth-father is," she said. "Caitlin's going to be sad about that. But, it is what it is."

"Happy birthday to me," Emma said. She chowed on pizza while she sat on the couch and flipped the "on" button for the new television she'd bought. The cats were stretched on the back of the couch. Thing 2 kept flipping his tail on her ear. The dogs were all sitting on the floor staring up at her as though the pizza was the key to their immortality. She could see the conspiratorial thinking going on amongst the three of them. Valentine was the only one who really had a chance at getting any of it. *Gotta keep my eye on the big guy,* she thought.

She hadn't told anybody about the DNA results, but she knew she was going to have to eventually. She just wanted to wait until tomorrow when it was no longer her birthday. Luella and Zoe had asked her out for drinks and a night on the town, but Emma figured she should pass. At least until Sam's jukebox got fixed. Both of her cousins had called to wish her a happy birthday, too. It was this day that she missed her Granny the most. Because without fail, Granny had always made her a chocolate cake. Even if Emma wasn't in town to eat any of it.

"Twenty-nine and holding," she said to Mutt.

Does that mean I get pizza?

"I'm going to be thirty next year!"

Does that mean I get pizza?

"All you think about is food," she said to him.

Does that mean I get pizza?

Marty came in the door then. "It's nice outside," he said. "It's gotta be thirty-five or forty degrees."

"Want some pizza?" she asked.

Mutt gave her a woeful look. *Traitor!*

"Nah, I'm good," he said.

"You want to play chess?" she said and switched off the television.

"Sure," he said. "Look, I know it's your birthday...but..."

"Oh, Marty, don't worry about it," she said. Surely he wasn't apologizing for not buying her a present! The man barely had two nickels to rub together.

"I been working on something for you, but I won't have it until tomorrow."

"Oh, you didn't have to get me anything," she said. "Don't be silly!"

He shrugged.

She put the pizza box on the couch and went to get the chess game out of the kitchen and that was when she heard the stampede and the box hit the floor and growling and barking and as she stuck her head back in the living room, she saw the pizza box fly through the air. "What is going on in here?" she said as she stormed back into the room.

All three dogs were covered in pizza sauce, but not one piece of pizza could be found anywhere. Emma looked up in horror at Marty, who looked as dumbfounded as she was.

"I'm standing right here and I still can't quite tell you what just happened," he said.

35

It was the day after Emma's birthday, a Saturday, and Emma sat on the couch surrounded by Luella, Zoe and Aurora. When she had stepped into the kitchen that morning and found the pile of pancakes sitting on the stove with a candle in it, she'd burst into tears. Marty had left her breakfast, which was great, but it made her realize that no matter how irrational it was, she'd been waiting to hear from Clancy all day. Surely, he wouldn't have let her birthday go by without getting in touch with her! That was when she realized she'd lost her phone.

"I...I can't believe he didn't even text me!" Emma cried. Then she hiccupped and snot went every which way, but nobody noticed because it was all mixed in with her tears anyway. She hugged her knees to her chest and took great joy in her misery. She had to wallow in it for a while before she could climb back out.

Luella, sitting next to her on the couch, shoved a bite of ice-cream into Emma's mouth.

"My birthday! And he just...*wham*. I no longer exist!"

"Well, now, baby," Luella said. "You did tell him not to bother."

Emma glared at her.

Luella had shown up on time to take her to the movies and found Emma in a puddle on the floor, tears everywhere and animal hair stuck to her face. She looked like a circus freak. Luella had sprung into action, calling Zoe, "Bring the double chocolate-chip."

And Aurora, "Cookies. Stat. I don't care what kind. Oh, and bring a box of tissues."

"Maybe he texted this morning," Zoe said.

"I can't find my phone!" Emma said.

"Open," Luella said. Emma opened her mouth and Luella shoved in another bite of ice-cream.

"How could I have been so stupid? Okay, do *not* answer that," Emma said.

"You're not stupid," Aurora said.

"I went over there last week to get Roy to eat food because apparently, Clancy can't control his own animals, and I...I saved Roy's life. I got him to eat. And when I left...nothing."

"Nothing?" Zoe said.

"He didn't even *look* at me," she said. More tears. More snot.

Aurora handed her a tissue. Emma blew.

"Of course all I wanted to do was run and hug him," Emma said. "You should have seen him. He was like a broken little boy when I first got there, lying in that pen with Roy. But no. He just *stood* there, stiff as a board."

Zoe looked up at the mantel on the fireplace to the eight by ten picture frame sitting there. Emma had just got around to setting out photos last week. "Is that you and Roy?"

"Yeah, I took that one day when we were walking over to Cl...to *his* house." Roy was smiling in the picture, showing all his teeth, and so was Emma.

"And who's this?" Zoe asked, pointing to another frame.

"That's my granny."

"And this?"

"My mom and my...f-father," she said. More tears.

Zoe handed the picture to Luella, who studied it a moment and took a bite of the ice-cream. Then Luella shoved another bite into Emma's mouth.

"Where on earth did you get a three-legged dog?" Zoe asked, looking down at Tricephus.

"Same place I got all of the animals."

"Where's that?"

Emma shrugged. "They found me."

"Oh, look," Luella said. "That bruise on your chin is turning a nice shade of green."

Aurora shook her head.

"Well, help me here!" Luella said.

"I brought some tobacco to smoke," Aurora said and pulled out a pouch.

"No!" Zoe said.

"Hell no, Aurora!" Luella said.

"Oh, I want to try it," Emma said perking right up.

"No you don't," Luella said. "Here, have some more ice-cream."

"You could have a vision quest," Aurora said.

"She don't need no vision quest, you crazy woman," Luella said.

"I...I...I have a confession to tell and a favor to ask," Emma said.

All three women grew silent, which was pretty wise, considering.

"I...I got the DNA results back," she said.

Nobody said anything.

She let out a banshee sounding cry and said, *"None of them are my f-f-father!"*

"Oh shit," all three women said at the same time.

"No wonder you're such a mess," Zoe said.

Luella picked up the frame holding the picture of Emma's parents and studied it again and said, "Well, there, there."

"Why do people always say that?" Emma asked. "It means nothing. There what?"

"So, what's the favor?" Zoe asked.

"I can't tell them. I just can't. I mean, I can, but..." she gestured to her messy face. "I won't be able to contain myself and I don't want to slobber all over them."

"So you want us to tell them?" Aurora asked, sympathetically.

Emma nodded.

Luella looked at the ice-cream container. "I don't think we have enough ice-cream."

"That's okay," Emma said. "If I eat anymore I'm gonna puke."

"Okay," Luella said. "We'll take care of it."

"You will?" Emma asked.

"Sure, we'll let them all know."

Emma burped. "I need to lie down."

The next day, Emma still hadn't found her phone and decided to go up to Winchester Hollow to buy a new one. It was a nice day. Sunny and almost sixty degrees. So, she put on a purple cotton dress that fell just below her knees, with her new red cowboy boots and a breezy white sweater and headed out the door. She was almost out of foundation make-up, too, because she'd used so much of it covering up that bruise on her chin, so she added it to her list of things to purchase.

She was better today. She really was. She hadn't cried in at least six hours and she was amazed that she still fit into her clothes after all the junk she'd eaten this week. That was always a plus. She'd gotten out her travel magazines and started looking for places to visit, because a trip would do her good. Maybe she'd take Luella along with her if she could find somebody to mind the café. Of course, she would just as easily go by herself. She always had.

She'd promised to meet Luella for lunch at the café at one, so she wanted to get an early start.

She wasn't sure where she'd left her phone, but she had a horrible feeling that she'd dropped it in Roy's pen and if so, she wasn't going over there after it. In fact, the next time that Clancy couldn't get Roy to eat she was going to just facetime her pleading. She was never stepping foot on that property again.

After she made her purchases, she stopped in a specialty shop and bought Jamie an adorable handmade sweater that was the same purple shade as the dress Emma wore. Then she bought Micah some toy horse figurines that came with a corral and a cowboy. Then she thought, *what am I doing?* They weren't her siblings and they'd probably never want to see her again. In fact, all three men probably knew the results of the DNA test by now. None of them would ever want to see her again. Sam and Jim weren't a problem other than the fact that she'd miss them. Marty, though, he had no place else to go and she didn't want him to leave.

She bought the gifts anyway. Why not?

"That's the spirit," Granny said.

When she was finished she headed back to Quail Bottom to Luella's café. Only as soon as she got there, Luella took her hand and escorted her out of the building and they got into Luella's Jeep. "Where are we going?"

"Sam's," she said.

The bottom fell out of Emma's stomach. "You told him?"

She nodded. "And he wants to talk to you."

"Uh-oh. Is he upset?"

"Nope."

"You sure?" she asked, feeling hope flower in her chest.

"Just wait until you get there and find out what he wants. You got, like, three and a half minutes so just chill. Three if I speed."

"Speed."

When they got to Sam's, Emma almost didn't get out of the car. But, whatever it was he had to say to her, she deserved. They walked across the dance floor up to the bar and she noticed that the jukebox had been replaced. The place was empty. He didn't open until three on Sundays. Sam came down the loft stairs and stopped when he saw Emma.

He'd shaved, although he still had his big ol' mustache, but he had no stubble anywhere else. His hair was clean, his jeans were pressed—*who presses jeans?*—and he wore a black cotton polo shirt with a red tie. "Emma," he said.

She almost burst into tears just looking at him.

He hurried toward her and gave her a big hug, then he took her hands and squeezed them and she winced because the right one still hurt a little. "We just want to say, Happy Birthday."

"We?" she asked.

"Surprise!" Balloons floated down out of the ceiling and the disco ball turned on, fracturing shards of light all around the room. Emma stepped back, gasping at the shock of people jumping up from behind the bar. There was Zoe, Aurora, Jim, Heather, Micah, Jamie, Brandon and Marty.

A couple of the workers from the restaurant rolled out a birthday cake on a cart. It said: *To Our Darling Daughter. Happy Birthday and many more. Love, Daddy Sam, Daddy Jim and Daddy Marty.*

Tears flowed down Emma's face, which surprised her since she didn't think she had any tears left. She glanced up and the three men she'd grown to love were all smiling at her. There were presents and there was suddenly music and there was food. She turned to Luella, "You're sneaky."

Luella winked. "I know. I ain't done yet. I've got a few more tricks up my sleeve."

Emma smiled through tears, wondering what in the world that meant.

Sam stepped over and raised a glass toward her. "Emma, you changed my life," he said. "You gave me strength and a new way of looking at things. Your outlook helped me let go of anger that I'd held onto for so long toward my son. And toward myself. I feel like a load has been lifted off my shoulders. And it's all because of you."

Emma was speechless. More tears welled up.

Then Marty raised his glass. "This is water, by the way," he said. "I don't think I have to tell you what you've done for me, but I'm going to anyway. When you met me, I was a pathetic excuse for a human being. But you saw a human being, none the less. I wanted you to be proud of me. And you let me use your address and your house so that I could get a job." He reached into his pocket and pulled out two items. "Two cards that represent my new life. My 12-step sobriety card and my driver's license. Something I haven't had in a decade at least."

Emma ran to him and hugged him. He squeezed her so hard she thought she'd faint. When she looked into his eyes she saw joy. She cradled his face in her hands and said, "I'm so proud of you!"

Then Jim stepped forward and raised his glass. But he could barely speak. Heather came forward to sign so that Micah would know what his father was about to say. Jim said, "At first...whew, I didn't think I'd be this emotional." He cleared his throat and started over. "At first, I didn't know what to expect when I met you. I thought maybe you might be after something. Money or maybe you just wanted to cause trouble. I was also embarrassed that I could have possibly fathered a child all those years ago. And Heather was just plain ticked off."

Heather elbowed him.

"But, I knew if there was a chance that you were mine, I had to do the right thing. My mother always told me that no matter what, do the right thing. So, I met with you and you were sweet and kind and...the difference you've made in Micah..."

He started crying. Aurora pulled a tissue out of her purse, Zoe fished around in her back pocket for a hanky, and Luella searched her boobs for hidden tissues.

"I just feel so horrible," Jim said. "Because it's like, you came here and gave the three of us the very thing we needed most, but we weren't able to give you what you needed."

More sobbing ensued. Emma ran to him and hugged him. Then she hugged Heather, who beamed at her and smiled. Then she kissed Jamie and Micah. Micah signed, *Don't cry! Are you sad?*

"No," she said and signed. "I'm not sad. I am very happy."

"It's like you were sent here to save us," Sam said.

She stood up then and looked out at all the faces that she'd grown to love. And she realized that she had found what she'd been looking for after all.

"We claim you," Sam said. "All of us. If you'll have us."

Emma stood there speechless, glowing with emotions that she couldn't define, when all of a sudden her animals came running into the room. Even Thing 1, who was looking really irked by the whole hullabaloo.

"Wouldn't be a party without them," Luella said.

Emma hugged her.

"I love you all," she said. "Every single one of you! This is the best birthday of my whole life!"

"It truly is," Granny said. *"It truly is."*

The music played and food was served and everybody laughed and ate and danced. Luella tried to teach Aurora some move out of "Flash Dance" involving a chair but Aurora told her to step back and watch how it was done. Aurora then proceeded to use the chair as her dance partner. Micah laughed and clapped, because even though he couldn't hear the music, he could feel the rhythm and vibrations.

Emma opened presents. Sam got her a fishing pole. Marty bought her a cookbook. Jim gave her five animal collars with Valentine, Mutt, Tricephus, Thing 1 and Thing 2 inscribed on them. Aurora gave her a beautiful beaded bag that she'd made. Zoe gave her more picture frames for her house. Luella's present was a tiny box wrapped in pink ribbons. Inside, it was empty. Emma looked at Luella, confused.

The door to the bar opened and Sam said, "Sorry, we're closed for a private party."

An older man walked in, cowboy boots, cowboy hat, big ol' belt buckle, and when he looked up, Emma saw that he had hazel eyes and brown curly hair. The man nodded at Sam.

"Ned?" Sam asked.

Ned Barstow? The man whose house she bought? Emma stepped toward him. There was something about him. Something in the eyes...

Ned nodded. "My sister called and told me I needed to come up and meet my daughter."

Sam looked to Luella, who was smiling sheepishly. For a full ten seconds everybody in the room just kept glancing at each other, wondering if the next person or the next would know what in the world was going on. Everybody except Emma. She only had eyes for Ned.

"You must be Emma," Ned said to her.

"Yes, I'm Emma," she said. "And who are you, exactly?"

"I'm here to take your DNA test."

The room went quiet, except for the music.

Emma whirled on Luella. "What is going on?" she asked.

Luella shrugged. "I suspected my brother was your biological father a day or two after I met you, but I didn't want to say anything, until I'd talked to Ned to see if he even remembered your mother or if he'd be willing to come up and meet you. Then when all the DNA tests came back negative and I saw that picture you have of your mom and dad, I became even more convinced that my brother was your father. I recognized that belt buckle. I called him yesterday and he got on the first plane from Florida."

Emma blinked at the empty box. "You're my aunt?"

"But..." Jim said. "Emma's not black."

"Well, I'm only half black," Luella said. "Ned's only a quarter. So, I guess there's not much left to show up in Emma."

"Ned's black?" Sam said. "I always thought you guys were just step-siblings."

Everybody stared at Ned. Emma would describe his skin as swarthy. His eyes were hazel. His hair, although definitely corkscrew curly, was light brown where it wasn't gray.

All eyes then went to Emma. "Well that explains my hair," she said and laughed. And she knew in her heart that Ned was her father.

Emma and Ned excused themselves from the party and went outside on the deck alone and talked for an hour or more, while everybody else continued to party and dance inside. What surprised Emma the most was that there had been no cloud-parting music. No rays of golden sunlight streaming through the sky and lighting him up like he was one of those kitschy angel paintings in a roadside gas station. They sat and they talked and he told her what he could remember of her mother. He held her hand and told her he was sorry for missing out on her life. No, there'd been no cloud-parting moment, but this time...this time she knew.

"You've got a really big family," he said. "They'll all want to meet you. Aunts, uncles, cousins, you even have a grandpa. And you've got three brothers and a sister."

"I bought your house," she said, dumbfounded. She'd been living in her father's house without even knowing it. "And Luella is my aunt. That is just blowing my mind. You can't even believe how much that blows my mind. Wait, I have a grandpa? I have *siblings?*"

"Yes," he said. "Lucy is about a year younger than you. Just a warning; she can be a bit intimidating at first."

"How so?" Emma asked.

"That girl is fearless. And weird stuff just happens to her all the time," he said.

Emma laughed while Ned just gave her a quizzical look. "What did I say?" he asked.

"Nothing," Emma said. "I can't wait to meet her."

He stood then. "I'm staying at Luella's for the next couple of days. I'd like to be the one who introduces you to the family, if that's all right with you."

Emma nodded. Stunned. She should have been born Emma Rose Barstow. Emma Barstow. It had a nice ring to it.

It was getting dark, so they said their goodbyes and Emma walked back into Sam's looking like, well, like, she'd just met her father for the first time. Sam came over with a twinkle in his eye. "That damn Ned," he said. "I'm more than a little jealous."

Emma smiled. "Don't be," she said. "You're a very special man, Sam Sherman. Nobody can replace you."

Then the door to the bar opened again and in walked Brad, Clancy's best friend.

"Bar's closed, private party," Sam said.

Brad shrugged. "I wouldn't stop this guest if I were you."

Roy clomped into the bar with a bouquet of flowers hanging from his mouth. "Aw, Roy came to say Happy Birthday!" Jamie cried out.

Emma was just about to go to the horse, when Luella handed her something. She looked down. It was her phone. Her brows knit together as she studied it. Confusion waylaying her. "W-what were you doing with my phone?" Emma asked.

"Trying to keep this whole thing a secret," Luella said. "Go to your Facebook page. Look at your notifications."

Emma tapped the screen, went to her page. She had a bajillion notifications. "I don't understand..." She clicked on them. *Clancy Stephens likes your photo.*

Clancy Stephens likes your status.

Clancy Stephens likes your photo.

Clancy Stephens commented on your photo.

Emma looked up, searching Luella's eyes for some answer.

She heard Clancy's voice. "I stayed up all night stalking your page. Experiencing your life."

Emma whirled around to find Clancy standing next to Roy, hands in his pockets, cowboy hat cocked back. Damn, he looked good for a man who'd been up all night. She couldn't speak. Her heart pounded so hard that it pushed the wind right out of her lungs.

Roy nudged Clancy with his nose. "All right," he said to the horse.

Roy shook his head, bared his teeth, whinnied, nickered, snorted.

"I got this," Clancy said.

Emma laughed. She looked up as Peri, Caitlin and Reuben stepped inside the door.

"I...I'm so sorry for being an idiot. I should have called, I should have said, well, I just should have been more of a man. More of a grown-up, really. So, um, I have a letter here from Zeus, if you'll allow me to read it."

Emma smiled and stuck her thumbnail between her teeth.

"Dearest Emma, I know I'm just a horse, but I want to thank you for not giving up on me. For being patient and kind and making me feel like I was special, even though I was being a big baby."

"You sure that's from Zeus and not you?" Marty said and everybody laughed.

Roy nudged Clancy a little closer.

"I got this, Roy. Sheesh."

A hush fell across the room. No music. No talking. "Um, and Roy, well, he says that he can't imagine a life without you. And quite frankly, I'm having trouble with that, too."

Emma's heart skipped a beat.

Roy nudged. Clancy went down on one knee.

"Oh my God," Emma said.

Roy flipped the hat right off Clancy's head with his nose.

"Emma Rose Gordon," he said.

"Barstow!" Ned said from the doorway. He'd snuck back in.

Clancy's eyes grew wide. "It's Ned? Ned is your father?"

Emma nodded.

"Oh, Emma, I'm so happy for you!" Clancy looked down at his shaking hands and smiled. "You bought your dad's house."

"Yes, but we can talk about that later," she said to him, impatiently. "You were saying?"

"Oh yeah." Clancy cleared his throat. "Emma Rose Gordon Barstow..."

"May as well add Sherman," Sam said.

"And Hollingsworth," Jim added.

"Don't forget Pepper," Marty chimed in.

Clancy took a deep breath. "Y'all are making me work for this, aren't you?"

Everybody laughed, but Emma just stood frozen.

He took a deep breath and said, "Emma Rose Gordon Barstow Sherman Hollingsworth Pepper...is that it? Anybody got any other names they want to add?"

"Just get on with it!" Heather said.

"I love you with all my heart. My horses love you. My family loves you. I adore you. Will you marry me?"

Emma looked up at Roy. He blinked at her. Then blew air out his nose and gave his big toothy smile.

"Y-yes," she said. "I love you. I love you!"

And the crowd went wild. And there was kissing and hugging and champagne and...

"Hey!" Ned called from the door. "Northern lights!"

They all stormed out onto the deck, squeezing and shoving their way through, which was a neat trick considering there was a giant horse to consider. Up in the sky the green light rolled across the horizon, lavender and magenta streaks dancing all through it.

And everybody oooohed and aaaahed and Clancy, who held onto Emma's hand, looked down at her with the oddest expression on his face.

"What is it?" Emma said.

"Are you really ready to give up all the craziness and settle down?" he said.

"Who says I can't be crazy and settled at the same time?"

She stood on her tip-toes then and kissed him. She kissed him deeply, softly, and then urgently. God, how she'd missed that. She'd missed the feel of his body next to hers. She'd missed his lips on hers. She'd missed the way he looked at her beneath the brim of his hat, the way he wasn't embarrassed about dancing by himself to a slow-moving blues song. She missed the way he'd made her laugh and how he checked on his elderly neighbors and how he valued all life and how he washed dishes. And now, she didn't have to miss it anymore. She kissed him again and again and he kissed her back, melding her body to his.

When they heard the music start up in the bar, they realized that everybody had gone back inside. Except Roy. He stood right next to them, almost between them, reared his head back and bared his teeth. See? Happy horse.

"I love you," Clancy said with the glowing sky behind him.

"I love you, too," Emma said.

And Granny said, *"They lived happily ever after."*

About the Author

 Rett MacPherson is the author of twelve Torie O'Shea books and a standalone novel from Word Posse, *Sleeping the Churchyard Sleep*. In addition to writing, Rett is a bead and fabric artist and loves all kinds of fabric, laces, buttons, and beads. She loves to be outdoors and she likes to run, even though she's slow and has to ice her knees afterward. In addition to reading—sometimes reading as many as fifty books a year—she also loves genealogy and is descended from a long line of English lords, Irish rascals, Scottish highlanders, Viking marauders, and French vintners and horse breeders. If time-travel were possible, she'd like to visit all of her direct ancestors. She's obsessed with British television and loves almost all music. She lives in St. Louis with her family, where she can often be found practicing yoga...unless she's at the winery.

Word Posse Fun Fact

Every animal Rett has ever shared her house with either found her or was a rescue. Currently, Rett is owned by a St. Bernard mix and an Anatolian Shepherd. She used to pick up strays and take them to shelters until that time she picked up a male and a female and neither had been neutered and chaos ensued in her backseat. That's just one crazy adventure that she used as inspiration for the main character in *Strange Bedfellows*. A few other adventures of Emma's are actually real-life escapades of Rett's that she mixed into the text, but she's not admitting which ones those are.

Made in United States
North Haven, CT
13 September 2023

41505161R00166